THE SECRET OF DREAMS

THE SECRET OF DREAMS

ARLENE ADAMO

Arlene Adamo

Copyright © 2021 by Arlene Adamo

All rights reserved. No part of this book may be reproduced in any
manner whatsoever without written permission except in the case of brief
quotations embodied in critical articles and reviews.

First Printing, 2023

www.arleneadamo.com

We are all ghosts when we are asleep
This is dedicated to all those ghosts who dream of justice

One

The crowd forces us along in the wrong direction. We want them to stop but they don't. They just keep moving. Mindlessly keep pushing. Sometimes even, in that chaotic flow, crashing into us. We do not feel them like they feel each other. We do not understand being in a crowd. For them, it is home. For us, it is hell.

Our flesh yearns. Our spirit yearns. For something else...something deeper...something meaningful. Not this place, where we are nothing more than strangers among strangers. And although we know we walk in grace, this place tricks us. We feel as if we only stagger and stumble. Tripping. Almost falling with every step. We want more!

Carrying this deep longing without promise, without hope, leaves us with nothing. The occasional blank stare of their strange empty eyes confirms this. Moving with nobody towards nowhere.

"Be nice" their voices say, while they bump into each other's bodies, spit in each other's faces and dine on each other's misery. All dressed to the nines they are—to the nines. Fashion is their religion of convenience. It seems to make them feel something. Or think they feel something. It makes us feel less than nothing.

What are we doing here?

One more crashes into us and we've had it! "That is enough!" we cry out to the openness of above. And then we stop. Dead in our tracks. And here *in this stillness we created, we begin to spin. Faster! Faster! Faster! "FREE-DOM!" we scream at the top of our lungs and the wind whips up into a furious tempest. Powerful! Powerful! Powerful! The world around us now a circular blur. An undefined spiral of colour. Then a silencing happens. And suddenly, we realize the crowd is gone. Carried away. Scattered across space and time. It is only at that point we stop. And the wind stops too. We now stand alone.*

At first, it makes us feel sad. The aloneness feels like a burden—a curse. But that doesn't last. We quickly realize we now have room to turn in any direction we want to go. No one is in our way. We are totally free. Stretching out our arms, we feel the glorious space around us. All options are now open. We turn and our eyes meet. For the first time. Staring with love. Then, warmly, we slip into each other. Flesh into spirit. Spirit into flesh.

And that is when I awakened into oneness.

∞◇∞

"Have you ever considered sponsoring an American refugee family? There are so many Americans in need and not enough is being done for them. According to the United Nations 80% of America's neediest are children. Please consider opening your hearts and homes today. Remember that these children are innocent victims who had nothing to do with their government's choices. As Canadians we have an obligation to help. They are our neighbours. They are our friends.

It's always easy to turn away but is that the kind of world we want? A cold uncaring place? So please, call today and sponsor a family in need. Simply contact us at the number below to give an American child the chance they deserve."

"Shitheads!" an old man suddenly shouted while shaking his fist at the screen. "I sponsored a family. A bunch of fat-asses! They took over my house—tried to tell me what to do. Goddamn Americans! Eventually I had to get the police in to take them away. Don't know what happened to them. Maybe they went for rehabilitation or maybe they sent them back. I don't know and I don't care. Just glad they're gone. Shouldn't allow them into Canada in the first place. They got what they voted for and now they can live with it."

Besides the old man and I, there were only four other people in the restaurant. It wasn't unusual for such places to be mostly empty. Not these days. People just didn't hang out the way they used to. Nobody seemed able to muster up much desire for social interaction anymore even with the threat of the viruses gone. Everyone just kept to themselves and went about their business as usual. It was easier not to seek out company or pleasure. It was safer. More secure. The world had gone numb.

For me, life didn't change much after what they often called "the great accident"—which wasn't an accident at all. Their intention was the same. It was just the target. The target was not intended. No, I had lost a great deal of hope for this world long before that happened. My existence had become just about moving forward—trying not to make too many mistake—keeping my distance—never letting people know too much—walking onward but never allowing myself to feel the ground. If I did that—if I let myself touch the ground, I might feel a part of this place. And that was something I didn't want. I didn't want to be a part of any of it. I wanted to stay above it all as much as possible.

The old man then suddenly stood up and walked over to a table where a young couple was seated. "Do you see what they're doing? They're trying to make us feel guilty," he said angrily while shaking his fist again at the TV. "Like we owe them. Like we were the ones who killed all those people. Well, I tell you, I'm not feeling guilty for living. Nobody should feel guilty for living."

The couple did not reply but just awkwardly smiled and nodded in agreement. They were obviously hoping he'd finish his tirade quickly and go away.

"I'm not feeling guilty for living," repeated the man who then abruptly turned and walked out the door.

It was silent after he left except for the TV which had now switched to a show about gardening. We seemed all in agreement about keeping the silence after that disturbing rant. Everyone just sipped their drinks and quietly listened to the benign droning of some gardening expert as if nothing had happened.

I looked down into my teacup and swirled the dregs that rested on the bottom. I could understand the man's point. Despite his angry outburst, I could understand his point. A man like him, who probably lived modestly his entire life, existed in a small world. He was of the generation ahead of me, so I understood something of how he thought. There were rules about how life should be lived. These rules had kept him alive so far, so he held to them. He didn't know how to adapt to new rules. He didn't know how to see what had happened to him in a different light. He only knew how to absorb his anger into his being to be used as a shield against any future encounters. But there are no real shields in anger. The truth is, he was just as vulnerable than ever. Maybe even more so.

And they did, after all, want you to feel guilty. This was true. Even before it all fell apart, they always wanted that. Guilt is a useful control. It paralyzes people while at the same time is also something people naturally try to foist upon others. Guilt is a burden people scheme to share. And as long as everyone was feeling guilty and, at the same time, trying to pass that guilt along, it meant a lack of scrutiny—people too preoccupied to ask any real questions. As long as everyone was in the middle of the square stoning the scapegoat to death, those who were truly to blame got away with it. It had been that way since likely the beginning of humankind. And it was one of the many ways corrupt power weasels itself into the fabric of things.

I stared at the gardening show on the screen. The easy-going man in the quirky broad-brimmed hat was demonstrating how to build a simple trellis out of sticks and twine. People still liked to do that...build little things in their little worlds. It was the same as they have always done. Little worlds. Little things. It was comforting to focus only on the smallest details. It's easy to get lost in the trivial and a good way to ignore the daunting things of the bigger world.

Suddenly noticing the small clock at the bottom corner of the screen, I realized time had gotten away from me and it was later than I thought. Quickly finishing off what was left of my shrimp sandwich then drinking down the last of my tea, I got up to leave. I could not be late for class. I already felt like I didn't fit in with the group and walking in late would only make everything worse. I had to be on time.

∞◇∞

"I have been working towards constructing an indisputable argument that will prove the existence of God. It is my opinion that St. Thomas Aquinas simply did not go far enough. His arguments were not enough to silence the skeptics. I intend to silence them forever." He then sat back in his chair and proudly adjusted his glasses.

God Almighty! What am I doing sitting here listening to some blowhard's fantasy of divine self-importance? And the professor is even worse—encouraging this. All of them pretending they're a part of something enormous—pretending they will alter the course of the world with their self-indulgence.

And why again did I decide to finish my Master's? How could I have forgotten what these classes were like. The endless sophistry. The teacher's pet. The simplest thinking dressed up in the rococo language of the hyper-educated to sound like a complex idea. There are plenty of other hobbies I could have tried. Knitting for example. Perhaps, I again just fell victim to the things this world has ingrained in me. We're taught that getting your Master's is a huge accomplishment whereas knitting a sweater is ordinary. Even if the sweater is far more useful.

I wanted more than anything to just get up and walk out but I knew I couldn't do that. For one thing, they'd notice my absence and talk. "The older lady is gone. I suppose she found it too difficult." And I just couldn't let that happen. Maybe it's my pride or maybe it's my obligation to the reputation of 'older ladies' but, for that reason alone, I could not walk away.

But beyond that I'd already spent the money and was more than halfway done. Plus, and most importantly, the professor, with whom I had nothing in common, was my accidental thesis advisor. Walking out on his class would not be easy to explain.

Despite my discomfort, it was clear to me I needed to persevere and finish what I started. So, I resolved to listen to silly arguments for the existence of God by people who supposedly believe in God but are incapable of imagining that Omnipotence could never possibly care about such piddly things.

And so, there I sat imprisoned in that cluster of dull convoluted conversations, nodding my head, playing the nice interested 'older lady' and pretending that I don't know things—things far, far beyond their comprehension. Yes, I would play my part in this boring farce. I would keep my mouth shut and my head down. And I would never let them know that I know secrets—secrets about them—secrets about all of us. I'd never let them even guess that I know the secret of dreams.

Two

"You've come back!" he sighed, warm tears of joy running down his face.

"Yes, I'm here," she replied. "I have returned to you."

"It's been so long," he said as he softly stroked her arm. "To feel you here again, after all this time. Why did it take so long? Why didn't you return sooner? I've waited night after night, but you didn't show. Didn't you even miss me?"

"I did miss you, but I'm just so busy with other more important things."

"You're the most important thing to me. Why am I not the most important thing to you?" he asked sadly.

"That would be difficult to explain. I'm not sure you would understand," she told him.

"I sang our song tonight. I sang it for you. I sang it with more passion than I ever have before."

"I know," she said. "That's what called me here. The song."

"And did you see the crowd! Did you feel them! The screaming, the crying, the cheering! They became a part of the wonder that is between us. We filled that space with love—with love!"

"We did," she smiled softly. "We did something good in that world."

"Are you now going to leave me again? If you do, I just don't know if I can take it. My heart shatters every time I feel you leave. My heart just shatters into a myriad of pieces!"

"I will have to go," she answered not wanting to deceive him. "As I've told you before, there is no forever for us, only moments. Secreted moments. Moments that hopefully can create something meaningful—something that changes things for the better."

"But you can stay! You have a choice. You can stay forever! Please, don't leave me again!"

"We will join here tonight," she told him. "In a precious moment borrowed from eternity. Like we have before. It's how we created our song. Do you remember?"

"That is all I will ever remember," he replied.

"Then will you join with me again?"

"Oh yes! That's all I want! All I've ever dreamed of. I want to join with you and then never part. Just stay like that forever! Complete contentment! Fulfilled! Just say you'll never leave me again. You know it breaks my heart every time."

"I know," she said. "I know it's difficult for you, but let's not think of that now. Let us instead savour the moment. Come closer my beautiful songbird. Come closer and feel all that I have to offer."

He knew he could not walk away from her. Why would he? She was life itself. Walking away would mean choosing death. So, taking in a deep breath, he then gently touched his forehead to hers. "Oh..." he softly moaned as he felt himself sink deep, deep into that calm living ocean. No longer did he feel any distress or fear. Suddenly, there was no future to worry about and no past to weigh him down. Only the moment. The perfect moment. Everything else was forgotten and the only thing remaining was the warm fog of ecstasy that lovingly enveloped him.

∞◇∞

"Issa, do I have a man for you," said Traci, my best friend of nine years. "This guy is amazing!" she beamed as we sat in her kitchen, while she poured us both a cup of tea.

I've never been one for keeping friends over long periods of time. We either just naturally drift apart, not having much in common to begin with, or I realize that I am less of a friend a more of a usable prop in their self-narrative, so I end up ghosting them. Traci has been my only exception. She's one of those people I call baby-souls, although I'm not really sure if they're babies or not. All I know is, she's innocent and wouldn't dream of ever hurting another human being. She's a little overly positive about everything but, at the same time, doesn't mind the hint of heaviness I carry. She's accepting and openhearted, but not excessively naive. And she believes in giving everyone a chance even the most lost among us.

"Amazing? That's what you said about the last guy," I tell her. "And he turned out to be a serial killer."

Traci laughed. "Oh Issa, you exaggerate! He was the CEO of his own company and was charged with embezzling, but that was after you already got rid of him. How were either of us to know. Anyway, that was seven years ago. It's not like I try to match you up every day, although I'd like to try." She laughed again.

It's true. If I allowed her, Traci would try to match me up nonstop until I finally gave in. She has been happily married for thirty years and feels sincerely sad at seeing other people alone. She wants everyone to enjoy the same happiness she found with Theo. Perhaps, that is her biggest shortfall. She can't imagine happiness comes in any other the way than the way she found it.

"Seriously though, this guy is great! He's an art history professor. Teaches at the university. He's interesting, smart and not bad looking. He's a friend of Theo's cousin and we met him the other day at a fundraiser for the American Refugee Project. He talked about how hard it was to meet single women his own age. Well, he is a little older than you, but not by too much. Anyway, I kind of told him about you...how fascinating you are and how you are working on your Master in Philosophy, and he seemed to be really interested.

Basically, he said he'd love to meet you. Please say yes...just this once...for me. You could just meet him over coffee, and if you don't like him, then that's it. Don't pass this one up. He could be the one."

The one? What would 'the one' even look like? The thought of having a serious relationship at this point in my life seemed absurd. When you're young, you're blind to so much. Getting involved with another person is easy. You don't really see them fully until you're all the way in. That's how I ended up married at a young age. But I had time back then. Time to shift and change and get divorced. Now, I'm older and time is more precious. Also, I know too much. I see too much. I'm less impulsive and more contemplative. I've built walls to protect myself. How do you start a relationship from behind a wall?

"Clarissa Comfort, you need to move outside of your comfort zone," declared Traci with a giggle. "Just take his name and number, and seriously consider giving him a call. I have a good feeling about this one."

She then slid a folded slip of paper across the table to me. Obviously, she intended on giving me this no matter what my answer.

"Alright, I'll think about it," I relented not wanting her to hurt her feelings. I picked up the paper and slid it into the pocket of my jacket.

"Yes!" she exclaimed somehow thinking this meant I'd do it.

After that we talked about other things for a couple of hours, but as I was leaving, she reminded me, "Don't forget about that piece of paper in your pocket. He could be the man of your dreams." Her face lit up with a large hopeful smile, making me feel obligated.

I hated being made to feel that way, but I also knew she didn't mean to be pushy. She was just hopeful for me. And perhaps this guy was alright after all. Who knows? I suppose meeting in the afternoon in a public place is not a big commitment. Perhaps I should do it for her. Was I lonely? Sometimes. But I also knew there were worse things in this world than loneliness. Much worse things. The occasional feeling of loneliness was something I could live with.

∞◇∞

"Authorities confirm that, yet another American rogue militia has struck this time in Alberta. On Thursday at around 3 o'clock in the morning a group of about twenty fully armed Americans swooped in on the sleeping residents of Whisky Gap. They terrorized the residents, pillaging homes and businesses. It has been reported that up to seven Canadians were killed and fifty injured. The seriousness of those injuries is not known at this time. This makes it the third such cross-border attack in four weeks. The Prime Minister is to issue a formal statement this afternoon regarding the ongoing problem of these roving gangs. It's rumoured she will be asking the Chinese government to assist Canada with border control..."

I switched off the TV as I tried not to think too much about the death and suffering. Of course, you have to know about it. You have an obligation to know and to feel and to care. But you can't let it consume you. That's the tricky part. To be attached and yet detached at the same time. To look straight into the heart of darkness while keeping faith. Faith. What was it Paul Tillich said about faith? Oh yes, "Faith is an act of a finite being who is grasped by, and turned to, the infinite." Did those people in Whisky Gap have faith? Were any of them grasped by the infinite? Or did they die only as finite creatures without spiritual form? It doesn't bear thinking about. And who am I to worry about such things anyway. I don't make those decisions from this world or the other one. Still, I feel for those who are left behind to wonder 'why'. Those who are left in grief—grasped and held in the suffocating embrace of the finite. Love has been ripped from them. Stolen from their earthly existences—the place where love is so badly needed. There is air, there is food, there is water, there is shelter and there is love. All of them essential. All of them necessary for temporal life.

But you can think and worry about others only so much before it always comes back to you and your own story. Like there I was, thinking of those poor people in Whisky Gap and all that they must be going through while at the same time looking at that piece of paper on the table. The one Traci had given me. There's the world outside with all its problems and all its tragedies, but always I can encounter it only from inside of myself. And that paper sitting there—calling me away from the vision of bodies in that tow—from the tears and the suffering. A paper with a name. A number. A question about what do with it. A whole human being waiting to be encountered. Perhaps a chance to bring more love into this love-starved world. I suppose, there is an obligation to at least try. Life goes on.

Three

It was a very nice little café he had chosen. Upscale but not pretentious. Artistic décor but not trying too hard. That was a good sign. Maybe Traci was right this time. He could be as interesting as she said. Although he was now almost twenty minutes late which could be a bad sign.

The waiter came over and set down a small copper coloured tray with a blue ceramic tea pot and matching cup in front of me. "Thank you," I said. He nodded, smiled politely and turned to leave. He's professional and not chatty. That's good.

I tore open the tea package and dumped the dried buds into the pot. As I sat there wondering how long I should allow the tea to steep, I glanced over at the door and saw a man entering alone. He was tallish with medium length grey hair and a matching neatly trimmed full beard. He had that professor look but not that stuffy professor look. He was not overweight, but it was clear he was one of those naturally skinny guys who, as he got older, also got a little wide around the middle. He did, however, put in an effort to hide it with an untucked shirt and casual blazer. His clothing was nicely coordinated—earthy complimentary colours—modern and with a sense of an artistic flare. He seemed alright. Unfortunately, however, he wore a silk auburn scarf wrapped loosely around his neck.

Perhaps, I was wrong to think it but a man in a decorative scarf just seemed a little too vainglorious.

He spotted me and smiled. I smiled back assuming that he must indeed be Crawford even though his photo on the university site looked quite a bit different. But I suppose that's true of most on-line photos.

He walked over the table. "Clarissa?" he asked.

"Yes," I said standing up to greet him. I thought we might just shake hands, but he went in for the full European hug with a kiss on both cheeks. I found it awkward. Ever since the viruses people just didn't do that anymore. Something I was glad of.

He waited to sit until I was seated then said, "It's so nice to meet you."

"Same here," I replied, realizing that I was feeling more nervous than I thought I would. How many years had it been since I was on a date? I couldn't remember exactly.

Crawford signalled to the waiter who was nearby. "A bottle of your house, with two glasses," he chirped.

"Thank you, but make that just one glass," I said. "I'm drinking tea." It seemed a bit strange to order a whole bottle of wine in the afternoon but again I heard Traci's voice tell me, "Don't be too quick to judge, Issa."

"Are you sure?" Crawford asked. "They have such a wonderful house wine here. It has a full rich nutty flavour with a hint of herbal zap. You really should try some."

"Thank you but no," I replied.

"Just a little," he insisted. He then told the waiter, "Bring two glasses anyway."

Crawford then turned to me and asked, "What kind of tea are you drinking?"

"Rose tea."

"Oh, I've never tried that before. Is it good?"

"I like it. Would you like the waiter to bring you a cup to try?"

"No. No thank you," he replied. "It would colour my palate for the wine. Another time perhaps."

I smiled and poured my tea.

The waiter arrived with a bottle and the glasses, setting one in front of Crawford and the other near me. Together with Crawford, he then went through the whole ritual of uncorking, smelling, swirling, tasting and then the authoritative nod of approval. Personally, I hate it when they do this in restaurants. It seems so silly—so fake. But I suppose it's expected by the customers. People have the urge to find meaning through rituals. I assume they feel those things give them power—control of life—filling them with self-importance. Rituals do that for people. Something I never quite understood.

"Ah yes! This is le pièce de resistance! Thank you, my good man," Crawford exclaimed.

Okay, that made the entire thing even more silly, but Traci says I'm sometimes too quick to judge so I tried not to hold it against him.

The waiter then filled Crawford's glass, but when he went to fill mine, I quickly covered it with my hand telling him, "No thank you. I'll stick to tea for now." He then smiled, nodded, placed the bottle on the table and left.

"So, your friend tells me that you are studying for your Master in Philosophy," Crawford said, then took a rather large swig of his wine.

"Yes, I am," I replied. "It's something I considered doing for a while and thought that the time was finally right to finish what I had started."

"Aww, nice," he said, then took out his phone and posed for a selfie while holding up his glass. "I just want to take a moment to share with the world how I am in the company of an intelligent beautiful and mature woman," he explained as he quickly typed something into his phone then returned it to his pocket.

I just smiled politely and took a sip of my tea.

"Well then," he said, "tell me, do you like this place? It's one of my favourites. They all know me here."

"It is very nice," I told him. "I like the eclectic atmosphere. It's very well designed. Very comfortable."

He then took another large swig from his glass, and at that point I noticed that he looked a little older than Traci had said. Was he not being truthful about his age? Or was he just the sort that aged quickly? Or perhaps, those were alcohol lines in his face?

"So, Clarissa," he said, "Let us now begin by journeying over the terrain."

I looked at him puzzled.

"Ha! I see that you're wondering what I'm talking about," he smiled. "Well, allow me to explain. I am a devoted follower of the teachings of Guru Durjoy. And not to brag, but I've actually achieved level five attainment. And that is no easy task."

"I've never heard of him," I said.

"Really! How could you not have heard of The Master? He's on the TV constantly. Celebrities, politicians—so many big names are, what we call, Followers of The Joy. I am a Follower of The Joy, level five."

Okay, so this was not what I was expecting. Was he going to try to convert me? Is that what this date was really about?

"As a Follower of The Joy, I am bound to the Sacred Tenets of Journey. When I meet someone with whom I could possibly become deeply involved, I am required to journey over the terrain of my past so that we may meet in honesty and truth in the present."

I didn't know what to say, so I said nothing. This didn't seem to bother him though, as he just continued on talking.

"The journey across the terrain cleanses us so that we might meet in a wholesome spiritual life-affirming place."

"Hmm...so, how does that work?" I asked, now growing more curious about where this exactly was going.

"First, I open the door by asking you a question about your past, and then, from your answer, I take the lead to journey openly across my terrain. Terrain is what we Joyers call the past."

I still wasn't sure what he was talking about, but I was willing to play along.

"Okay then, ask me a question," I said.

Crawford quickly drank back his wine then refilled his glass. He seemed to have forgotten all about my empty glass and his previous insistence that I try the wine. That was fine by me.

"Your friend told me that you were once married. What made you decide to get married, and do you have any children?" he asked.

Actually, that was two questions, but okay. "I don't have any children," I answered. "And I married because I was young. I was young, short-sighted, starry-eyed, idealistic, vulnerable and very lonely. All the typical curses of youth."

"Now that is honest," said Crawford. "I appreciate that, Clarissa. We are getting off to a good start."

"Thank you," I said, wondering what could possibly come next.

"Now, as I open a path before me, you will share in the journey of my terrain." He closed his eyes, swept his arm over his head then down again and rested it upon the table. He opened his eyes and stared directly at me. "I too married young," he began, "I was a graduate student at the time. So was she. Same field—art history. At the time, I felt she was the love of my life. So beautiful. She reminded me of the Lady of Shallot by John William Waterhouse. Are you familiar with that painting?"

I tried to answer but couldn't as he continued talking.

"I thought we'd be happy forever, but she changed after we

married. She became more demanding, unpredictable and jealous—very jealous."

"Did she have a reason to be jealous?" I couldn't help asking. Surely the Lady of Shallot would have had good reason to be jealous.

"Shhh..." he said. "You are not supposed to interrupt a journey of the terrain."

"Oh, sorry," I quickly apologized then took another sip of tea.

"So yes, she changed. And I, in my discontent, began to wander. As a TA I had constant temptations. Young bright women fascinated by art history would throw themselves at my feet. Eventually I did give in to these temptresses. And after three years of a tumultuous union, we did indeed divorce." He took another large swig of wine, and I wondered if that was the end of 'the journey', but he kept going.

"Of course, I did go on to become a full tenured professor, as you know. And the temptresses never waned. Every year would bring a new group. If we got along well, the relationship could last even longer than a year, but each one always seemed to fade much like a cut flower. For me, love was always such a fleeting thing."

I sat there in stunned silence unable to believe that this stranger had just casually confessed to me about years of preying on his students.

"So, my most recent serious relationship was with a young woman who showed so much promise. She was my protégé. Everything was wonderful until she got pregnant. In my haste to do the right thing, I married her. It was all quite good for a while. Until the child was born. Then everything went downhill from there."

"You are married!?" I exclaimed.

"Shhh...you're not supposed to speak yet. But I understand and forgive you. I'm in the final stages of the divorce. It should come through next week or maybe the week after. Anyway, to get back to my journey—once the child was born, my soon to be ex-wife had changed. She became less her wonderful free and open self. She became but a mere stranger. So, at that point, I made the decision that it was over." He stopped there, went silent then finished off his glass of wine.

Is he done? Can I speak now?

"I must confess that have always preferred younger women," he suddenly continued, pouring himself more wine. "They always seemed more open to my ideas and easier to get along with, but they do change, and the entire thing turns into a big mess. It is only recently that I came to realize that I should date women my own age who are less likely to change so there are no surprises."

"Actually, I'm younger than you," I told him.

"You know what I mean," he replied. "In a certain age group. The age where women are more set in their ways, so you know up front what you are getting. There's no bait and switch with a mature woman. She knows who she is and what she wants." He then quickly gulped back some more wine from his glass.

I wasn't sure what to say at this point.

"So that is where I stand today," he said. "This is the journey across my terrain. You now possess the knowledge of the true place in which you meet with me."

Not knowing how to respond to any of it, I simply replied, "Well, that was different."

"It most certainly is," he agreed. "And now it's your turn. We need to now journey across your terrain."

"But I'm not a Follower of The Joy," I told him.

"Well, that doesn't matter. You can still experience the wonderful freedom that comes from following the Master's teachings. Just try it. You'll find it so freeing. Let us journey across your terrain," he insisted.

"I'm not really comfortable with this," I said, wondering if I should just get up and walk out.

"Oh Clarissa, it's not about feeling comfortable. It's about freeing yourself. Sometimes that's not always the most comfortable feeling. As a student of philosophy, you must know that. There is a price to freedom."

It was obvious that he was not going to let this go, and if I stayed, he was going to try and force some sort of confession out of me. At that point, I wasn't sure what I should do.

"It's completely unfair that I should give you a gift of my journey and you then give me nothing in return. It would be so wrong of you," he said in a slightly pouty voice.

This was now too much, but it had also become too tempting. He was, after all, begging for a story. I felt a little guilty considering it, and I'm not normally a game player, but he was pushing me into it, so what choice did I really have?

"Okay then," I began. "The journey across my terrain begins just after my divorce, when I found myself young and alone and needing to make money fast. So, I fell into exotic dancing. But not your seedy strip-club. No. I worked in an exclusive club. The kind that has no street sign—no advertisement—only a discreet address and word of mouth referral. Such places are known only to the most elite clientele.

"Now just to keep it clear, I was not a prostitute. They had women for that, but I was not one. They only came to watch me dance. My dancing was so hypnotic that millionaires and billionaires from all over the world would fly in just to see me. I was called Aurora because watching me was like watching the dance of aurora borealis in the night sky. I could draw them in with the swing and swirl of my hips, the grace and beauty of my flowing arms, the allure of my shapely legs, my hair long and silky as the milky way. I could draw them in like no other dancer. I was a silent siren.

"And it was there, in that club, that I met Francois. Francois was a multi-billionaire but unlike most of the other men who frequented the establishment, he was young and handsome and clever. So, to make a long story short, we fell in love.

"We were about to embark on an incredible life together when, unbeknownst to me, he had angered the CIA. I didn't quite understand it at the time—the relationship between the extremely wealthy and the CIA. And he said very little—only that he had done something which they found unforgivable. So, three weeks before we were to be married, they shot him dead. A clean shot straight through the head. I knew it was them and of course, you know, from all the reports in the news these days, just what horrors the CIA were capable of.

"So now, with my Francois gone, and my heart shattered, what was I to do? Francois did, in his thoughtfulness, bequeath me enough money that I might live comfortably for the rest of my life, and not have to return to dancing. I was grateful for that. For although I loved dancing, I had grown tired of the leers of dirty old men. What young woman wouldn't?

"After all that, I could not even look at another man and thought this would be my fate for the rest of my life. That is, until today when my good friend convinced me to meet with you. And now here I am. And that is my journey of the terrain."

Crawford was silent. He then drank back all that was left in his glass and said, "Clarissa, that is truly a remarkable journey! Don't you feel so free after sharing it with me? Also, do you still dance?"

I just barely kept myself from bursting out laughing. "Only in the privacy of my own home," I told him. "In private, I still dance in honour of my beloved Francois."

He poured the last of the wine into his glass. "You are far more interesting than your friend indicated," he said, slightly slurring the word 'interesting'.

It was then that I realized he had forgotten Traci's name.

"I live just a couple of blocks away," he said. "Perhaps, you would like to come to my flat and see my art collection. I had it secreted out of the home just before I left my wife. It is a remarkable collection indeed. And perhaps, if you would be so generous, you can show me a little of your art—your exquisite dancing."

Oh no! I had laid it on too thick. Now this cretin was overexcited and, to make matters worse, he was drunk too. I knew I had to get away from him as soon as possible.

"I'm so sorry but I have an appointment," I told him. "Perhaps, another time."

"Don't tell me that," he smiled in a way that I suppose was meant to be seductive but just looked lecherous. "Surely you can cancel. We are just getting to know each other."

"Oh no, I really can't cancel. It's with the American Refugee Project," I said, thinking quickly for any excuse. "They have an emergency situation, and I promised I'd help out. They need me to come in today."

Crawford tried to pour more wine into his glass, but the bottle was already empty. "Both beautiful and benevolent," he said. "I'm so glad I met you. I must confess, I had second thoughts. Maybe a mature woman was more trouble that she was worth, but I must say that you have changed my mind. I really like you Clarissa...and I mean really."

Okay, time to leave. "It was lovely meeting you, Crawford, but I do have to go. People are depending on me," I say rising from my chair.

Crawford leapt up from the table, almost losing his balance. "Adieu, sweet lady," he said, as he grabbed my hand and kissed it. "May we meet again very soon."

"Umm...yes," I said, not sure what else to say at this point. I didn't want to say anything that could possibly prolong the conversation.

As I then quickly headed for the door, I heard him behind me calling out to the waiter for another bottle of wine.

Four

"You sang so beautifully," she told him as she stroked his forehead.

"And you, along with me. The magnificent sound of your voice with mine—it melted their hearts," he said.

"It's nice to be here with you. I did miss you. I did miss this. There have been many times when you have been my sanctuary."

"You are my whole world," he responded. "There is nothing but you!"

His declarations of love were always enough to restore her and fill her with joy, but this time there was something else. Something was not quite right. He was different. There was a confusion. A confusion that left him feeling a little frightened. Was he gaining a new level of awareness?

"Something is bothering you," she said. "What is it?"

"I can hide nothing from you," he replied. "You know everything."

"But I don't know what's bothering you," she said, gently taking his hand in hers. "Tell me what it is."

He hesitated for a moment then tried to explain. "I'm not sure and I don't understand. I just can't figure it out. There we were on the stage. Singing. Beautifully singing. Powerfully singing. The audience was going wild. And then, after that, I remember nothing. I remember nothing much before and nothing much after. All I know is that now we are here. And I'm not sure how we got here. There's a blank. Is there supposed to be a blank?"

"Yes, my darling. There is supposed to be a blank. There are many blanks."

"Is it drugs?" he asked. "Have I been taking drugs again? I thought I gave them up. I remember giving them up."

"You did," she answered. "When they almost killed you, you gave them up."

"Then why are things so fuzzy. Why is it all dark outside of the light that you and I give? And you are so bright. So much brighter than me. Are we supposed to give off light? How can we do that? What is going on?"

"You've never wondered about any of that before," she said. "Why now?"

"I don't know. It's just...I was on stage...we were on stage...and now here we are? Where are we? What is this place?"

"Do you really want to know the answer to that? It could spoil things for you."

"Would it make you go away?" he asked. "If it would make you go away, then I don't want to know. In that case, don't tell me anything."

"I would still come to you," she reassured him. "It's just that it would complicate things for you. Are you prepared for that?"

"I'm not sure," he said. "Would it be painful? It couldn't be anymore painful then when you leave me. Maybe you'd stay forever if I knew the truth. Would you stay forever if I knew the truth?"

"I already told you many times that forever is not something between us. Only these precious moments. You should not hope for more."

"I will always hope. But for now, please tell me why it is like this. Why is everything so strange? So confusing? I need to know."

She was not sure why he now suddenly wondered about things when for so long he never questioned any of it. But for this to have happened, it must be important. It might have to do with something she'd been noticing about him recently. Something troubling.

"It's simple," she told him feeling that the best thing she could do now was to be honest. "The reason why everything is so strange...why it is all so confusing, is because we are asleep."

∞◊∞

"Oh, I'm so sorry he was such an idiot," Traci apologized. "I really am sorry."

I had invited her over for some afternoon tea to fill her in on my 'big date' as it just didn't feel right telling her over the phone. She had been so excited thinking she had done me a such great favour and was the kind of person who would feel extreme guilt upon hearing it did not go well. I wanted her there, face to face, so I could reassure her that there was no harm done.

"He really did seem okay when I met him," she tried explaining. "I mean, I didn't speak to him for a long time, I suppose, but in the time I did talk to him, he seemed nice enough. Very sophisticated. Educated. Suave. He knew a lot about art. How could he have been such a jackass?"

I laughed. For Traci to use the word 'jackass', was akin to someone else cursing. "We can't see inside of people, Traci. We only see their public personae. Who they really are, is not that clear. Sometimes it can even take years to see someone's true colours. Don't worry about it."

"I know," she said. "But I just can't believe that, when you finally after all this time, agree to let me set you up with somebody, it turns out to be with a guy like him. I really am sorry. I feel like I just ruined everything for you."

"Stop being so hard on yourself," I told her. "It wasn't all that bad. And to tell you the truth, the entire thing was kind of funny. In fact, it was really funny. And come to think of it, I should be thanking you. So, thank you. Thank you for setting me up with that moron."

"Why would you thank me?" she asked in confusion.

"Because, that ridiculous date made me realize just how bored I was. You're right. I've kept to myself for far too long. I've been too isolated. I need to get out and meet people. Have conversations even if it is ridiculous. You go ahead and feel free to fix me up anytime. Fire away with your match-making."

"Are you sure?" Traci asked. "I don't think I trust my judgment anymore. Why is it that I always seem to miss the red flags? I'm so naïve. I try not to be but then..."

"Because that is who you are," I tell her. "In fact, that's one of your best qualities. A quality I admire. You mostly only see the good in people. Always filled with hope. You're a baby soul."

"A what?"

"You're a baby soul. You're innocent and open to the world in a way that many of us are not. I call people like you baby souls."

Traci started laughing. "I'm a baby soul? That's so funny. But aren't babies the most self-centred people on earth? At least my babies were. Both of them. They still are sometimes."

I didn't want the conversation to veer off towards her children. It was too painful for me. She shared a wonderful relationship with both her now grown children, and it only reminded me of what I had lost—what had been stolen from me. And I never told her my secret. No one who knows me now has any knowledge of it. I kept it hidden away because it helps me pretend it never happened—at least it helps some of the time.

"Anyway," I say to change the subject back, "Just in case you run into Crawford again, I told him that I was meeting with the American Refugee Project. It was an emergency, and they needed my help. That was my excuse to get away."

"Oh perfect!" exclaimed Traci. "Because I wanted to talk to you about that. You know how I've been doing volunteer work for The Project...well, I've just been so shocked at how many needy Americans are out there just waiting to come to Canada. Nice families who suffered so much and have even lost loved ones in the great accident."

There were those words again. "The great accident." It wasn't an accident and I wish the media would stop calling it that.

"Theo and I have already applied to sponsor a small family to stay in our empty bedroom and expect a match to come through any day now, but I was thinking of you—of your carriage house."

Oh no! She's going to ask me to sponsor a family! "Well," I tell her, "It's not a carriage house. I mean, look at it!" I pointed out the back window at the red brick structure sitting in my backyard. "It's an old backyard garage that someone once converted into a very small one bedroom apartment. It hasn't been used in years and I'm not even sure if the plumbing works. I barely use it for even storage anymore and can't remember the last time I've gone inside. It's dirty, grimy, probably full of spiders and not fit for human habitation."

"But that's not a problem," she said. "It's a good solid brick structure and we have teams of volunteers that can fix that place up in just a few days. We'll even furnish it, all free of charge. It has four lovely big windows, so lots of light. It could be easily transformed into a really nice place."

"Oh, I don't know. It seems too complicated," I told her honestly.

"Listen Issa, we are just so desperately in need of sponsors and homes for these people. Many of them really have nowhere to go and it's becoming so dangerous down there. As the border talks continue, the militias have become more and more violent. And there are so many children at risk. Can't you please help?"

What was I going to say to her? I wasn't heartless but my world had become one of self-preservation and, I suppose, a lot of distrust. How was I to honestly welcome a family of strangers into my backyard. It would be an invasion of my private space—a space I spent years ensuring was free from any type of troublesome interloper.

"You've been so blessed, Issa," Traci continued. "When it's such a tough time out there for so many, you don't have to worry about money. You have your home and your security. I know that you like your privacy, but this family will only be staying for a year maximum—just until they get on their feet. And the program doesn't just dump these people on you and leave. We work with you. If there are any problems, we are there. And we are in constant contact with the family to ensure that they have loads of support too. Really, you don't have to do much other than supply them with a safe place to live. How much you get involved with them is up to you."

"But it's only a one bedroom. How can a family be comfortable there?" I asked, searching for any excuse.

"Some families are small," Traci replied. "A couple or a single parent with one or two children would be quite comfortable. Won't you help out? I promise that if, for some reason, it's just not working, we will move them to another home. You've really got nothing to lose, Issa. And there is some family out there that needs you."

I didn't know what to say at this point, and the truth was that I did feel guilty. Traci was right that I had a secure place in a world while, for so many others, their places had been torn to pieces. Outside of my comfortable walls that enclosed me, there were people just hanging onto the edge of nowhere trying desperately to survive.

But yet, this was my space. My treasured space. And I needed my space for my own sanity. I needed the quiet in my awake world to balance out the intensity of my dream world. Would I be able to deal with strangers complicating things? Would they unbalance everything?

"Give me a couple of days to think about it," I told her, not knowing what else to say.

"Great!" she exclaimed. "Take all the time you need to think about it, and I'll email information to help you decide. But I really hope that you'll help us out. It's getting harder and harder to find sponsors and there are just so many good Americans who are desperate to come here. And if you do this, you won't regret it. I promise you. People need you, Issa. Just think about that."

Five

"Border talks resumed today between Canada and Mexico. There is continued disagreement regarding where exactly they will draw the new Mexican-Canadian border and what compensation each country will receive from the UN. Mexico is arguing that by accepting the remaining Southern States, it is taking on a far greater burden and should receive more funding. The budgets of both countries have already been stretched by security issues."

I turned off the TV, not wanting to hear anymore. Why did it have to be like this? Those fools! I couldn't stop them. I couldn't save all those millions. Why did my dreams fail me? Was it predestined? Is this the only way it could have happened? Does God allow human beings to smash things to pieces because it's the only way to put it all back together the right way? I wish I had the answers. I wanted to understand the meaning of this world, but some days it just seemed so meaningless.

What I knew for sure is that I felt it coming but could do nothing. At the time, it felt as if a massive, vile monster was poised and ready to pounce on the unsuspecting masses. And I saw it was coming but what could I do? There was no one I could warn. No one who would possibly listen. So, I just helplessly waited and then watched it unfold like everyone else. I watched video after video of the land crumbling and those people dying. Unable to do anything, I watched the world as I knew it, fall to pieces.

∞◊∞

"I am here," she said, her light blasting through the darkness.

"Oh, thank God!" he replied. "Thank God you are here. I've been so lost without you."

"How do you know that I am not lost too?" she laughed.

"You are not lost," he said, taking her hand in his. "You always lead the way. When you're around, I always feel secure. You know things. Things I may never know."

"Do you still love me?" she asked.

"More than anything. More than my own life." He gently squeezed her hand.

"That's why I return to you," she confessed. "You still have that unfailing love. I need to feel that when there is so much darkness. Too much darkness. I need to keep this little protective bubble of love between us. It helps give me strength."

"Oh, to know that I mean anything at all to you, makes me so happy! I just want to feel happy with you! That's all I have ever wanted! Just let me lie back and float in your beautiful sea of love."

"I understand," she said. "And I feel your love, but there is also something else, isn't there? You're trying to avoid it but there is something else. It's mixed in with your love...diluting it. It's an uneasiness. An uncertainty. You are still suffering confusion."

"Yes,", he admitted. "I do feel confused. It is true. I'm not the same as I was. Things have changed for me, and I need you to explain. Since your last visit, I have become even more unsettled. There are questions. Questions that bother me."

"Ask me anything," she said, gently running her fingers across his brow.

He trembled at her touch. How could he ask her for anything when she had given him so much already? But the questions were there. And they weren't going away. He needed answers. "The last time...the last time we met, you said something," he began. "Something so strange. I don't understand it, but I want to. I want to understand what it is about. If I knew what it was about, perhaps love could even become a forever thing between us. You said it was not a forever thing but perhaps it could be. If I had the knowledge, perhaps I would know what must be done to make this love eternal. I would understand everything then."

"That is a wonderful thought," she replied. "The idea that such knowledge could transform us into a forever thing. And you ask for answers in the spirit of innocence and honest yearning. You have indeed changed and the need to know is now within you. So yes, I will answer any of your questions truthfully. But you must be warned that knowing the truth could possibly ruin things. If it does not go right. If you do not want to or cannot believe my answers, it could go very wrong, and I might not be able to return to you after that. Do you want to take that risk?"

He thought about it a moment. Losing her would be the worst thing to ever happen. How could he even go on after that? But on the other hand, something absolutely wonderful could be gained. They could become a forever thing. He'd never feel alone again. Just the mere thought of that possibility filled him with joy, and he knew what he had to do. "If it brings us closer, then yes!" he exclaimed. "I want to take that risk. I would risk it all to avoid the heartache of you ever going away again."

"Very well then," she agreed, suddenly realizing that the pain of not knowing would not only hinder his love but also threaten his very existence. It was necessary to answer his questions. "What would you like to know?"

He was silent for a moment as he tried to put his thoughts together and then asked, "The last time you were here with me, you said that we are asleep. How did you mean that? How are we asleep?"

Still not entirely certain if he was strong enough to handle the truth, she sighed then told him, "A part of us is sleeping. The awake part. We are here now because we are together in dreams. We exist in dreams. This is why it always feels so confusing for you. Thoughts moving around. Things appearing…disappearing. Snippets of memory. Me, coming and going. We connect in dreams."

He was silent for a moment as he thought about it, then asked, "You are saying that right now we are dreaming? This is only a dream?"

She could feel his anxiety rising and knew this would not be easy for him. Still, he had come this far, and there was no going back. He needed to hear the full truth.

"Yes," she answered. "We are dreaming. But dreams are not just dreams. They are much much more."

"Then what is real?" he desperately asked. "Is this real? Is a dream real? I'm so confused. Awake or asleep, which is it? Which is real? And when I sing? All the time I sing. I sing our beautiful song over and over again. If this is a dream, do I really sing at all? When I sing on the stage in front of all those people, is that just a dream? Did I imagine those people? Are they just part of a dream?"

"No. That is not a dream. But this, at this moment, this is a dream. Dreams are real. The awake-world is real also."

"Then I'm even more confused than before. I mean, I sing. I know I sing. I sing for crowds—great cheering crowds. So, are you saying that when I'm awake, I sing for those crowds?"

"Yes, you are a singer in your awake-life."

"But I distinctly remember you there with me on stage tonight. I felt you there, singing with me. Your love—your strength carrying through on every note. How can that be if we only meet in dreams?"

"Although you were awake on the stage and singing, I was asleep. Sleepers often inhabit those who are awake," she explained.

"Really? You inhabited me? When I was awake? Is it like a spiritual possession? Did you possess my awake-self? Are you a spirit who possesses people?"

"It's similar but it's not a possession. I don't take control of you. It's more like a visitation. Just being there. Holding your hand. Feeling you and you unaware but feeling me. It is what we all are. You as well. All those times you remember when things do not seem to make any sense. Those times when you did not feel like yourself. Instead, you felt like some-one else. A person in a different place with a different identity. Those are times when you were inhabiting others. You experience them and hopefully help them in their waking lives. They in turn may come to experience you. But neither of you realize it is happening, awake or dreaming. You just experience. You are not aware awake or asleep."

"So, you are saying that I sometimes inhabit others? Is this the truth?"

"Yes, sometimes you inhabit others in your dreams. Not now. Right now, you are here with me. But other times when you find yourself in peculiar situations and places not recognized. Most of those times, you will be inhabiting those who are awake."

He thought carefully about it for a moment and then said, "Yes, now that I think about it, there are times when I do suddenly appear in strange places, and I am not myself at all. I feel like someone else. Someone differ-ent. And the people around me are people I know, and yet, they are also, at the same time, people I don't know. And many of those times I have stage fright or anxiety because the show is not going well even though I know I have never had that problem. Are you saying it isn't me? It isn't really my experience?"

"Those are the lives of other people," she told him. "You inhabit them—share in their painful emotions and then hopefully help to support and guide them. Even the most selfish among us are forced to live this helper-existence in dreams. The dreamworld is a different sort of place."

"And so, you helped me when I was awake? You helped me when I was on stage? Is that why I felt you when I sang?"

"Both in your awake-life and in your dream-life, I have helped you. I made it possible for you to write that song that launched your career.

That song has kept you afloat all these years. In some ways, I made you what you are."

"Oh, it is strange but yet somehow that all makes perfect sense. Yes, I feel it. This is the truth. I understand now, and it's so beautiful! No wonder I love you so much. I owe everything to you! In some strange way you created me! You sort of created the life of my awake-self, didn't you?"

"And therein lies the problem," she said with a sigh.

"How can that be a problem?" he asked. "How can there be a problem in something so amazing and so beautiful? Much of my awake-life was created by the vibrations of love between our two lights. I think that is wonderful!"

She looked at him sadly. He was so full of hope and now she had to explain everything to him. She had to make him fully understand what was going on. "In my quest for love in this world," she told him, "I gave you a song that changed the course of your awake-life. As I said before, I made you what you are in your awake-life."

"But you don't seem happy. Why does that not make you happy? It makes me happy. How can that possibly be a problem? I'm so confused. Please explain!" He suddenly felt frightened and held her hand even tighter.

She could feel the desperate need for truth in his touch and knew, that no matter how hard it was to say, she could not keep this from him. Truth is salvation even when it is not good news. And she had to respect his honest desire for knowledge. He was afraid and yet he still wanted to know. That was courage and courage must always be respected. He had to be told and it was her obligation to tell him. "I will be blunt with my answer so that you understand just how serious this is," she said. "It has become a problem that I have made you what you are because your awake-self— the self you only really know a few things about—the self in the awake-world who sings that magnificent precious song of love—stirring souls and moving people to tears—that self is a shameful man."

Six

"Alright Traci, you've made me feel guilty enough. I will sponsor an American family."

I had only intended to tell her 'maybe' when I called her. My real plan was to stall longer and hopefully get out of it. But somewhere in the seconds between the sound of her phone ringing and when she picked it up to say hello, something happened. Perhaps, it was all those commercials with the faces of sad American children finally getting to me. Or perhaps, it was just wanting to see Traci happy. Or perhaps it was just my dream-self with her forceful compassion. But regardless of why, that's what I did. I impulsively said 'yes'.

"Really!? Oh, that's great! Thanks so much, Issa! You won't regret this. I promise. Theo and I are having such a wonderful time being sponsors. The Cohens are such a sweet old couple and a delight to have around. It's a rewarding experience and you'll be a hero for helping a family in need!"

"I'm not a hero," I tell her. "I'm just tired of you making me feel so guilty all of the time."

Traci laughed. "Okay, believe what you want but you will be making such a big difference in someone's life."

As long as it doesn't change mine, I thought. I don't need changes right now. No big changes anyway. Just easy monotonous sailing. That's my philosophy.

"How soon can I send a crew out to fix the place?" she asked.

"Anytime is fine, I suppose," I said, imagining the entire thing would take a while to put together. "I'll give you the key, so they can start even if I'm not home." I actually preferred not to be there when work was being done. The idea of fixing up the old apartment seemed so arduous and chaotic. And I didn't like the thought of chaos. The noise. The garbage. Breaking things. It all seemed too much.

"How about tomorrow? Is tomorrow okay with you. We have teams ready to go. I just have to email you the forms. You can fill them out and return them today, and then the crew will be there tomorrow."

"Tomorrow?" I exclaimed. This had suddenly become all too real.

"Yes, we have to act fast. Some of these families are in immediate need. Is it okay if they start tomorrow? They'll arrive in the morning somewhere between eight and nine. This is a crisis, Issa. It requires urgency. We have no time to lose."

No time to lose. Time is of the essence. This situation requires your immediate attention. I hated the tension in urgency. Urgency breeds chaos. It leaves me flustered. Uncertain. Like I'm stuck on some horrible game show. That's why I try to build a life without it. Everything at just a slow easy pace. Everything well planned. Everything happening as expected. Calmness. Order. Peace.

I thought about telling her that tomorrow would not be a good idea to at least give me a little more time to get used to the idea. But instead, I replied, "That's fine. Come tomorrow. We might as well get it over with. I'll just leave the key under the flowerpot outside the garage door so they can start whether I'm around or not."

"That's the spirit, Issa! You won't regret this. So many of our sponsors have found it such a rewarding experience. I know you will too."

At that point, I remembered the ranting old man in the restaurant. He said he needed the authorities to get the obnoxious Americans out of his home. Will that be me in a few months? Ranting to strangers in restaurants about my horrible experience? I hoped not. I just hoped this was the right decision.

∞◊∞

"Bonhoeffer expressed the spiritual qualities of music. He said it purifies us and provides us with a constant fountain of joy. But what is music? What is it really? It's a universal need. We know that. Humankind thrives on it. Desires it. It nurtures us. Heals us. Even the deaf experience it. Perhaps we could say that music, especially when done in honesty and love, is one of the languages of God."

There was a long moment of silence before he replied, "Well that's very interesting. Thank you, Clarissa. Does anyone have any reflections on that particular thought?"

I suppose, I couldn't have expected any other response from Professor Wagner. Those were the words he used whenever he was unimpressed or in disagreement. And I knew he wouldn't like it. Before I even said it, I knew he wouldn't like it. And I also knew he didn't consider Bonhoeffer a real philosopher. Wagner had a very stringent view of philosophy and theology. He wasn't open to fresh ideas. Real philosophers respected only the traditional ways where Aristotle was king. Also, I don't think he liked having women in his class. Especially a woman close to his own age. It threatened him. It was an invasion of his masculine territory, a land where all the males knew and understood each other. Their pecking order carefully set out and commonly agreed upon. There was no room for a woman in that place.

For a moment, we all just sat awkwardly waiting for someone to speak. You did get extra marks for speaking in class, so usually there was someone trying to take advantage of that. Finally, the young man who planned on proving the existence of God said, "I don't understand the idea of the languages of God. Since we are made in His image, wouldn't He speak as we speak?"

"Do you mean spoken language?" I asked him.

"Of course," he said, with a slight condescending air. "That's how we, who are created in the image of God, communicate. Langue, the tongue."

"Spoken language is only one form of language," I explained. "And easily subject to misinterpretation. It's also an expression of a particular time and place. It's highly temporal in so many ways...disappearing upon delivery and only existing in faulty memory. It can be recorded, but simply recording it does not make it impervious to time. All spoken language is subject to a temporal existence. How could such a limited easily misinterpreted thing be the only language of the Omnipotent? How could a singular limited finite mode of expression be the only means of Infinite Expression?"

I could see Mr. Prove-the-existence-of-God didn't have an answer, and that hurt his pride. Would he try to pull rank on me? Him, a young man with his whole life ahead of him, a man on a career path, a valued member of society, versus me, a woman past child-bearing years, considered in our culture to be of little value. A woman on her way out. Is this where he would go?

"Perhaps the idea of languages of God is more of twentieth century type thinking," he said, really going there. "I believe we've moved past such things as flower-power thinking long ago and onto something more concrete, more intellectual. More based in tradition instead of fad."

Before I could respond, Professor Wagner interrupted, "Well, as interesting as this discussion is, time's up, and I need to be somewhere. Please note that there will be no class next week as I am travelling to the United States to visit with my daughter. Because of the unpredictable process at the border, I will not be able to guarantee making it back in time and for that reason am cancelling the class. To make up for this, there will be an additional on-line class at the end of the semester. The exact date will be worked out.

"In the meantime, I will email you a selection of articles which should be read in preparation for the next class in two weeks. Please come prepared and ready to discuss them."

As I packed up my things, I thought about how much I hated this class and how unfortunate it was that Wagner was indeed my thesis advisor. I didn't choose him exactly. It just happened. My first thesis advisor, the one who originally taught this class, was a dull but humble professor. He was very traditional but also did not hold any extremely rigid or prejudiced views. He was generally accepting of new ideas and respectful of all his students. Unfortunately, his age caught up with him and he developed severe health problems which left him bedridden. His class and the role of my advisor were then taken over by Wagner. Initially I had accepted Wagner because my original thesis advisor recommended him. I didn't know much about him other than what I had learned from reading a few student reviews online. The impression I got was that he was rigid but fair. It was only after several weeks of dealing with him that I realized just how judgmental and arrogant he was. By then it was too late, and I was stuck.

I did consider just altering my ideas and playing along...giving the professor what he wanted and ignoring my own learning. Isn't that what most of academia is about? Like so many things in life, it's about suppressing your own thoughts and feelings, and following the script no matter how untrue. And there were some days I felt that I should go that route. Make it easy on myself. But in the end, I couldn't because it wouldn't actually be easy at all. It would be hard work to pretend to be someone I wasn't and repress the things I knew. And it would be an affront to my love of learning. It was already challenging enough to have to pretend everyday...to hide my secrets. In this instance, I had to be true to who I was and the truth I knew. That was important not only for my own emotional well being but also for the health of my dream-self. I always had to think about my dream-self and what my decisions in the awake world could do to her. Keeping some level of truth was essential to keeping my light shining as brightly as possible.

Seven

"I don't know why you would return to me, after what you said about my awake-self. Is it true? Am I really that terrible? As you put it, 'a shameful man'? Is that why you always go away? Do you secretly find me repulsive?"

She felt bad for him. He was so confused and distraught. His feelings were all over the place. To know the truth, a dream-self must be ready. He wasn't ready but circumstances meant that it had to be done regardless. There was no waiting for a better time. He had to be told. "I'm sorry," she said. "I know it's difficult. Sometimes the truth is difficult."

"But how can it be? I'm not horrible, am I? Here you are with me. If I were so horrible, why would you come here at all? How could you possibly be in the presence of someone who is that horrible?"

It was sad to see him in such a state, but she knew there was no other way. "No, you are not horrible," she tried to reassure him. "Your asleep-self is wonderful," she told him. "You are wonderful. A wonderful little light of love."

"Oh!" he exclaimed, feeling better at hearing her call him 'wonderful'. "But if I am a wonderful light of love, how can this be the truth? How can I be wonderful and horrible at the same time? I don't understand."

She could now feel his pain. This had opened up a new and frightening world for him. A world he had never known before. His emotions needed to be stabilized and the only way to do that was to enter into a more honest relationship. She had to move this thing forward. She had to move him forward. Knowledge was his only hope as it is everyone's hope.

"Think back to that long ago time, when we wrote our beautiful song together. Do you remember what you were like?" she gently asked him. "Do you remember what your light was like?"

"What do you mean? Was I different then? Are you saying I was different back then?"

To make certain he fully understood, she knew he had to see for himself. He had to know without a doubt what the truth was. "You need to see it," she told him. "You need to know just how serious a matter this is. Look back. Look back through time and see. You know how to do that. Will yourself to travel back to that point and you will see it in your memory."

He felt a little nervous about what he might find but reached back into his memory anyway. In an instant he was there again. Existing in that beautiful time when she had first appeared, and they created that song together. How wonderful and comforting it was to be there again. A place of pure joy. The words and music manifested as incredible shining droplets of love brightly circling the air around them. Like countless dancing children reflecting the living lights they were born from. It was so beautiful! So bright! So amazingly bright!

"Look at me," she told him. "Look at me in your memory and tell me what you see."

He looked at her and sighed. "Your light is so magnificent! So, nurturing! It fills me!"

"Do you think I was brighter back then than I am now?" she asked.

"No," he answered without hesitation. "If anything, you are even brighter now. Actually, I'm quite sure you are brighter...more bright, more beautiful!"

"Now look at yourself in the past and what do you see?"

He looked down and was surprised by the brightness. "I am bright!" he exclaimed. "Not bright like you, but I am bright."

"*Look and think. What do you look like today? Do you still shine like that?*"

He thought for a moment and then cried out, "Oh no!" His voice was shaking as he suddenly realized the truth. "How can this be? Please tell me that I am remembering wrong! Tell me that I am just as bright as ever and am just remembering wrong!"

"*You are remembering correctly,*" *she told him.*

"*But if it's true and I am darker now, then why did I not notice it? Wouldn't it be something that I would know was happening? If I were losing light like that, I'd have to know.*"

She could feel the intense fear growing within him. This was no easy lesson, but he had to learn. "Time can be a great deceiver," she explained. "Over time you simply didn't notice how much you had changed. It was gradual, so you just didn't notice."

"*But how? How did this happen? How have I lost so much of my beautiful light? Please help me! You must help me!" he pleaded. "I want to shine again like I once did!*"

The absolute terror he was now feeling made her want to flee the deluge of that negative energy, but she knew she had to stay. She had to be strong for him. "It's true that you were brighter back then, and so much more beautiful. And it was that brightness that drew me to you. It made you open to creating our song. It made the song possible. I was able to connect with you in a purer sense at that time, and, in that purity, we were able to create something wonderful that will continue perhaps forever. But over the years you have dulled. As time went on, your light became darker and darker. That's why you could never again write such a great song. Your light was not strong enough to connect with me at that level. That degree of intimacy was gone."

"*But why?" he cried out. "Why did this happen? Why am I fading? What's wrong with me? Am I ill? Am I dying? I don't want to die!*"

She could see he was now even more distraught, and his emotions were brutally slicing through the harmony between them. It was painful and she wanted to get away more than ever. But she knew she could not simply abandon him. They still had an important connection. A love. Not an eternal love but still a love. And love is the essence of all existence. She had to try and save him, and if there was any saving him, he had to know the whole truth.

"There is nothing wrong with you," she told him. "You are not ill, but you are in great danger. It is your awake-self that is the problem. Your awake-self is killing you."

∞◊∞

A memorial service is being held in Ottawa today to remember the thousands of Bahamians who lost their lives in the great mistake. It is being organized by the Bahamian Canadian Society to honour all those who perished on that fateful day...

I turned it off. Now they are calling that murderous act "the great mistake". I didn't like it, but at the same time I suppose I understood it. Partly, they just didn't know what to call something that horrible, and partly they didn't want to inadvertently cause a backlash against all those innocent Americans who were struggling. After all, many of them would become Canadians in a few years if the border talks went according to plan.

I turned back to fixing my usual breakfast—avocado on toast with fresh tomatoes and orange slices on the side. Laying it all out decoratively upon my plate, I thought about the care I now took for such small things. The news on the TV was sad—tragic. That was big. Balancing it all out was important. Concentrating on the little things in the present was a necessity. Of course, it was critical not to lose oneself in the trivial—use superficial things to avoid reality like so many people do. And it's also critical to always carry the truth with you no matter how uncomfortable. But focusing on those precious tiny comforts in life have often kept me from falling into the void of despair. Sometimes little things made precious were all I had to keep my eyes fixed towards the Light. And keeping one's eyes fixed towards the Light is the ultimate survival in both worlds.

I placed my plate on the table and was just about to sit down when there was a sudden loud bang. It sounded like it had come from the backyard. Hurrying over to the window, I looked out and could see four people in work gloves and hardhats picking up pieces of wood and other debris from in front of the garage. As they carried the garbage towards the front gate, more pieces of debris came flying out the open door landing in a jumbled heap in the grass. It was, of course, the crew from The American Refugee Project. How did I forget they were coming? Traci said they would be arriving early that morning, but somehow it had just slipped my mind. Perhaps my dreams from the night were interfering with my memory in the day. I hoped not. I had to stay alert and aware in both worlds.

I watched from my kitchen window, surprised at how swiftly the men and women were working. They seemed to be very well organized with each individual sticking to an assigned task. I could hear things being smashed and broken inside the garage. It sounded like they were ripping the entire thing apart and for a moment I worried the whole building would come crashing down on them. But I knew better. It was solid. It may be shabby looking, but the construction was solid. The workers were safe.

As I stood there watching them, I suddenly realized that none of it was bothering me. Here was a group of strangers in my backyard tearing things apart but it didn't bother me at all. I had worried about that. I thought it would cause me anxiety with all the chaos, noise and people. But no. It didn't feel like chaos at all. It was organized change. A refreshing change. This was a good thing...having all those people in my yard fixing things. This was a good shift.

I stepped out the backdoor and was immediately approached by a broad-faced smiling woman in a hardhat and carrying a tablet. "Hello!" she said cheerfully. "You must be Clarissa. It's so nice to meet you. I'm Lenore. I'm basically in charge of this little project."

"Good morning," I replied. "It's good to meet you too."

"So, just to let you know, the next three days are all planned out," Lenore explained. "Today is mostly the wrecking crew but we'll also be repairing and painting anything salvageable. Tomorrow, we plan to install the new kitchen and bathroom. The good news is that all the plumbing and electrical seems sound, and the windows are good. We'll replace the front door but that's not a biggie. Most of what needs to be done is purely cosmetic. By day three, we'll be finishing up the final touches and bringing in the furniture."

"Wow!" I said, "you work fast."

"We have to," Lenore explained. "The need is too urgent. Everyday we have a thousand new applicants and no place for them to go. When something like this comes up, not just a room in a house but a complete separate unit, we count ourselves lucky."

"I'm glad I can help," I said, meaning it. I should have listened to Traci and helped sooner.

"I'm glad you could help too," she replied. "Well, I should get back to work now. If you have any concerns or worries, just let me know. I'm on site every day."

"And if you or any of the crew need anything at all, let me know," I said.

"I'll do that," Lenore replied. "Oh, and just one more thing. On the form you filled out you stated that we were to throw out anything in the apartment that isn't usable. Is that right?"

"There's nothing but junk in there," I told her. "Throw it all out."

"Great. I just wanted to double check on that," she said. "Well, I best get back to work. Have to keep on schedule." She then smiled, tipped her hardhat and headed back towards the garage.

As she was about to enter, I watched her stop, move to one side and then gesture for someone inside to come forward. That was when I saw a man coming out of the door walking backwards while carrying something large and heavy. Then another man appeared at the other end of the object trying to push it forward. As they manoeuvred it successfully through the doorway, I wasn't sure what it was they were carrying. It was only when they got closer that I recognized it. It was the old couch, now dusty and faded. That flowery blue couch from so long ago. I forgot it was in there. When I first moved to this house, I must have stuck it in there and then somehow forgot all about it.

As they carried it past me, I froze. Suddenly I could see him—there on those blue flowers. As clear as day, I saw my little Matty there, laughing and jumping from one end of the couch to the other. He was dressed in those dinosaur pyjamas he loved so much. So full of joy and innocence. Making my heart explode with happiness at every leap.

"Matty, should you be jumping on the furniture like that?" I ask him playfully.

"Jump, jump, jump," he happily chirped. "Me jump."

I hug him and wrestle with him on the couch, making him fill with wild laughter. "Who's the best boy in the world?" I asked, grabbing him up and holding him tightly in my arms. "Who's the best most beautiful boy in the whole world?"

"Me!" he shouted. "Me the best!"

"I love you Matty-Matt!" I say, nuzzling him.

"I wuv you Mommy," he says as he throws his tiny arms around my neck and kisses my cheek with the warm softness of his baby face.

Then suddenly, he was gone. My Matty was gone, and I was left watching as the men carried the dusty old couch through the side gate. Quickly, I turned back towards the house, tears streaming down my face. I hurried back inside knowing I couldn't be seen like this. Closing the door behind me, I slumped to the floor and wept aloud. Why!? Why did I have to see that? Why did I happen to be there when they brought it out? I could have been easily anywhere else. I could have easily missed seeing it. But no, there I was. Standing alone, completely unprotected from the suddenness of it all. Wham! And then for it to trigger that memory. And to remember so vividly. Beautiful memory! Cruel memory! The terrible horrible cruelty that can reside in our most beautiful memories!

Eight

"You've been gone so long," he cried, clutching at her arm. "I've been here waiting...hoping. I need you more than ever now. I'm scared."

"I know you are," she replied. "But it really hasn't been that long, and I've had some very important things I needed to finish."

"But I'm being murdered! You said so yourself. What can be more important than that?"

"Someday I may be able to explain to you what is so important, but not now. For now, we must focus on you. Our time together is limited and there are so many others I must help."

"There are others?"

"Yes, many others," she answered honestly, suddenly realizing that it had never occurred to him that there were others.

"Are they like me? Do you wrap them in your embrace as you do me?" he asked, unsure if he liked the idea.

"Some are like you...the music makers. The songbirds. Music is important."

"How many? How many other music makers?" he asked.

"I don't know," she told him. "Hundreds. Perhaps thousands."

"Thousands!" he exclaimed in surprise.

"Yes, music is important."

Suddenly things were different for him. He was not the only one. There were many whom she made feel that way. At that moment, he couldn't help but feel a little jealous.

"Do you love them as much as you love me?" he asked.

"It's not really about that," she explained. "It's much bigger than that."

He didn't quite understand what she meant but at the same time knew that her answer was the truth. And as he thought more about it, he found himself beginning to find comfort in the knowledge that there were others. He was not alone in his painful longing. There were many others who suffered in the same way.

"Are some of the others dying like me?" he asked.

"Some," she said. "And too many of them, I cannot help. They are beyond help now. I tried to turn them back. I tried to keep them from being killed by their awake-selves, but it doesn't always work. Awake-selves can be ruthless."

"And so, what happens to them. When their lights go dark, will they disappear forever? When their lights go out, is that the end?"

"Yes," she answered sadly. "They are gone forever."

"I see," he said trying not to panic. "And when the light goes dark, does the awake-self die too?"

"That's not quite how it works," she explained. "A light will not go completely dark while the awake-self is still alive. It simply cannot. The light is life itself to your awake part. Long before the awake-self was created, there was the light. There is no life without some degree of light."

"Then I am safe as long as my awake-self stays alive, but at the same time my awake-self is killing me? How can that make any sense?"

"I know it's confusing but let me explain. The body will eventually die. And when the body dies, the awake mind will be absorbed into its light. Once this happens, the light must be bright enough to sustain itself. If it is too dull to do this, by one way or another, it will be extinguished forever."

"So then, if my awake-self weakens me even further, I will be extinguished when he dies. Both of us will be dead forever?"

"Yes," she answered truthfully. "No part of you will continue."

"*But I don't want to be extinguished!*" *he loudly cried. "You have to save me! You can't let my light go any darker! Please save me!*"

She could feel his intense anguish. He was hurting in a way that was so different than the pain he felt whenever she left. That pain came from love and was hopeful. This, however, was a dull dark ache that tore at his very existence. "That's why I'm here," she said, wanting to give him hope. "To try and save you. But so far, me giving you love is proving not to be enough. It's not working. Your light is still fading and I'm not sure how to help you."

"I have an idea!" he exclaimed. "If my awake-self is killing me, why can't your awake-self go find him and tell him what he's doing. Your awake-self can do that, can't she? I feel that you and she are connected in ways that I am not connected with my awake-self. You can have her explain things out there in the awake world. She can face him and when he sees her, he will surely melt with love like I do. He'll listen to her...to you. And he'll know that you speak the truth. Please go find my other self! Please talk to him and save me!"

At that point, she wasn't sure how much she should tell him. Was he really capable of handling the full truth? But he had to be told. He had to understand how impossible his suggestion was.

"I wish it were that easy," she began. "I wish I could simply walk up to your awake-self and explain, and everything would be fixed. But that's not how it works out there. Even if by some fluke, I was able to reach your awake-self, he would not recognize me. He would look right through me as if I didn't even exist."

"That's not true!" he exclaimed, upset at the mere thought. "He would melt with love. He would see you. How could he not? You, who mean the world to me. You, who I love more than life itself. That doesn't make any sense."

"Your awake-self is you but not you," she tried to explain. "He is so different. To him I'd just be a crazy woman living in a crazy fantasy. He wouldn't know me, and he certainly wouldn't believe me."

"I can't accept that!" he cried. "I can't believe my awake-self would ever think like that! How could he? But yet, I know you aren't lying to me. I can feel it. I know you're telling me the truth. I'm just so confused right now." He looked down at his depleted light and wept.

At this point, she was worried that it was all too much for him. She never had to reveal this much knowledge to such a weak light before and was now suddenly unsure if it would have a terrible effect. If he could not progress and instead devolved into a permanent state of denial, that would certainly kill him quickly.

Just then he looked up at her and said, "It is the truth though, isn't it? No matter how hard it is to believe, it's the truth. That's what he is. My awake-self. He is a blind creature who could look at you and see nothing. He would look at you and never be able to see your beautiful nurturing light that has sustained us."

She could sense how sad that truth was to him, but it was a great relief that he had not entered a self-destructive state of denial.

"Perhaps," he said, "there is another way to get through to him. Perhaps we could trick him. What if you didn't tell him the truth at first? What if you simply charmed him—seduced him? You could win him over and then make him see. I'm sure he'd believe you then."

She almost laughed at this suggestion but stopped herself. His life was on the line, and she must show respect for that. "Such a thing would never work," she told him.

"Is it not worth a try?" he asked.

"There would be no point," she said. "You see, even though your awake-self is somewhat older than my awake-self, my awake-self is not thirty years younger than him, and neither is she part of any elite group. These are the things he lusts after. These are the things he uses to prop up his ego and his illusion of power and control. My awake-self, without any of this, would be nothing to him."

"Oh no!" he cried. "How can that be? How can he be so awful? So blind? What am I to do? Why...why can't I get through to him? Why can't he feel me?"

"He does feel you," she explained. "Everyday he feels you fading away. He feels your pain and your anguish. But he only transfers that anxiety into other things. He tries to heal it with more stroking of his ego and filling up his life with empty things. In this way, he feels brief moments of relief, but it doesn't last and only works to diminish your light further. His weakness and shallowness are killing you."

"What do we do?" he cried. "I want to live! I don't want to die! How can we stop him? There has to be a way to stop him!"

The thought of him disappearing forever distressed her. The truth is that she would miss him, and it would be such a tragic waste of life and light in a world that needed more light not less. If there was a chance to save him, it had to be taken.

"At this moment, I'm not sure about the way forward," she told him honestly. "But I will try to come up with something. You still do mean a great deal to me. When I came to you, those many years ago, my awake-self was in great trouble. A sad terrible thing had happened, and she needed me to find more ways to give her strength and keep her going. Making music had always given her strength so I searched for someone new. That was when I found you. Being with you, loving with you and writing that song made her hardship bearable. Even though, at that time, she did not know about me or her dreams or any of that. In her mind she knew nothing, but she could feel it. She could feel that strength I was sending through that healing power. It kept her alive. It kept her from giving up. You see, her life is not only important to me but is also important to this world. How that works is too complicated to explain right now, but I wanted you to understand that you are important too. That you played a role in things so much bigger than both you and your awake-self. I cannot let you die without a fight. And I will fight for you. I just have to figure out how."

∞◇∞

These days, when I wake up in the morning, I remember most of what went on during the night. Not all of it but most of it. The encounters. The other dreamers in the world. Those awake whom I visited. The changes I made happen. It was a sudden yet gradual thing...this remembering dreams...this knowing. For most of my life, I was just like everyone else. I slept. I dreamt. I woke up. And none of it had much meaning. Dreams were just funny little things. Just unimportant gobbledygook. A common meaningless experience.

Now, there is so much meaning that some days it threatens to consume me. The intense feelings. The intense sensing of others. Throughout my waking days, I often try to stay focused on little things. The little chores and decisions that distract my mind. The sanctuary of the mundane. A way to keep my sanity through it all. Maintaining my balance while straddling two worlds.

This is why people aren't usually meant to understand the true nature of their dreams. The truth is so huge that it can destroy a mind not ready for it. For a consciousness to become one with its core being—with its soul—is an experience that can liberate the prepared or destroy the unprepared. It's a process of learning to fly, not just randomly jumping off a cliff.

And I try to choose carefully in my waking life to keep the process steadily building. It is the choices in the waking life that determine ultimate life or death. Those choices alter everything. The mind will either feed a soul or kill it. This is not something to be taken lightly. It's a daunting reality. I remember how someone once told me that if you only think about your own desires, the entire world will be destroyed. Perhaps that is correct to some extent. The world needs souls in order to survive—good strong souls.

Although I'd never wish to go back to ignorance and blindness, I must confess that some days I envied those who are oblivious. Their worlds are small, compact, easy to understand. There are no big questions, only the everyday-ness of everyday. They are not without their troubles, but they take comfort in their imagined stability. And they are all in it together. They are not alone in the worlds they imagine to be real and lasting. Like herd animals, they find security in their throng and never begin to imagine the vastness of it all. Oh, to be a herd animal, content and unthinking.

Truth, on the other hand, is solitary. It can be a very lonely place in the awake world. The more you know, the less you fit into the herd. It's not an easy path but it is the right path. And it's the path we all need to eventually walk if we are to live forever.

I am not yet completely one with my core, but I am moving closer to it. I still falter. I still sometimes choose unwisely. Perhaps I will get there in my lifetime. Or perhaps in the next one. I only wish it were clearer—the division between right and wrong choices. Everything in waking life is just as blurred and confused as it is in dreams. None of it is easy no matter how close you are to fully achieving the great union of your divided self.

Sponsoring a refugee family gives me one more thing to focus on in my waking life. I'd like to think it's the right choice—the good choice, but the truth is that I don't know. Often charity is only about placating the ego. A task to make you feel important—feel superior. Every act of charity is suspect. What I am sure of, however, is that taking on this refugee family is indeed a distraction. Just like working on my thesis. These are distractions when compared to my other life. Yes, perhaps they can help me in building a unified-self, but they are still secondary. My waking life is, in so many ways, the unreal part. While my dream life is everything.

Nine

It was after dark, and I had spent nearly the entire day working on arguments to support my hypothesis. I was mentally exhausted and planned on going to bed early. Also, there were so many things that needed to be done in my dreams. Important things.

Looking out my kitchen window, I noticed that the lights were still on in the garage. The team from the Refugee Project was still working. Their work was now into day five, past their planned three day deadline. Regardless, it was still amazing to watch how quickly they were transforming the old place. They were even working into the night to ensure the fastest possible completion. Their devotion was admirable.

And although I had yet to look inside, being afraid that something about what they were doing might trigger me like it did with the couch, I was very pleased with what they had done with the outside. The renovation really did improve the view from my window. Although the rustic old garage had given the yard a kind of quaint country garden feel, it definitely looked better now. More defined. Less patchy. The old wooden window frames, which were once speckled with peeling and cracked white paint, were now a smooth soft rich green, and the old grey wooden door had been replaced with a more secure white metal one with a half-moon frosted lite. They had also installed a new wall lantern which significantly brightened the front entrance. No longer was it a tired looking garage. Now it resembled a quaint cottage. A fresh clean cottage. Perhaps I should stop calling it a garage and start calling it a carriage house after all.

As I stared out the window, I saw Lenore step outside. She, in turn, saw me and waved. I waved back. She then gestured for me to come outside to join her.

Opening the backdoor and stepping out, I took in a deep breath of fresh fragrant air. It was a lovely late spring evening that felt more like midsummer. Everything seemed so vivid and alive. The kind of night that offered a sense of calm along with the gentle welcoming of hope and wellness. Most would compare such evenings to a dream, but I knew that, although wonderful, it did not begin to even compare to a beautiful dream.

As I walked up to Lenore, she greeted me with a huge warm smile, "Sorry about staying so late but...good news, it's finished! And sorry it took us a little longer than we said it would, but good things come to those who wait, and the crew has done a terrific job. Come on in and have a look."

"Lead the way," I replied, as I followed her inside, now eager to see what they had done.

When I entered the apartment, the first thing that struck me was how bright and clean it was. What was once uninhabitable was now a very inviting living space. The crew from the Refugee Project had done an amazing job. The rich cream coloured paint and updated lighting made me see how the apartment was so much bigger than I had thought. It really was a roomy place.

The kitchen had been fitted with updated white cabinetry and the counter was a grey faux granite. There was also a sizable island to be used as a work and eating area. The old worn linoleum floors had all been replaced with clean white-oak laminate and in the main living area was a large aqua-marine couch, a couple of grey padded chairs, a coffee table and a TV. Everything was just so nicely coordinated and certainly inviting.

"It's beautiful!" I exclaimed. "You've really transformed it!"

"And we replaced the old tub in the bathroom with a walk-in shower," she said.

I walked over to the bathroom and looked in. They had actually replaced everything including the old, outdated tiling. "It looks incredible," I told her. "I can't believe you've done all this in such a short time."

"Now, have a look at the bedroom," she said.

I walked over and peeked inside. The walls had been painted a light blue and were covered with silver star decals. There was a single bed, a nightstand with a starry night projector lamp and a couple of dark blue dressers. On one of the dressers was a brand new ball and an action figure still in the package.

"This is for a boy?" I asked in surprise. Just the night before Traci had told me that the final decision on the family had not yet been made. There were a couple of applicants they were considering but she couldn't tell me anymore than that.

"That's right. This family consists of a boy and his father," Lenore explained. "The sofa in the living room is a pullout sofa. It's not ideal but it's good enough. The place will still be comfortable enough for the two of them. I'm sure they'll be very happy living here."

"How long will they stay?" I asked, suddenly worrying again.

"It depends," said Lenore. "Sometimes it's a couple of months and sometimes it can take up to a year for the family to get on its feet. But you should know that we at The Project don't just drop them here and leave. They get complete support, and we do everything we can to help them reach the goal of total independence."

That didn't seem so bad. And it's not like they would be my complete responsibility. There were supports. Perhaps this would work out just fine. "Okay, it all sounds great. Is there anything else you need from me?" I asked.

"Now that you mention it…," she said, walking over and picking up a tablet from the kitchen counter. "I need you to sign off on the work done. It's just a formality really, to confirm that you have no objections to any of the work we've done on your property. It protects the agency from unscrupulous claims."

"I have no objections at all," I told her, taking the tablet in my hand and signing the form. "You've done a wonderful job. I'm very impressed."

"We aim to please," she smiled. "Oh, and before I forget, here are the keys for the new locks. Give a set to the family and keep one for yourself."

She dangled the keys in front of me. "Thanks," I said, taking the keys in hand.

"Oh, and just one more thing," Lenore added as she took the tablet back, "although all this work was done for free and we do know that you have very generously given up your space and agreed to pay all utility bills, we would still be very grateful for any sort of donation you may be able to give. Most of what we do is paid for by kind donors like yourself."

"Already done," I told her. Actually, earlier that week I had made sure to make a sizable donation to cover all their costs plus more.

"That's great then. The family will be arriving tomorrow evening around eight o'clock."

"Tomorrow!" I exclaimed in surprise.

"Is that a problem?" Lenore asked.

"Uh…no. No of course not. It's not a problem. Tomorrow evening is fine. I'll be home." I really did not expect things to move that quickly, but it was what it was. I needed to try to adapt and not be so rigid in my ways.

"That's great. I'm going to be moving on to another job site so

I won't be here, but Traci will arrive with the family. She'll do the introductions and walk you through it all."

"Sounds good," I say, still unsure about everything that was happening and at such a fast pace.

"Alright then. I'd better get home, or my cat will be mad," she said chuckling.

"Good night," I tell her.

"Sweet dreams," she said happily as she walked out the door.

Now alone in the apartment, I looked around and thought about my new guests who would soon be living here. They'd be cooking here. They'd be sleeping here. This would be their home at least for a while. Would they turn out to be a problem? Would they be traumatized people that I wouldn't know how to deal with? How would I know the difference between problems caused by trauma and just ordinary problem people? And if they were traumatized, how could I help? Did I even need to help, or would it be better to keep my distance? Give them space? Did I have a role other than just providing them with someplace to live? Suddenly, this all seemed so much more complicated than it did a few minutes ago. Now filled with uncertainty, I just hoped I was doing the right thing.

∞◊∞

"Justice, justice, justice," she sang as she flowed softly through their many minds—swimming in that living ocean of spirit, leaving each one with a sweet droplet—a warm comforting feeling—strength. Each mind, under the weight of its individual existence—the burden of its individual circumstances was now offered a truer sense of the way to turn—of the way to go. "Justice, justice, justice," she sang, spreading the seeds of justice everywhere.

Then suddenly, she felt a small tug, so she stopped to welcome it in. At first it was soft and then it became a little stronger. She was being pulled.

Pulled by the current of the Light of Lights. This was the call she knew. The call that it was time to do something. Something big. So as always, she went. She went to where she was needed. Drawn there to that uncomfortable disturbing spot, she swam to one of those many places where earthly power rises to a head like a pus-filled boil on the skin.

And it was there that she saw him. His tiny weak dream-self. A squeak in a universe full of thundering voices. Such a far cry from the powerful figure he was in the awake world. In the awake world his feet pounded against the earth and his impulsive selfish demands shattered across cities. But here, he was his true self, and she could see just how dull his light had become. It was very dull but not yet darkened to the point where reaching him would be impossible. He still radiated enough light that she could work with him. It was not easy work, but she could still interact with him. Still influence him. And in the wasted state of his soul, influence was all that he had left for her to work with. Not his salvation. He left no room for that. She was not his saviour. But she was the saviour of those he could destroy.

She moved up close against him and he moaned in relief. Dull lights are always desperate hungry lonely lights.

From there, she knew what to do. It had already been told to her in the pull and in her willingness to follow. Her desire for justice and peace made hearing it possible. She had the instructions. Instructions on what to do next. Instructions that could have only come from the Light of Lights.

"Choose the hard path," she whispered softly into his ear. "Choose the hard path."

"Be here with me," he begged. "Oh beautiful, beautiful stay forever."

"Choose the path of offence," she bid him again. "Be unmoving."

"I love you," he whimpered. "I want only you. Don't go away. Don't ever go away."

"Remain immovable," she told him again. "If you love me, you will choose this path."

"I will," he relented, wanting to do anything that might make her stay.

"The hard path is the path I choose but only for you. Stay here with me. Please stay."

"The hard path," she said.

"Yes, the hard path," he repeated. "The hard path is the way I will go."

At that point, it was done. She knew that the thought was now imprinted in his mind and could not be rooted out. It was a part of his whole being now. Her work here was finished so she quickly darted away.

Even though she was too far away to hear it, she knew that he was now crying out for her. They were always heartbroken when she moved away, taking her light from them. And even when he awoke, he'd not be entirely free from this. He'd feel a sense of painful longing that he could not explain. For relief, he would pop one of those pills beside his bed to dull his emotions. He wouldn't remember anything about her, but the essence of her light would remain like a sweet fragrance on the wind. And he would indeed choose the hard path, thinking this was the good choice—the right choice. He'd never know that it was she who told him to make that decision—the decision that would ultimately bring a final end to his power in the awake world and open the door to a new, fresh and better way.

Ten

So excited that she forgot to knock, Traci came bounding in through the backdoor. "They're here!" she happily exclaimed. "Come on Issa! Come outside and meet them!"

I had been standing at the sink, busily cleaning up the last of my evening dishes. I knew they were coming but for some reason it still surprised me. They were real and they were here.

"Come on, come on!" She pulled on my arm just barely giving me a chance to dry my hands on a tea towel and grab the keys to the apartment.

I followed her out to the backyard and for the first time saw my new guests. Even though I knew I was getting a father and son, I was a bit surprised to see a tall African American man in his early to mid-forties and a small skinny pale blonde boy around nine or ten. They were certainly an unusual family.

"Zeke, come and meet Clarissa," said Traci, grinning from ear to ear. She always told me how much she loved working for the Refugee Project and now I could see just how true that was. It felt good to see her enjoying this moment. I loved seeing Traci happy.

"Clarissa, I'm so glad to meet you," said Zeke, as he walked over and offered his hand. "We are just so grateful for your help. Aren't we Jake?"

I shook his hand and said, "It's not much. I'm glad I could help."

The little boy came running over and stood beside his father. "My name is Jacob. My father's middle name is Jacob. Everybody calls me Jake for short. They call him Zeke for short, but his name is Ezekiel. I want to be an archaeologist. That's somebody who digs up old stuff. Old stuff is important. We can learn a lot from it. Important things. Thanks for helping us. I'm eight years old, but in three weeks I'll be nine. So really, I'm closer to nine."

I laughed and replied, "Hello Jake. I'm so glad to meet you."

It was such a relief that they seemed like such nice people. In between dreams, I had woken a couple of times in the night worrying that I might have taken on more than I could handle. Was I making the right decision sponsoring refugees? The thought of finding myself stuck in an intolerable situation caused me some anxiety. But standing here now, I had to admit that, over the years, my solitude and monotony had become things I perhaps cherished too much even if they did help to centre and balance me. Having these strangers, not only living in my backyard but also depending on me, would certainly disrupt things. Complicate everything. But maybe it was time for me to accept a little disruption in my life, and meeting Zeke and Jake reassured me that disruptions could be a good thing. I found myself feeling glad they were here.

"Would you like to have a look at your new home?" I asked them.

"Yes, please!" exclaimed Jake. "I want to see my room! I had a room in Washington. That was my first real room. This will be my second real room."

I led the way to the apartment then unlocked the door. Opening it, I gestured for Zeke and Jake to go in first.

"Wow!" shouted Jake as he skipped across the threshold.

"It's very nice," said Zeke. "Much more than we were expecting."

"Where's my room?" asked Jake. "They said I get a room!"

"Through that door," I said, pointing to the only closed door.

He ran over, pushed the door open then squealed with delight. "Dad, look! Come and see this! My own room! And there's toys? New toys! There's a superhero! Is that for me? Are those things for me? Can I open the package?"

"Yes," replied Traci. "Open the package. That's for you. For you to keep."

"Thank you! He can be a superhero archaeologist!" he exclaimed as he ran over and grabbed both toys from the dresser.

Zeke walked over and peered into the room. "It's incredible!" he said. "Best room ever! Except for my room, of course. My room has a fridge and a TV."

Jake's eyes lit up in excitement. "Where is it, Dad? Where's your room?"

"Right here," said Zeke, walking over and slapping the couch. "This is a magic sofa that turns into a bed when the sun goes down."

"Wow!" said Jake, running over to examine the mysterious furniture. I was surprised that Jake had never heard of a pull-out couch before.

"That's right," said Traci. "And it's a very comfortable design. We have one like it at home in the basement, and our overnight visitors have always told us it's the best night's sleep they've ever had.

Jake put his toys down on the couch and threw his arms around Zeke's waist. "Thanks, Dad! Thanks for bringing me to Canada! It's awesome!"

"We need to thank Clarissa and Traci," he replied. "They made it possible."

"Oh no need to thank us. It's our pleasure," said Traci.

"Thank you anyway!" insisted Jake. "This is the best ever!"

"You're welcome," said Traci. "Now, we just have to get your bags from the van, and then we'll let you settle in. It's been such a long day for the both of you. And just to let you know, the fridge and cupboards have been fully stocked and we'll be delivering groceries once a week. There's a linen closet and the bathroom has everything you'll need. If you find there is anything that we forgot, just phone me and I'll personally see that it's taken care of."

"Or you can ask me too," I added. "And if I don't have it on hand, I'll be happy to pick up things for you when I go shopping. Just knock on the backdoor anytime. I'm home most days and most evenings. There are times when I'll be at the university but other than that, I'm usually home."

"Thank you. Thank you so much," said Zeke. "Your generosity is overwhelming!"

"It's nothing," I tell him. "I'm just glad I could help out. These are difficult times and people need to help each other."

"Not everyone is so kind," replied Zeke.

Now I was feeling extra guilty that I had not done this sooner. "These are your keys," I said, offering them over. "There's one for this front door and there's one for the backdoor that leads out into the alley. Just use the front door though because it's much nicer. The backdoor is really just a fire exit. Also feel free to use the back-yard...which would be your front yard. There's plenty of room for Jake to play and I have some garden furniture that I'll put out. Make yourselves at home."

"Thanks," said Zeke taking the keys and jangling them in his hand. "Let me know if you need help with the furniture."

"It's alright," I tell him. "They're light pieces. I'll get them out of the shed tomorrow."

"Okay," said Traci to Zeke, "let's get your stuff from the van and you and Jake can get settled in."

"Yay!" exclaimed Jake who then ran out the door.

Zeke laughed and said, "I'd better go after him, or he'll be trying to drag those heavy suitcases through the yard by himself." He then disappeared out the door too.

With them gone, I turned to Traci and said, "They seem very nice."

"Aren't they adorable!" she happily chirped. "And you are doing such a good thing, Issa. Really, it's a wonderful thing you're doing! And remember, if there are any problems just call me and I'll fix it. But really, I don't see how you will have any problems at all. They really are good people, and of all the applicants we had, I think they are the perfect match for you."

The perfect match. What does that mean? Is such a thing even possible or is it simply a meaningless expression? What are we but confused and flawed individual spirits drawn to each other in a world that is in constant unpredictable flux. When we do come together, we come together clumsily. Awkwardly. Full of misunderstandings and miscommunications. Nothing ever fitting perfectly. We are not perfect, any of us, but then again at least we know the word. We know the word 'perfection' and, in some vague way, can somehow conceive of the idea. We are not perfect, and we have never witnessed anything perfect. But we are trying. And in the end, perhaps trying counts for an awful lot.

Eleven

"Oh, you have grown so dark since last we met," she cried. "Poor, poor thing. He is now destroying you even more quickly."

"Please," he pleaded. "I don't want to die! Please find a way to stop him! You must stop him!"

"I'm trying," she said. "Being with him on stage—singing with him used to help but now not even that seems to be doing much of anything anymore. Our awake-selves can be such monsters."

"Can you at least hold me?" he asked. "I know that will help a little."

She wrapped her arms tightly around him, and he settled into her. His light then glowed a tiny bit brighter. "Is that better?" she asked him.

"Yes," he replied. "It gives me hope. But I fear that once you are gone, it will start again. I don't know how to stop him."

"I wish we could write another song," she said. "That could help a lot. But your awake-self is too far gone to be able to connect in that way. It would only work if you both can feel it. He can't feel new songs anymore. Not real songs. The songs that change things."

"I feel so trapped," he cried. "Why is my awake-self so foolish—so selfish? I'm at his mercy, and he has no mercy."

"You should know that I am working on something," she told him. "There may be a way to make him change, but it's risky. It could mean the end of both of you. Do you understand this?"

He thought about it a moment and then replied, "If it's my only hope, it's my only hope. How can the risk of death matter when the alternative is death anyway?"

"That's very true and I'm glad you see that. But I do need your consent if I am to do anything."

"You have it," he said. "I agree to anything that might save me."

"Are you certain you want me to proceed with my plan even though it is very risky?"

"Yes, I am certain! Anything is better than this slow death. Feeling my light grow dimmer and dimmer and not being able to do anything about it, it's awful. If you know of a way to stop this, it must be done."

"Alright," she said. "It will take a little time to prepare. Many things have to be put into place. Calculations must be made. One thing out of alignment and you would both be lost. But I assure you, this is something I've done before successfully, and I believe I can do it again."

"As long as it saves me," he replied. "I just want to live. I want to keep on shining. I want life."

"Very well," she said, resting her head against his to try and comfort him. "I'll do my best. I won't abandon you. You were one of my early loves and that still means something. I will do whatever I can to try and save you. But I must go now and make those preparations. You are fading and there is no time to lose."

Then, just as she pulled away from him and was about to leave, she felt a sudden strange sensation. It was an odd feeling she had never quite felt before. Where was it coming from? It was not coming from her songbird. She knew that. No. There was another. There was another nearby. She then looked around and spotted a strange twinkle in the distance.

"Look there!" she exclaimed in surprise.

"Where?"

"Over there," she said.

He looked in the direction she indicated. "Is that a light?" he asked. "It looks like a light."

"Yes," she replied. "Someone is over there. I see him. I feel him too."

"But what is he doing here? This place is only for us. Is he trying to steal you from me?" he asked in concern.

She looked directly at this strange light and tried opening to him. Any other light would have come running over to her, but not him. In fact, he was blocking her. "He's trying to hide—trying to hide from me," she said. "But how is this even possible? How did someone make it into our dream? A dream that is just between you and me. This has never happened before!"

"You!" she then shouted at the stranger. "Who are you?" She began to move quickly in the direction of the light, leaving her songbird behind. The new light seemed startled, paused for a moment then turned and ran in the opposite direction. "Stop!" she yelled. "Stop and tell me who you are. How did you enter this dream? What are you doing here?"

She knew he heard her, but he didn't stop. He didn't even slow down. He just moved away even faster until he was out of sight.

At that point, she knew she had lost him. Outside of an individual dream, the pathways were infinite. Without knowing anything about him, there was no way to find him. No markers to follow. It was impossible to know where he could have gone. She stared off into the darkness hoping that he would reappear to explain himself, but he didn't.

"Where did he go?" asked a voice from behind her. She turned to see her songbird limping towards her.

"I don't know," she answered.

"What was that about?" he asked. "Who was that?"

"I have no idea," she replied. "Such a thing has never happened before. No one has ever infiltrated a dream between me and another. This is very strange."

"Do you think he'll come back?" he asked.

"I don't know, but I hope so. I want to be able to understand what has happened here. How he was able to do this. I also want to know what it is he wants."

"Perhaps he wants to write a song with you," he said.

"No, that's not it. It's something else entirely. I could feel it. There is something he wants, but I just don't know what it is."

"Well, whoever he was, he's gone now. Can you hold me again before you go? I don't want to be selfish like my awake-self, but I'm still very afraid."

"Of course, I will," she told him. "I'll help you increase your light a little more, and you try your best to hold on to it while I'm away. And rest assured, I'll be back as soon as I can, and I'll also try to hurry my plan along."

"Thank you, my beautiful love," he whispered softly. "I need you now more than ever."

∞◇∞

When I opened my eyes, the first thing I remembered was that distant light. The light that was trying to hide himself. How could I make sense of this? Who was he? What did he want? How on earth did he manage to find his way into my dream? If he appears again, I need to catch him and force him to explain. There is a sensitive balance to dreams that must be maintained. Is he a threat? Did he come to try and sabotage my work? Does any spirit even have that power? Just when I thought I knew everything about dreams, something like this happens.

I stretch out in my bed and say the same small prayer I say every morning. "Lift up the oppressed and cast down the wicked." This is how I pray not only because it is important to say those words aloud each day but also because sometimes, I do see evil in my dreams. Most people would call them nightmares. They see them as mere illusions from their unconscious most likely brought on by anxiety. But I know that's not the whole truth. Those visions are the real evil out there in the world. Those nightmares are the real thing. And the reason we see them is because we need to be there. We need to stand with those who witness evil or who are subjected to it. We help them face the terrible reality head-on. They are not alone because we are there. Within their very being. And hopefully that will be enough to make things a little more bearable. It's neither easy nor pleasant, but nightmares are often work that needs to be done.

I get out of bed, throw on my robe and go downstairs to my office. That is what I do first thing every morning. I go to my office and log onto my computer to see how my dreams may have affected the world. I need to witness things my dream-self has done. Part of me already knows that whatever was done was successful, but I need to see it in this world. I need to see it manifesting to reassure myself. Only then can I rejoice in the progress—in the battles won. That is what sustains me. Gives me hope. Keeps me going. I need to be reminded that what I am doing is important. And it is true that ever since my awake-self and dream-self have become more unified, I have been able to do greater things—much greater things.

This morning, I search for the word 'massacre'. Nothing relevant comes up. I try a few more search words but still nothing. I try again using a different search engine. Still nothing. There was no massacre anywhere in the world. It worked!

Last night after I left my songbird, I was quickly drawn to a place where my help was needed. Plans had been made and they were preparing. They were preparing for murder. Mass murder. I'm not even sure where it was. I'm not even sure who was to be killed or who was to do the killing. I only knew that it was wickedness and that it would be happening soon. The bombs were already being loaded.

That is when my dream-self called out for help. Calling out to the Light of Lights. "Remember your mercy, O Lord, and your steadfast love!" My dream-self does that sometimes. In extreme situations she cries out words from sacred texts. Perhaps there is an eternal sacredness in some words. They somehow hold an essence of the Holy that transcends worldly divisions. I wonder this because it always works. Whenever she pleads for help like that, help is given.

And then, I'm uncertain how it happened but the massacre was abruptly called off. It's all quite fuzzy now, the way dreams can be. Those in charge, those who had planned on killing thousands, had backed down. It may have been that better people among them found their conscience. Or it may have been that something happened to confuse those in power. Or it could have been a whole combination of things. I don't know exactly how it happened. All I knew for sure was that something had suddenly occurred which prevented it from going forward. The attack was called off. Mercy was given.

Leaning back in my chair, I took in a deep breath and thought about all those people. What I knew about them was limited but I did know that they had been in their land for a very long time. Those men, women and children would now go on living—living in their homes like their ancestors had lived for centuries. Evil was pushed back. Today was a good day, and it called for a celebration. Perhaps I would go to my favourite café and order a slice of their delicious homemade apple pie. When something important has been accomplished like that, when suffering and death have been averted in the world, I always give myself a secret little party. Sometimes I'll go on a little trip, or I'll treat myself to something delicious. A trip is out the of the question right now, but a treat is something I could do. Yes, some hot apple pie with a scoop of vanilla ice cream is just the thing for my secret little one person gala.

I was just about to shut down my computer and go have my morning shower when I noticed a new email in my in-box. It was from the university, so I opened it:

Dear Ms. Comfort,
It is with deep sorrow that we inform you of the passing of

Professor Wagner. Last Thursday, while visiting his daughter in the United States, the Professor was among a group of people who were attacked by an armed militia. Although, a small contingent of the Russian Army, who happened to be working as nearby support, was able to subdue the attackers and save many lives, Professor Wagner, tragically was not among the survivors.

Professor Edgar Wagner was a great asset to both the University and the Department of Philosophy and will be deeply missed by both staff and students.

All classes taught by Professor Wagner will be cancelled for the next two weeks and grief counsellors will be made available to all those requiring assistance.

Please contact us if you have any questions or concerns. We are here to fully support our students at this difficult time.

I stared at this email and found myself casually thinking "So, Wagner is gone".

What do I make of this? Am I supposed to feel something? Intellectually, I know that it was sad such a thing happened, but I felt nothing sitting there. The truth was that Professor Wagner will not be missed by me. There was nothing he did that I could see had any value. He was hard, judgmental and somewhat misogynist. But then again, he was a human being. Does that make me cold-hearted, or does that make me honest? Do other people lie about what they are really feeling when someone who was unkind to them passes away?

I had just saved thousands of lives. In that act, I treasured human life. Yet, many of them may have been like the Professor. Vain. Arrogant. Close-minded. Prejudiced. So, what is the difference?

Wagner was a man I knew. I heard his voice. I looked at his face. He looked at mine. He was loved by someone—by his daughter at least. And he's dead and I feel nothing.

Perhaps, it's about the potential that would be lost. For the people I saved, it's about a collective future secured. A community kept from being shattered more than it has been already. It's a pathway. An opening for all the individual lights to shine and to grow. It's the bigger picture. It's allowing for the possibility of an exodus out of darkness.

And I don't know what Wagner's light was like, but I suspect it was quite dull. And I'm not the judge of what is to be done with a dull light when the awake-self has depleted it. But what happens to such souls is not something I like to think about. I only know that sometimes terrible things happen to them...horrible things. If I could have helped Wagner when he was alive, I would have. But to him, I was an object of disdain. Something he wanted to go away or at the very least to subjugate. I guess I shouldn't feel too bad about not feeling anything for him. He had the power. He set the boundaries between us. All I could do was exist within that hostile space. How he related to me was his own choice and his choice alone. He gave me nothing to feel for. He blocked off all pathways.

It's then I decided I was not going to waste anymore time thinking about it. I shouldn't feel guilty for not feeling bad. No, I should reserve guilt for when it is justified. And I didn't believe it was justified in this instance. So instead, I decided to simply proceed with the day by concentrating on my thesis and all the other little everyday tasks that needed to be done. Also, I'd get out to enjoy some homemade apple pie.

Twelve

Just as I had walked into my kitchen to brew some after-dinner tea, there was a knock at the backdoor. I looked over and saw Zeke smiling and waving through the window.

These past two weeks I hadn't seen much of either Zeke or Jake. In the evening I noticed their light on, but they didn't seem to be around much in the day. I simply assumed they were busy working with the volunteers at the Refugee Project who would be helping them get adjusted.

I opened the door and smiled, "Hi Zeke. How are you?"

"Am I disturbing you, Clarissa?"

"No, not at all. Would you like to come in?"

"Thank you."

Zeke stepped inside and I closed the door behind him. "Would you like to sit down?" I asked him, gesturing toward the table and chairs.

"Thank you," he said again then went over, pulled out a chair and sat down. He seemed a little nervous as if he wasn't sure what to do or say next.

"Would you like something to drink?" I asked him. "I was just getting ready to make some tea for myself."

"Uh...do you have any coffee? Coffee would be nice, if it's not too much trouble."

"Yes, I have coffee and it's not too much trouble," I said as I went to the cupboard and pulled out my French coffee press and a small package of ground coffee I kept mainly for guests. I'm not much of a coffee drinker myself as caffeine keeps me awake at night.

"Are you and Jake settling in alright?" I asked, turning on the tap and putting water enough for two into the electric kettle.

"Yes. Yes, we are. The volunteers at the Project have been great. Traci especially has been so much help. She's been with us every step of the way. Jake's now enrolled in school and loving it, and they're helping me look for a job."

"That's wonderful!" I said as I pull out two cups from the cupboard. Opening a canister on the counter, I took out a chamomile teabag and placed it in one of the cups. "And are you liking the city?" I asked pouring some of the coffee into the press then turning to look at him and leaning my back against the counter.

"It's nice—peaceful. It's nice not to have to worry about what could be waiting around the corner."

"Where were you before this?" I asked, wondering if they were in a particularly violent area.

"Washington," he said. "Washington D.C."

"Was it bad there?"

"Let's just say it wasn't good. There was a lot of security around but there was also a reason for that. You just didn't know what was going to happen, and I worried every time I had to drop Jake off at school."

"That must have been difficult."

"It was unnerving a lot of the time. I mean, I'd never be able to leave Jake in the apartment watching a documentary like I'm doing now. He knows where I am by the way and he's a responsible boy. But this kind of freedom just wouldn't have been possible in Washington. Not with everything going on there."

"Well, I'm glad you're both here and safe in Canada," I said meaning it.

"So are we. I'm just so thankful you opened your home to us."

"It's nothing," I told him.

"Oh, it's something," he replied.

The water had now boiled so I turned back to face the counter then carefully poured some into the coffee press and teacup. "I haven't seen much of you or Jake since you moved in," I said, turning back to face him.

"It's been a real whirlwind," he said. "We've just been so busy. But it's good. We're happy to be here."

"That's nice to hear."

"Yes, Canada was definitely the right choice. There were other countries we could have applied to, but I think this is the best place for me and for Jake."

"I'm sure you made the right decision," I told him. "We have our problems too, but overall, it's a good country."

Zeke shifted in his chair and said, "You must be wondering about us. About Jake and me, and who we are. We are after all strangers living in your backyard and we do make an unusual looking father and son."

"It's not really any of my business," I replied. "You seem like nice people. That's all I care about."

"Still," he said. "You must have some curiosity. You must want to know our story. I would if I were you."

"Being curious isn't the same as believing one has a right to know someone's story. I don't have that right."

Turning back to the counter, I removed the teabag not wanting it to steep too long then put the coffee press and the two cups on a small tray. I carried them over to the table and sat down across from Zeke. "Would you like anything to eat? I have some cookies or maybe some fruit?" I asked.

"No, no thanks," he answered. "Just the coffee is fine."

"You're sure?"

"Jake and I had a big dinner. I only have room for coffee," he laughed then nervously tapped his fingers on the table.

"So, like I said, don't feel you have to explain yourself to me," I tried to assure him.

"You're a good person, Clarissa," he said. "I can see that. But would you mind me sharing our story with you anyway? You've been so good to let us stay here, and I think we owe it to you. It must have been strange to see us two show up on your doorstep."

"That's okay," I tell him. "You don't owe me anything. You don't need to feel obligated to share things that you don't want to share. You're Zeke and your son is Jake. That's all I need to know."

"But I want to," he said. "I'm a talker, you see. I need to talk. I need to share. It makes me feel better...makes me feel like things really matter. I'd like you to know our story. I'd like you to know who we are and how we came to be here."

"In that case, feel free to tell me whatever you would like. I'm all ears."

"Okay," he said, then paused to take in a deep breath before continuing. "First off...and I don't tell you this lightly, but I need to be completely honest with you. And I don't want you to accidentally hear it from anyone else and then have you think I was being deceptive. But I also don't want you to be alarmed or think badly of me when I tell you."

"Tell me what?" I asked, now becoming curious.

"Okay, cards on the table." He then took in another deep breath and said, "I used to work at the Pentagon."

"I see," I said not sure how to feel about it with everything that had happened. What exactly does it mean he worked for the Pentagon?

"Yes, you see, I'm an engineer. That's my profession. It's always been my profession. And I worked at the Pentagon for all of my career. I was recruited right out of school. But let me make this perfectly clear, I was not in any way, at all, involved in the making of the weapon. I had nothing to do with it or with the making any weapons for that matter. My job was always small things...mostly gadgets. Many of them silly gadgets. For example, we had this one general who'd lost his hand in a yachting accident. He had a drinking problem and did something stupid and lost his hand. Anyway, we spent a lot of time working on custom prosthetic replacements just for him. He'd request that these have all kinds of ridiculous things built into them. He thought of himself as some kind of Hollywood movie secret agent and wanted us to build crazy things like a hand that shoots lasers. What can I say? It was a job and it paid well. We did make him a hand with a built-in flashlight. It was a good flashlight."

I laughed then said, "Sorry but that is funny."

"No need to apologize. It is funny. Sometimes my job was completely ridiculous."

"I suppose a lot of people worked for the Pentagon," I said, trying to make him feel more comfortable.

"Yes," he replied. "A lot of people worked there; my wife, Tara included. We were both engineers working in the same department. That's where we met. We met at work and then we worked side by side for all the time we were together. Most couples couldn't do that—work all day together and then be together at home. But Tara and I weren't like most couples. We were closer than most."

Zeke went silent as he began to tear up. I quickly got up and grabbed a box of tissue from my pantry and placed it on the table in front of him. He pulled out two of them and wiped his eyes and nose. "I'm sorry," he said. "I didn't think I'd break down like that."

"You've got nothing to be sorry about," I assured him. "If it's too much, don't feel you have to go on. We can talk about other things."

He was then silent for a bit, so I took that moment to ask, "What do you take in your coffee?" as I plunged down the filter of the coffee press turning the murky water instantly to a dark rich brown.

"Just black," he told me as he took two more tissues and wiped his eyes some more. "Tara and I always took our coffee straight up." He tried to smile a little and I poured the coffee into his cup then placed it in front of him.

Holding out my hand, I said, "Let me throw out those tissues for you," as I could see he was feeling awkward holding on to them not wanting to set them on the table and unsure if he should stuff them in his pocket.

He apologetically handed me the bunched up tissues and I discarded them in the can under my sink.

Returning to the table, I sat down and picked up my tea. Only then did he pick up his cup. He blew on it a little and took a small sip. "Mmmm, that's good. Strong. Just what I needed," he said.

"I'm glad you like it," I told him. "As I'm not a big coffee drinker myself, I'm never sure of my coffee making skills."

"It's good," he assured me. "The best I've had in a long time."

I didn't know if he was telling the truth, but I appreciated the compliment.

"Tell me Clarissa, are you alright with this? Am I making you uncomfortable? I'll go if it's a problem. After all we barely know each other and here I am breaking down in front of you. If it's too much, I'll just leave."

"No, of course it's no problem," I told him. "You are no problem. If you need to talk, I'm quite happy to listen. Listening is one of my greatest talents. Speeches, I'm not so great at. But listening, I'm a pro."

"That's good to know. Thank you. I want to talk. I need to talk. It's how I feel better...talking."

"You tell me as much as you would like," I told him. "I'm listening. And if you need more tissue, I have plenty so don't feel embarrassed about that."

Zeke sighed and said, "Thanks. I appreciate it." He then took another sip of his coffee before continuing.

"So, about my beautiful Tara..." There he paused again and took in a deep breath. It was obvious how painful it was for him to talk about her. "Yes, my Tara.... Just to let you know, I didn't lose her in what they're calling 'the big accident'," he explained, "but we did lose both of our families...our entire families. We were from Florida, you see, and that's where they all were when it happened. Our mothers, our fathers, my brothers, her sister and brother, nieces, nephews— they were all there and we lost them all in one day."

"I'm so sorry," I tell him knowing that I could not even begin to imagine how devastating such a thing would be.

"Yes, they were all gone. In an instant, gone. And we were heart-broken to say the least," he sighed. "Just heartbroken. But on top of that we shared this survivor's guilt. You see, we should have been there. We were planning to be there that week but were held up by something at work. It wasn't even an important thing. It's just that someone in charge decided it was important, so we had to stay. We were expected in Orlando because my brother was getting married, and we were planning to be there a week early to be with family and help out. If the weapon had been deployed a week later...the week my brother was to be married, we would have gone with them."

Zeke was quiet for a moment, and I worried that he was wishing he had perished with his family. He must have those moments. Who wouldn't?

"So, after a few weeks," he continued, "when the whole damned country fell apart because of a decision made by a few fools with more power than brains, we decided to drive down there. It was what they were all doing. People from all over were travelling to the edge and holding memorials. They were coming together for support, and we felt a need to be a part of it. We needed to mourn somehow. So much lost...so much lost. The whole thing was just so incomprehensible.

"And going down there did help some. We talked with others who were going through the same hell as us, and we got to say good-bye to those we loved. We had a quiet little service with just us and we also participated in a memorial with a big crowd. It still hurt bad, but it hurt just a little bit less. And we still had each other.

"It was on our way back as we were travelling through Georgia that Tara saw Jake. He was such a skinny frail looking little thing, just out there begging on the streets. Things were bad everywhere and lots of parents were sending their kids out to beg by then, but Tara, for some reason, thought that this little guy was alone. And she was right. He was alone. His name wasn't Jake, it was Thor. His parents were extreme survivalists. They call themselves the Nordic Thunder. Do you know anything about the Nordic Thunder?"

"I'm not sure," I said. "But they sound familiar."

"Among the survivalist movements this group is the absolute worst. They mix ancient Nordic practices with that of the Spartans. They believe only the strong, or who they imagine are the strong, should be allowed to survive. When everything fell apart, they decided that Jake was a burden...that he was a weakling, so they dumped him. They drove into the city and just dumped him out on the street. They told him, that in the new world, he would only drag them down. The ironic thing is that that boy is smarter and stronger than the whole lot of them. Jake has a brilliant mind. And that is what was keeping him alive when we found him. He was living in a makeshift shelter in an ally and scrounging whatever he could find, often from the garbage. When he couldn't find anything to eat, he'd beg strangers for money. That's how we met him. He approached us begging for spare change."

"That's terrible!" I exclaimed. "How could anyone do something like that to their child—to any child?"

"It's beyond me how anyone could do that. But I can tell you that my Tara had the biggest heart a woman could ever have. She was a natural mother. Nurturing, kind. As soon as she saw him, she didn't even ask me," he laughed. "She just took that boy in, cleaned him up, fed him, and then decided for the both of us that we were taking him back to Washington. "We are going to adopt you," she told him. "We will be your mother and father." And that was that.

"Somewhere along the way back home, Jake decided he wanted to change his name. He said, he didn't like the name Thor and never liked it. He wanted to share a name with me, since I was his father now, but was worried that if he was also named Zeke people might start calling him Little Zeke and he didn't like that." Zeke chuckled. "So, I suggested that he might like my middle name, and he decided he liked it a lot. From then on, he became Jake."

"When we got back to Washington D.C., we still had a place there but with everything continuing to fall apart and with the American banks frozen, we weren't sure for how long we would survive. Nobody knew from day to day what was going to happen. That uncertainty was hard to live with.

"Tara and I had already been approved for adoption before everything fell apart so adopting Jake was quick and easy. Some government offices were still operating so we were able to file the appropriate paperwork. Without that, I don't know if I would have been able to get Jake across the Canadian border that easily.

"So, we lived there for while, and Jake was just such a wonderful blessing at such a difficult time. He gave us something else to think about other than our own pain. It was good for a while. The three of us became a real family.

"We wanted to get out of Washington for a lot of reasons but mainly because it was becoming a more dangerous place. There were too many militias wanting to target the government—what was left of the government anyway. So, we applied to join one of those Little Africa Sanctuaries. Have you heard of them?"

"I don't think I have," I replied.

"With so many dangerous militias about and a lot of them racist, many of my people began to organize for protection. One group created a foundation that worked to set up communities in abandoned or mostly abandoned towns. They called themselves The Little Africa Sanctuaries. These towns were created to provide safe havens for Black people to start over. It's a very well organized charity, and they are very thorough. You have to apply and go through a screening process before you're allowed to join a community. We told them straight up about Jake, but they were more than willing to accept him too. All three of us were set to go when Tara got sick. It was the YAMA-13 virus."

"She didn't get the vaccine?" I asked in surprise as I knew there was a massive push to ensure everyone was vaccinated and surely people working at the Pentagon would have been at the front of the line.

"But she did," he told me. "She got what she thought was the vaccine but remember how, shortly before the devastation, it was uncovered that the government was being sold fake vaccine along with the real vaccine. It turned out that Tara must have received one of the fake vials."

"Oh my God!" I exclaimed.

"God had nothing to do with what those devils did. Those greedy...! They killed my Tara!"

I could see that Zeke was ready to break down again and wasn't sure what to say. I didn't want to say the wrong thing. I didn't want to make it any worse.

He closed his eyes and took in a deep breath. We were both silent for what seemed like a long time before he opened his eyes and continued. "So, afterwards it just didn't seem right to go to Little Africa without Tara. That was our dream for the three of us. Being there would only constantly remind me of her absence. I just couldn't do it. I couldn't take that pain. That's when I applied to come to Canada. I thought it might be a good thing for me and Jake. A completely fresh start. Something new."

I felt like crying. How horrible, all this man and child have been through!

"And as for Jake—I'm just so grateful for him. He kept me going. I couldn't give up with him depending on me. Tara would never forgive me if I abandoned him like his parents did. When she was sick, she made me promise that no matter what happened, I'd keep going for Jake. He's God's mercy. A small skinny little mercy. But never underestimate the power of small mercies. Blessed be the small mercies."

We then sat there in silence sipping our drinks and trying to absorb the insanity of it all. All this anguish and suffering caused by something as cheap and stupid as the selfish arrogance of a few people.

"What's it all about, Clarissa?" Zeke suddenly asked. "Why is there so much pain in the world? Why are good-hearted people like Tara taken from us? Why is it so unfair? Why? What's it all about?"

O' the lamentations of Job! How do you answer Job's age old question when even God did not answer? Still, I had to say something. I had to give him something even if it wasn't much. "I wish I knew," I told him. "Is it to make us push harder for a painless and just world? Maybe to force us not take goodness for granted? Is it a test? I don't know. I just don't know. I wish I did. I wish I had real answers for you, Zeke. I really do."

"Well, that's not bad," he replied. "That's something isn't it? To make us push harder for a painless world and to not take goodness for granted. I'll hold on to that. It's better than nothing and it helps give it some meaning, and I need meaning more than ever these days. Thank you, Clarissa. I appreciate it."

Zeke then drank back the rest of his coffee and set his cup down in front of him. "Well, I'd best get back to Jake. His documentary should be ending soon. Although, he'll likely just start watching it again for the millionth time," he chuckled. "So anyway Clarissa, thank you again. To be honest I was feeling a little down tonight thinking about my Tara but now I'm feeling better. Talking always does that for me. Thanks for listening and for the coffee."

"You're very welcome," I tell him. "And if you or Jake need anything, just let me know. I'm here for you."

"You've already done enough by giving us a safe place to live. Without that, I don't know where we'd be. That's primary—a safe place. Everybody needs a safe place." He then got up and headed towards the door. I followed after.

He stepped outside, then turned and said, "Clarissa, I just want to say that I'm glad you didn't look down on me for working at the Pentagon. Many people would have said it's karma—that I deserved everything I got."

"Oh no!" I exclaimed. "Of course, you didn't deserve what happened to you. You didn't make that weapon and you certainly didn't deploy it. You were a victim the same as so many others. You, Tara, Jake and your families—you are all the victims of those once powerful people who made that cruel horrible decision. You did nothing wrong, Zeke. You are innocent."

Zeke smiled a little. "Thank you," he said. "I guess the high and mighty do teach us to carry around guilt for sins that aren't even ours just so they can walk around blame free. You're right. That's no way to live. That's letting them re-victimize me from inside my own mind and I'm not going to give power to those thoughts again. Thank you. You've given me a lot to think about. Have a good night."

"You as well," I said as he turned and headed towards the apartment. I closed the door and watched him through the window as he disappeared inside. At that moment all I could think about was Job's question to God:

What is mankind that you make so much of them,
that you give them so much attention,
that you examine them every morning
and test them every moment?

Are we? Are we being tested every moment? All of us? Every single moment? That's overwhelming to think about. So, was Job right? Is everything in our lives just a test? A testing of souls? Separating the spiritually weak from the spiritually strong? There is that. I know that from dreams. But at the same time, it can't be that simple. Suffering must never be embraced. It must be fought against. It must be deplored. It must be held in contempt and subjugated by the want of a painless world. Perhaps that's where Christianity went wrong. They obsessed over the suffering—turned suffering into a perverse fetish instead of something to be reviled. Instead of marvelling at the courage of Jesus to bring truth to power—at his strength to never fold and give in to temptation—to never loose sight of the glory and goodness of the Divine no matter how much darkness threatened him—at his ability to rise above everything, they focused on the suffering. And it was this that made them vulnerable to the same type of evil power structure that crucified their Messiah. It was this sickening embrace of affliction that corrupted them.

No. Suffering must always be rejected. No matter how much is heaped upon one person, it must be looked upon as a loathsome intruder. It must be seen as something to be eliminated. And it also must be carefully examined for its true source. For those who cause suffering should not be allowed to shirk the blame. They must carry their guilt and shame for what they have done. They must be punished, and the innocent must be allowed to walk free.

Thirteen

"We should just bomb them! All the trouble they're causing! They murdered the professor! Why don't we just bomb all those American troublemakers? Why do we put up with it?" declared Mr. Prove-the-existence-of-God. He seemed to have a couple of others agreeing with him.

I just sat in my chair at the table wondering if I should say something. If I did, would anything I had to say make any difference at all? Would I just be wasting my time and making myself a target for their anger? Giving them an opportunity to put the mark of scapegoat on my forehead? But I couldn't let this go on. Someone had to say something, so I said, "That's not very Christian," knowing he viewed himself as extremely devout.

Everyone turned their eyes on me, but I said nothing more. What I said was already enough to shut him up.

Suddenly, the door opened and a dark haired woman I had never seen before marched straight to the front of the classroom. Without a word, she took out a dark blue marker and began writing on the whiteboard. We all sat silently as we read:

There is a light over every person, and when two souls meet,

their lights come together, and a single light emerges from them to feel the universal generation as a sea, and oneself as a wave in it.
   -Martin Buber

She then turned to the class and announced, "Hello everyone. My name is Naomi Comay and I will be teaching this class going forward. Please let me begin by saying just how sorry I am about the tragic loss of your professor. Although I did not know Professor Wagner personally, being new to the faculty, I understand he was very well respected and liked by both students and staff. I also understand that this is a very challenging time, and if any you find yourself requiring grief counselling, I want to remind you that it is available through student services. If you have any other concerns as we go forward, please do not hesitate to let me know. You are in the unique situation of having now a third professor for this class, and you may find that my teaching style differs from both of your previous teachers, which of course could add even more challenges to this already difficult situation. If this is the case and you find it confusing, feel free to come and discuss it with me. It's not easy changing professors not once but twice. I will be emailing all of you information about my office hours, and you are welcome to drop by if you need to talk. Also, where is Clarissa?"

I raised my hand.

"Hello Clarissa," she said. "I've been asked to take over the many duties of Professor Wagner including that of your thesis advisor. I understand this is all very sudden so, take some time to think about it and if you have any questions, I'll be happy to answer them."

"Thank you," I smiled, knowing that there was nothing for me to think about.

"And if you can stay for a few moments after class, we can discuss a few things that may help with your decision."

"Certainly," I replied.

Pulling out a chair at the head of the table, she then sat down and said, "Now, as Dietrich Bonhoeffer once said, 'We are not to forget but to overcome'. So, let us not forget Professor Wagner as we move forward."

I looked over at Mr. Prove-the-existence-of-God and could see he was not happy at all. As for me, I was overjoyed.

∞◊∞

Hitting the rewind button, I watched again as my little Matty-Matt took his first wobbly steps then fell into my open waiting arms. "You are so amazing!" the young me exclaims as she wraps her arms tightly around her baby. "You walked, Matty-Matt! All by yourself! You walked! I'm so proud of you!"

There was then a close-up of Matty-Matt's happy chubby little face. My bottom lip began to tremble and then tears started streaming from my eyes. Why am I doing this to myself? Why am I watching these videos again? Why am I torturing myself?

If I hadn't caught sight of Jake playing in the backyard from my kitchen window, I wouldn't be here now—crumpled on the floor, my back against the couch—weeping uncontrollably.

If only I hadn't seen him out of the corner of my eye and, in that instant, thought 'it's Matty-Matt', I'd be busy now with other things. I'd be calm.

But no. I had seen a blur of boy running after a ball. Matty-Matt running after a ball as he had done hundreds of times before. Matty-Matt! Oh, my beautiful Matty-Matt!

And when that split second was over and I realized it was only Jake, it was too late. The wall I had carefully built between my brain and my heart had instantly crumbled and I could feel Matty-Matt wrapped tightly, painfully around my heart—squeezing it. And then I had to put the old video on. I had to see him again. I just had to.

"Who's my best boy? Who does Mommy love more than anyone else in the whole world?" chirps my young self. I look at her and envy her for all that unlimited hope. She doesn't know. She doesn't know what is to come or even how lost she really is in the moment. All she knows is the overwhelming love she feels for her child and how that makes the universe shine alive and bright. If only that were enough. If only her intense happiness in that moment could wipe out the future. But life isn't like that. So now here I am. On the floor. Broken and weeping.

"Come to Mommy, Matty-Matt! Come to Mommy!"

∞◊∞

"It's going to happen very soon," she told him. "I have put everything in place and there is a very good chance that this may save you."

"What if it doesn't? What if it doesn't save me?" he asked.

"It has to. This is our only option. It has to save you," she told him.

"If it doesn't," he said, "please know that I love you. I love you so deeply. So purely. All those times I bathed in the joy of your beautiful light. I'm just so sorry, I couldn't have been more for you. I'm sorry my awake-self is so terrible. If it had been just me, without my awake-self dragging me down, I would have shone a love that could heal not just me but the entire world. That is how much I love you."

She didn't know what to say. This was perhaps his final heart-felt declaration. It was both noble and sincere. If only love would have been enough. But somewhere between dreams and awake, love gets twisted around. It can't find its way. It's lost in the chasm between worlds. Love, our primary building block for life, is so formidable in our dreams and yet so fragile when we're awake.

"You just hold on," she said. "It's coming soon. Help is coming soon. It will come in the awake world. You won't know it's happened until it has

happened, and even then, you will wonder. Just have faith. Faith can carry you a long way."

"I'll try," he said. "I'll try to keep going. I'll try to have faith."

It was at that moment there was a strange flash from the corner of her eye. "It's him again!" she exclaimed.

"He's back? The interloper?"

"Yes, over there in the distance. Do you see him?"

"Yes," he replied. "I see him."

"I need to find out who he is and what it is he wants," she said. "I must go now."

"Why would that stranger matter? I need you. I need you, now. Please don't go!" he pleaded.

"I must. This is important. I feel it. His presence speaks of urgency. For him to be here, in a dream that is not his, is unprecedented. For him to do that twice, is a serious matter. I have to find out what is going on and what it is he wants. Don't worry. That which is planned will happen very soon. The next time we meet, things should have already begun to change for you. Have hope. Hold on to hope." She then gave him a small kiss and left him as she ran off in the direction of the light.

As she got closer, she slowed down afraid that coming up to him suddenly may make him run off again. She then stopped, still some distance away, and tried sensing his intent. This time he did not block her. He was now waiting for her.

She moved cautiously towards him although not because she was afraid. Light is not anything to ever be afraid of. She simply didn't want to move too quickly because she could feel his nervousness. If he dashed away again, she might never know what this was about.

When she was close enough to see him more clearly, she wondered at his brightness. He was one of the brightest lights she had ever encountered. She immediately felt drawn to him and found that she had to hold herself back from getting too close. "How did you get here?" she asked bluntly. "How did you get into my dream?"

"He's beneath you, you know. That dull little light," was his only reply.

"It's not about that," she admonished him. "Your light shines brightly. Because of that, you know things and you know it's not about that. It's about saving lights. We don't do that here. We don't judge like that."

"Yes, of course not," he said a little ashamed. "I don't know why I said that. Perhaps it was my awake-self leeching in."

"You know about your awake-self?" she asked in surprise. Never had she ever come across another light that knew about their awake-self.

"Yes," he replied a little sheepishly.

"Does your awake-self know about you? About dreams?"

"Yes," he answered again. "My awake-self knows the truth about the dreams, but it is new knowledge. I have only been fully aware for a very short time. I'm not sure how it happened but I think it was my awake-self that brought me to this awareness. I thought of you. I thought of how I needed to find you and somehow, I was brought here. It was him who helped me find you."

She wasn't sure what he was talking about but was trying her best to understand.

"That first time I saw you in a dream," he continued, "I was shocked. I was shocked that it had happened. I wanted so desperately to talk to you, but I became afraid. This was all so new and so strange. So, I ran away. But now I am back. I came back to find you again."

"You came to find me?" she asked. "How did your awake-self even know about me? You're a stranger. I don't know you in the awake-world. I'm certain of that. How could you possibly know me?"

He ignored her question and instead exclaimed, "I came to you because I need your help! You are the only one who can help me! Please you must help!"

"Help to do what?" she asked. "Your light is very bright. What do you need my help with?"

"It's not me," he replied. "It's not for me or my awake-self. It's much bigger than me. It's much bigger than both of us."

She was so confused. This entire situation was something she had never encountered before. Here was another being, like herself, whose awake-self and dream-self were aware of each other. Someone she did not know, claiming to know her. A stranger entering her dreams when she had always been the stranger entering the dreams of others. "What is it? What is so big that it brings you to me?" she asked.

"It's about the future of the awake-world. It's about stopping evil before it happens."

"What are you talking about?" she asked. "What kind of evil?"

"It's a second weapon. They have a second weapon," he told her. "And they intend to use it."

Fourteen

I could not finish my breakfast as those words kept turning in my head. "A second weapon." Someone has a second weapon, but who? And where was it? The news reports had always claimed that there was only one weapon created. They assured us that there was nothing more to fear.

Taking my dishes to the sink I thought back to before the devastation. I remembered how it had all unfolded and how no one saw it coming. How could they?

With the Cold War escalating to the point where nuclear war seemed a real possibility, the Americans suddenly had a huge change of heart. They began to seriously talk about bringing the world together where all nations worked in harmony with each other. They initiated a global campaign that included events and festivals – all in support of a unified planet. They set up the World Peace Talks including both Russia and China. It seemed such a hopeful time for everyone, and the world appeared to be on a new and better path.

They also began to close down many of their military bases abroad. Every week more and more troops were coming home to fanfare and celebration. It really seemed sincere—turning from violence and militarism to peace and democracy. As a well-publicized goodwill gesture, they even evacuated Guantanamo. The world was elated. Finally, there would be a real movement towards security and safety for everyone. No more living under the threat of nuclear annihilation. This was a new age.

What no one knew was that there were dark horrible forces on the move. The Americans had secretly developed a new weapon of mass destruction—a seismic weapon. I'm not exactly sure of the specifics of how it worked but it was designed to cause earthquakes and tsunamis. The purpose was to weaken other nations through these supposed natural disasters to the point where they could be completely dominated.

Because of their long-standing animosity towards Cuba, the U.S. decided that would be their first target. Also, because it was an island, they believed the weapon could be easily deployed there. It would be planted underwater not far off the coast and Cuba could be basically shaken into submission. They didn't intend to destroy the entire land mass but merely to cause enough death and devastation to bring the nation to their knees. They wanted complete control no matter what the cost.

The U.S. had become increasingly frustrated that they no longer controlled areas of the world they had previously dominated. They were bitter beyond reason and wanted to prove that they were still the greatest force—the most powerful nation on earth. Cuba would be their new Hiroshima. They would destroy it without risk.

All this was planned to be done covertly, of course. They didn't want other nations to know immediately in case some of them banded against them or tried to retaliate. Also, they were still concerned about their image. And this was only the first stage of their plan. That's why seismic disruption was their primary choice of attack. A nuclear bomb would be obvious and bring immediate retaliation, but with the seismic weapon they could claim that it was simply an act of God. They could claim innocence. At least until they had gained enough power in the world that it was safe for them to reveal the truth.

After Cuba had been dealt with, they had a master plan in place for gaining complete U.S. hegemony. The details of that plan had been trickling out daily in the International Criminal Court trial. It involved every nation on earth.

So much time, effort and money had been spent on the weapon, but it had one significant flaw. Everything hinged on it working effectively. What they didn't understand was, just because their weapon worked in theory and in small tests, it did not mean that it would work in the real world and on a such a large scale. They were too arrogant to even consider the complexity and mystery of the tectonic plates. All they wanted was to destroy those they perceived as their enemies and were blind to the idea that they would not be successful.

When they detonated the weapon in those dark ocean depths, the Bahamas, Florida, a large section of Georgia and the coast of South Carolina instantly cracked apart like shattered eggs. There was no warning, just instant 'BOOM'. It was then that the sea came pouring in. Leviathan swallowing up the broken land and all life upon it. Now, where once people laughed and loved, there was nothing...only the raging sea covering a mass graveyard.

The weapon also resulted in seismic activity in other places within the U.S. There were several eruptions in Yellowstone Park, and because of that, parts of Montana, Idaho, and Wyoming had to be evacuated. Those people will never be able to return to their homes. Not in their lifetime. The area is considered too unstable until they know more about the long-term effects.

Ironically Cuba remained completely untouched. Not so much as a stone was moved from its place on that tropical island.

After the weapon was deployed, the United States fell into complete chaos in a matter of weeks with the United Nations having to step in to try and restore some degree of order. And almost immediately people began to talk. Racked with horrible guilt, scientists and others came forward to confess and let the world know the truth. The U.S. had created a seismic weapon and, in deploying it, had essentially destroyed itself.

The President, along with all the major players in his administration, were arrested and eventually sent to face charges in the Hague. An interim government was quickly put into place but with the country so fractured, that government had little power. It was finally decided that it would be nearly impossible to try and put the U.S. back together again and that it should be completely dismantled and divided up between Canada and Mexico. The division would be overseen by the U.N. And so, that's where we are now. The nations of the world trying to somehow clean up the worst man-made disaster in human history.

And knowing all that, I was now faced with some horrible knowledge. That stranger in my dreams telling me there was a second weapon. And I know he can't be lying. The awake world is full of liars...constant, constant liars, but in the dreamworld, we are all naked. There is no room for lies. Your light either shines bright or it shines dull. That's it. You are seen as exactly who you are. No one can fake it in the realm of the non-temporal. He wasn't lying. There is indeed a second weapon, and someone out there intends to use it.

∞◊∞

"What is wrong?" he cried as he walked towards her carrying a lifeless body in his arms. "Who is he? Why am I carrying him? Is he dead? What does this mean? Will I soon be dead too? Please tell me what this means!"

"It's alright," she tried to reassure him. "It's your awake-self as he would appear in dreams. And he's not dead. He's just in a coma."

"A coma? I don't understand," he pleaded. "This is all too confusing."

"I realize that. It's about what has happened in the awake world. There was an accident," she explained. "Your awake-self was in a car accident and is now in a temporary coma."

"So, he is not dead? And I am not about to die?"

"No, you are both alive."

"Was this the plan you spoke of?" he asked. "The last time we met you talked about a plan."

"Yes, this was the plan. It took a little time because I had to put guardians in place."

"Guardians?"

"Guardians are those who no longer have awake-selves. They are lights that were bright enough not to die with the body. I had to put them in place around your awake-self to protect him. This was done so that he would not be killed in the accident. He is badly wounded but he's not dead."

"Guardians? What guardians? I've never seen any guardians before?"

"Sometimes you do," she told him, "But you just don't realize who you are seeing. The guardians are mostly the souls of people your awake-self once knew. Mothers. Fathers. Some are even ancestors who lived and died long before your awake-self was born. They protect those once connected to them whenever they can. And there are others whom your awake-self was never connected as family but who shared a common experience in life. Guardians are plentiful and everywhere. Everywhere they are allowed to be."

"So, if I understand it, my awake-self is still alive because guardians protected him?"

"Yes, this is correct."

"Then please tell me, what do I do now?" he asked. "Is there something I should be doing now other than just carrying him around? Is there a way to try and wake him? How can I help myself?"

"No, there is nothing else you need to do. You just need to be patient. He will eventually regain consciousness and when he does, he will simply disappear from your arms. You won't even necessarily notice at first but then you will realize that you are no longer carrying him. At that point, your awake-self will be interacting in the world again and things should start happening. If this plan works, your light should no longer be fading, and you should actually begin to shine a little brighter."

"I'm so glad," he sighed in relief, as he held the body tighter in his arms. "I just want this to be over. It's been so frightening knowing that I was dying and feeling so helpless to stop it. Thank you! Thank you for all you've done! You are love! You are life! I owe everything to you! Oh, beautiful, beautiful light how blessed I am that you found me! How blessed I am that you gave me song!"

His declarations of love and gratitude warmed her, and she felt happy she had saved him. At least there was a good chance she had saved him. Only time would tell if this were true.

As she prepared to kiss him to help his light along, they were suddenly interrupted by a flash in the distance.

"It's him again!" she exclaimed realizing who it was. "I must go. It's extremely important that I talk to him."

"I wish you could stay a little longer. I feel so much better when you here with me and I don't really like being left alone with him," he said indicating to the body in his arms. "How do you fully face yourself...forgive yourself when he did so much damage? I feel confused."

"I wouldn't leave so soon if this wasn't urgent," she explained. "But there is an urgency in this. It's imperative that I talk with him."

'Yes, of course," he sighed. "You know more than me and I know that when you say it is important, it is important. And I do feel stable now with my awake-self in a coma. He's not making me any darker. I'll be fine until you come back."

"I know you will," she said, giving him a quick kiss on his forehead. "I'll come back to check on you as soon as I can." She then turned and ran in the direction of the strange light.

∞◇∞

As she approached the light, she noticed again how brightly he shone. So much brighter than any light she'd ever seen before. Moving closer, it amazed her how warm and inviting his presence felt. It was wonderful wading into his glow. This was a new experience for her. Prior to this she had only ever encountered much dimmer lights, and her focus was mainly on saving them. This was so different. He didn't need saving. Instead, his essence washed over her with a sense of freedom and peace. Was this what the dimmer lights felt when she came near them? Is that why they always begged her to return? But there was no time to think too much about that now. There were important matters to be discussed.

"You told me there was a second weapon," she said, getting straight to the point.

"Yes, this is true," he replied. "There is a second weapon."

"How do you know this and what is it you want from me?"

He hesitated for a moment and then said, "I need to be honest with you, Clarissa."

"You know my awake name?!" she exclaimed in alarm.

"Yes. Yes, I do," he confessed. "It's because of knowing your awake-self that I found you here."

"Do I know you in the awake world? I'm sure I don't. I don't know you," she said more confused than ever.

"This is true," he answered. "You don't know me, but I know you."

"You know me? How do you know me? Tell me how you know me!" she demanded.

He sighed and she could feel his reluctance. He didn't want to tell her the truth, but at the same time he knew he had to. "If I tell you how it is I know you, you may not help me," he said. "And if you don't help me, I might not be able to stop them. They might detonate the weapon."

"If it meant stopping death and destruction in the awake world then I

would have to help you," she told him. "I'd have no choice. That is who I am, and I can be no other. So, tell me how is it that you know me?"

He looked down pausing for a second and seeming ashamed. He then lifted his head, looked straight at her and confessed, "I'm the CIA agent who has been spying on you for years."

"The what?!" She couldn't believe what he had just told her.

"Well of course, an ex-CIA agent now, as the CIA has been disbanded. And it was your awake-self. I spied on your awake-self...on Clarissa. At that time, I did not know about you or this world. Only recently did I come to know the truth about dreams."

For a moment, she just couldn't comprehend it at all. How could any of it be real? His light...his light shone so brightly. How could his light be so bright if he had done something so despicable in his awake-life?

"You know I'm not lying," he told her. "We can't lie to each other here. In this place we are revealed to each other."

"I...I don't understand," she said. "Why would a CIA agent even spy on someone like my awake-self? My awake-life is so boring."

"It was about the things you said on the internet," he explained. "There were people who didn't like the things that you had to say. You and other people like you. Names were gathered and then sent to our department. Yours was among them."

"Why?" she asked. "What could Clarissa have possibly said to interest the CIA?"

"You were just one of many. It didn't take much to get on the list. Those who were critical of the U.S. government and their policies went on the list. You were among millions. The entire thing was ridiculous."

"So, if you know my awake name, what else do you know about me?"

"I know most things about your awake life. I know about your son?"

She felt a knife in her heart. Even though he was Clarissa's son, she still felt the pain.

"I'm sorry," he said. "I can feel your heartache. I'm not sure how, but I can feel how much it hurts you – hurts Clarissa. I wish I could lie to you

so you wouldn't know what I did. I wish I could tell you a made-up story. But neither one of us can lie here."

"What's your awake name?" she demanded. "The least you can do is tell me that."

"It's Jonah—Jonah Ellis."

"Well Jonah Ellis, you need to tell me more. I need to understand what all this means. I have so many questions."

"I can't right now," Jonah replied. "I need to wake up soon. They are expecting me, and I mustn't be late. I can't do even the slightest thing that might make them suspicious."

Before she could say anything else, he quickly said, "I'm sorry, Clarissa. I'm sorry about the past and all that I've done. Later I'll be able to explain in more detail, but right now, I have to go. Please don't be angry with me. I need you. So many lives are depending on us. Please stay open to me so I can find you again. I need your help." It was then that he suddenly dashed away and disappeared into the darkness.

Finding herself now alone, she tried to understand all that had just happened. It was unnerving to say the least. Never had she ever been that confused in the dreamworld. This was a world she knew better than the awake world. The awake world was full of confusion, deceptions and masquerades. The dreamworld, on the other hand, was honest and infinite —full of winding paths and billions of wandering lights looking to realize their full potentials. She found the kind of hope there that she couldn't find in the awake world. Now everything had been turned upside down. Here was someone, like her, whose awake-self and dream-self were well aware of each other. But this was not just anyone. This was someone who would be her enemy in the awake world.

Fifteen

"Clarissa!"

I turned around and was surprised to see Zeke hurrying up to me. "Hi Zeke," I said wondering what he was doing on campus.

"Are you going to or coming from class?" he asked with a big smile. He was obviously feeling very glad to bump into me. It was then that I realized, not only was I his sponsor, but I had become one of his only friends in a new and strange country. That was more responsibility than I had been expecting and I wasn't quite sure what to think about it. My initial plan to keep my sponsored family at an emotional distance did not seem to be working very well.

"I just finished class and was debating on whether or not I should spend some time in the library or just go home," I answered.

"If you have some spare time, would you like to go for coffee? To be honest, I need to unwind a little. I've just been to my first job interview. An important one here at the university. It was only a preliminary interview and I think it went alright. It's been a very long time since I had to do that. I was so nervous. I just hope I was able to hide it. I'm usually much more confident."

"That's fantastic that you've had your first interview already and I'm sure you made a great impression," I said, trying to reassure him. "Also, I'd love to go for coffee. There's a little café just around the corner. Personally, I've never tried their coffee, but I've heard people rave about it."

"Sounds like just the thing!" he happily exclaimed.

As we headed in the direction of the café, I asked him, "So, you've applied for a position at the university?"

"Yes," he said. "The Refugee Project set it up for me. They have a program that tries to match applicants with the most suitable job opportunities. This is for a teaching position. I've never taught before, but I know I can do it. It would also involve some research work in robotics which is my area of expertise."

"That sounds wonderful!" I said as we reached the café. He opened the door for me, and I walked in.

"Where would you prefer to sit?" he asked.

"The table near the window is nice," I replied. "Is that alright for you?"

"Sounds good. The window seat is always the best in the house," he said, gesturing for me to go ahead of him.

I walked over, set my laptop bag down on the floor beside the chair then turned to Zeke.

"What can I get you?" he asked before I could offer.

"Oh, let me get these," I said not wanting him to be out of pocket.

"No, I insist. You've done enough for me already. Just sit down and tell me, what you would like."

Even though I knew that he was on a very limited budget, his income being only a small allowance from the Refugee Project, I could also see that this was a matter of pride for him. He had just been to his first interview and needed to hold onto a feeling of confidence and control. I had to forget about the money and allow him this.

"Well, if you insist, a lemon tea would be lovely," I answered then pulled out the chair and sat down.

"Lemon tea, it is. And of course, I'll be having a nice strong cup of coffee. I need it. Be back in a minute."

As I sat alone looking out the window, I thought about the class I had just finished. It had been such a welcome change. The professor was really fuelling some interesting conversations and we were no longer being marked on simple participation. When someone asked about it, she said that it only encourages meaningless input and that she preferred we not feel pressured to fill the space with random words. Because of that, Mr. Prove-the-existence-of-God was mostly silent now which was an improvement.

Casually watching people walk by the café while paying no real attention to any of them, I suddenly caught a glimpse of someone familiar. By the time it dawned on me who it was, it was too late to try and hide. He saw me, smiled and waved. He then headed straight for the door.

"Clarissa!" Crawford exclaimed as he walked over to my table.

"Hello," I said, trying my best to be polite and not sure what to say next.

He was just about to sit down on the chair opposite mine when Zeke appeared carrying the drinks. He set them on the table then turned and smiled at Crawford. Before I had a chance to introduce them, he jumped straight in. "Hi, I'm Zeke."

Crawford did not smile back and paused a moment before saying, "How do you do? I am Professor Crawford Kravitz."

"Crawford works here in the Art History Department," I explained, trying to smooth over the awkwardness of it all.

"I might soon be working here myself," said Zeke who seemed to be enjoying the situation.

"Oh, really," said Crawford who then looked over at me. He was obviously not happy.

Zeke then picked up his coffee and took a sip. "You were right Clarissa. This is the good stuff,"

Before I could say anything more, Crawford suddenly said, "Well, I don't want to intrude, and I can see now why you were too busy to meet with me. So, I'll just let you alone with your young man and be off." He then abruptly turned and left in a huff.

"Is he your ex?" Zeke asked as he sat down.

"Oh no!" I exclaimed, feeling a little embarrassed at the thought. "No, we were never together. One time we met for coffee and that was it. He's been texting me for weeks trying to arrange a date, and I've been trying to gently let him know that I'm not interested. He hasn't been getting the message though and I wasn't sure what to do to make him understand."

"I think he understands now," laughed Zeke.

"One can only hope," I said.

"I just don't know why you wouldn't want to go out with him again. He would have had me at that purple scarf," Zeke said, making me laugh.

I removed the tea strainer from my cup and placed it on the saucer. I then sipped my tea, its warm tarty flavor passing over my tongue.

"Tea good?" he asked.

"Yes, it is. Thank you," I replied.

He then said, "Anyway, I'm so glad I ran into you, and not just because you're such great company but also because...and I'm being totally upfront with you, I do have something I wanted to ask."

"What is it?" He seemed so hesitant making me wonder what it could possibly be.

"You've done so much for me and Jake already, but I need to ask a favour of you? Just know, I wouldn't ask if it wasn't important."

"Of course, I'll help," I told him. "Whatever you need I'll help."

"Okay...so, as I said, the interview today was just preliminary. This coming Saturday they want me to come in for what amounts to a series of interviews with a number of different people. I think because of where I used to work, they're being extra cautious. The entire process will go from nine in the morning to about four in the afternoon."

"That is a very long process," I said.

"Yes. Yes, it is. The problem, you see, is that Jake will be home during that time, so he needs an adult to watch him. I could get someone through the Refugee Project, but they'd be a stranger. Now that wouldn't ordinarily be a problem, but Saturday, you see, is Jake's birthday. Normally, I'd be there for him no matter what, but these interviews are crucial if we're going to have a future in Canada. I just can't pass this up. I thought that, because he knows you and trusts you, it would be easier on him if you could look after him. He's just been through so much already and I don't want to do anything to make it worse. Would you be able to watch him, please?"

"Oh, of course!" I said without hesitation, although I secretly worried. Having Jake around was already making me think too much about Matty. Entertaining Jake on his birthday could be a challenge. It might just be a painful reminder of birthdays that were and of birthdays that weren't. "Of course, I'll watch Jake for you. I didn't have anything planned for Saturday anyway other than doing a little housework and it's nice to have an excuse from doing that. It's no problem at all. I'll take care of Jake."

"Oh, that's great!" exclaimed Zeke. "That's just great you can help us out! I was so worried about leaving him alone on his birthday. Tara used to put so much into making him feel special. She'd decorate and have loads of surprises. His biological parents never really celebrated his birthday. Instead, they'd put him through a series of physical challenges. If he passed the tests, then he got to eat dinner. The whole thing was cruel. It made Jake so happy to finally have his birthday celebrated like an ordinary kid."

Poor Jake, I thought, knowing that I'd have to put my feelings aside and be strong for him. I couldn't let that boy down.

"After the interviews, I'll be able to celebrate with him," Zeke said. "I can't do it as well as Tara, but I'll cook his favourite meal, give him his presents and then we'll have the special cake I ordered. I just need help with those few hours during the day."

"I'm sure Jake is going to love all the things you have planned, and I'll keep him entertained in the daytime. Maybe we'll go to amusement park or the museum. You don't have to worry about anything. You just concentrate on those interviews."

"Thanks, Clarissa! This really takes a load off my mind. The last thing I want is for Jake to feel abandoned on his birthday. He was so badly abused and then losing Tara. It's all still so hard on him."

"Well, between your efforts and mine, I think we can make sure he has a wonderful birthday," I told him. "If you like, I'll decorate the yard—order balloons. That sort of thing."

"He'd like that," replied Zeke. "And that would be so generous of you. Thanks!"

"No problem at all," I said. "It'll be fun."

Despite my personal concerns, I reminded myself that this was a good thing to have happened. The best kind of distraction. The kind where you get to do something for someone else. The meaningful distraction. I wish there were more of those in my life. But is that greedy? The desire to help others is sometimes just another form of greed. I've seen it. The want to fill your ego with self-importance. Play the saviour. There's a fine line between the selfless good deed and plain old self-indulgence. And it's not always easy to guess where that line is. But so many things in life are fine lines. I suppose it takes constant reminding to continuously re-examine everything no matter how emotionally exhausting that may be. That's the only way to help ensure you always stay on the good side of that line.

∞◊∞

He came bounding up to her and happily chirped, "Oh look! Look at me! I'm no longer burdened with carrying him and I'm brighter! I'm so much brighter!"

"Yes, you are," she agreed, happy to see him once again so full of hope.

"You did it for me! I love you more than ever!"

"I'm glad. I'm glad I could help. We've known each other for a long time. I didn't want to see you fade away."

"This means he's awake and healing. Is that right? Am I right about that?"

"Yes, he is awake and healing. Although at this point it's unclear whether or not he'll sing again. But none of that matters. It's a better path he's on and how that is giving you strength is the important thing."

"Will I be able to write a song with you again?" he asked. "If I am brighter, will I have what I need to write a song? It would be so wonderful if I could. Even if he can't sing again, I could still write."

"I don't know," she answered him truthfully. "Perhaps. But even though you are brighter now than before when you were fading away, you are still far behind what you used to be. Also, my light has grown over the years. I am much more than I was when I first came to you all that time ago. A connection like that may no longer be possible even if you do grow brighter."

"That makes me so sad," he wept. "I lost you, didn't I? The greatest love of my life and I lost you because I couldn't keep up. My awake-self was not strong enough. Oh, my angel, my angel, my angel, my angel! Where have you gone? A part of me has been ripped away!"

She smiled, "Do you think of the word 'angel' often these days?"

"All the time. Why?"

"It's not 'angel'. It's Angela," she explained. "Angela was the girl your awake-self left behind. She supported you during those early years and, in so many ways, helped make your career possible. Your awake-self, blinded by the trappings of money and fame, left her behind. When the accident happened, she came to help him. She came back into his life, and it was

her face he saw when he woke up. That old love was reawakened in that moment, and it's that love that stopped him from killing you."

"Angel, Angela, Angel. Yes, I believe what you say. I feel it is true. I am alive thanks to Angela. Thanks to you bringing Angela to him. But I still love you more than anyone! You are my saviour! How could I not love you more?"

She smiled at him, and he glowed a little brighter. "You will be fine for a long time now," she told him. "But I'll still come by to see you when I can. Perhaps, if he heals well, we can even sing together again one day."

"That would be so wonderful!" he exclaimed. "I will wait for you. I will wait forever for you. You are all I ever want and all I ever will want. My everything. My everything."

Softly reaching out and touching his hand, she watched as her touch made him glow even brighter. He was no longer fading. He would go on. He was saved. Barring something horrible happening he was safe from forever death. And by the power of salvation, light and love have been increased in the world. Hope and possibility have been birthed. All things were better because of it. "Take care," she softly whispered into his ear then dashed away.

Sixteen

"Issa, it's me Traci."

I don't know why she always did that. I knew her voice. I always knew it was her and she knew that. But for some reason she always felt the need to introduce herself, and it made me chuckle every time.

"Hello, Traci. What's up?"

"Well, I don't want to pry. And I wouldn't ask but you are my best friend and best friends have to look out for each other. And I want to tread delicately here. And maybe it's none of my business, so I hope you won't get mad."

"What are you talking about Traci? Just tell me what it is."

I could hear her sigh on the other end of the phone and then she said, "Theo and I decided to eat out last night and who did we happened to bump into but Crawford."

"You did?" I laughed wondering where this was going.

"He kind of mentioned you and suggested I should be worried."

"Really? And why does Crawford think you should be worried for me?"

"I don't know how to put this, so I'll just say it outright. He said you were dating a much younger man and suggested that the man was some type of gold-digger—that he was trouble."

I laughed. "Oh Traci, he saw me having coffee with Zeke. I don't know where he got the idea that I was dating a gold-digger. That man has far too much imagination."

"So, you aren't dating a younger man?" she asked.

"Of course not."

"Oh," she said, sounding a little disappointed. I secretly laughed about that.

"Zeke had finished a job interview at the university, and I had just finished my class," I explained. "We ran into each other and had coffee. Crawford happened by and then became all whiny because I was with Zeke, and he assumed too much. It's all so stupid—so childish. Also, the fact that he thought a younger man would be dating me only for my money is kind of insulting. Not to mention his disapproval is very ironic coming from someone like him. And then, to assume something like that about Zeke sounds a little racist. If you ever run into that man again, just ignore anything he has to say."

"So, it was just Zeke?"

"Yes, it was just Zeke."

"Well, I suppose I can see how Crawford might have gotten the wrong idea. The dating part, I mean. You could possibly be dating. After all, Zeke's not really all that much younger than you and he is very handsome," Traci said.

"Just stop right there Ms. I-want-a-romantic-ending-every-time. I will agree that Zeke is ridiculously handsome, but he is also a little too young for me—not to mention that the poor man is in very deep mourning for the love of his life. That's just not going to happen. We are friends, and friends are a good thing. I like having friends."

"Yes, of course," said Traci, "you are just friends. Oh, you know me. Sometimes I just get carried away. I just want you to be happy, Clarissa. I really do."

"I am happy. I'm happy with my life the way it is."

"Okay," she said, not sounding completely convinced.

Traci had a highly developed empathic intelligence. I knew she always sensed there was something painful I carried with me. But I also knew that she only assumed it was loneliness. I suppose it's because that is what she feared the most. She had no idea that I had conquered loneliness years ago. Being without a partner didn't bother me at all. I was okay with being solitary. Paul Tillich once said, "Loneliness expresses the pain of being alone and solitude expresses the glory of being alone." I had reached the place of solitude —well mostly. There were of course moments, but such moments also happen for people who are not alone.

And I couldn't tell her the truth of what really pained me—that thing she sensed. I couldn't tell her about the secret burden I carried. Traci was a safe place, away from all that. If I brought that in, where would I find sanctuary? She could never know about Matty. No one who knew me now could ever know about Matty.

∞◊∞

Jake sat on my living room couch watching a children's TV channel. I got the sense that he wasn't even really watching it. He just wanted to sit there and stare and try not to feel anything. "Are you sure you don't want to go somewhere?" I asked again, hoping I could find something that would cheer him up. "There's the amusement park or the aquarium or the museum. They have mummies there. Anywhere you want to go."

"No thanks," he said not taking his eyes from the TV.

"I have a present for you," I told him hoping that would help. "Would you like to open it now?"

"That's okay," he replied. "I just wanna wait for my dad to get back."

I could see that nothing was working. Zeke was right to be worried about him.

After his dad had left for the interview, I had a service come in and professionally decorate the backyard with balloons and streamers as a surprise. But when I brought him outside to show him, it seemed to make everything worse. I think it only reminded him of Tara and what he had lost.

"But it's your birthday, Jake," I said. "It's *your* special day. Wouldn't you like to do something special to celebrate? Just name it and we'll do it. Anything you like."

He turned from the TV and said, "That's what my mom said. She called it my special day. My real mom—the one married to Zeke. She's my only real mom. The other one was my fake mom because she wasn't a real mom. I wish she was here now. My real mom, not my fake mom."

My heart broke for him. To find such love and comfort in his adopted mother and then to have that ripped from him. It was tragic.

"Why did she have to die? Why?" he asked, tearing up.

"I'm so sorry Jake. I'm so sorry she's not here with you today. I can see how much you miss her."

"Dad says she's an angel now. Do you believe in angels?" he asked me.

"Yes," I told him. "I most certainly do believe in angels."

"Do you think my mom is an angel?"

"I know your mom is an angel."

"How do you know that?"

"Because," I explained, "why wouldn't she be? She was an angel in life—full of love for your dad and for you. When she was such an angel in life, why would she not be an angel in the other world? While she was in this world, she put so much of her love into you and into your dad. When she left, that love not only stayed but it grew. It grew between you and your dad. You both had to double your love for each other to fill that empty space she left behind.

She took two people and made them love twice as much. That's one of the magical things angels do. They make people love extra hard. And it's love that makes people strong enough to become angels."

"Do you think she can see me?" he asked. "Even if I can't see her."

"Yes, I'm sure she watches you all the time. She makes sure that you're okay. She watches over both you and your dad."

"I just wish I could see her," he said sadly, turning back to the TV.

It was then that I suddenly had an idea. It was not something I wanted to do. In fact, it was the last thing I wanted to do, but this little boy was suffering and needed a distraction, and this was the only distraction I could think of.

"Jake, did you know that this house has a secret basement room that I've never even been in," I told him.

He turned from the TV. "Really?"

"Yes, it does. I bought the house from a very mysterious old woman. She had already left to go live in a nursing home, so I personally never met her, but neighbours said that she was very strange, and a few of them were even frightened of her. They said that she knew things—magical things. When I first looked at the house, I did inspect the basement and noticed a strange door, but it was locked, and no one had the key. I thought maybe I'd break it open when I moved in but then, once I was living here, I just never felt comfortable doing that. I mean, I don't know what's in that room. But then a few weeks ago, I found a key in the back of a cupboard, and I think it's the key for the secret room. I did take it to the basement and put it in the keyhole, and it does seem to fit, but I couldn't bring myself to open it. I'm just too nervous. What could be in that room, Jake? What could be hidden there?"

"I'm brave!" declared Jake. "I'll go look for you!"

"Really? You would do that for me? You are definitely braver than I am. I'll tell you what. Why don't we turn off that TV and we'll go together? I really need someone brave like you to help me."

Jake switched off the TV and jumped off the couch. We then headed for the basement stairs. As we descended, I just hoped the entire thing wouldn't be too overwhelming. I couldn't break down in front of this child. He was already having a bad day without seeing that. No, I had to be strong. I needed to give this little boy, who had suffered so much, a happy birthday and if this was the only way then I had to do it. I had to sacrifice.

"Are you okay, Clarissa?" Jake asked. "You're not too scared, are you?"

"I'm just glad you're here Jake. You being here, makes me feel better."

When we reached the bottom of the stairs, I switched on the hallway light. "It's that door over there. Do you see it?" I asked.

"Yeah," he said as ran over and tried to open it. "It's locked alright. Where's the key?" he asked.

"It's hidden along the left-side of the door frame in a little space," I told him. I'm not sure why I did that—locking the door and then hiding the key beside it. Perhaps it just made me feel safer. Painful secrets locked away and the key hidden but always there if I needed to get in. It's funny the little things we do to trick ourselves into feeling more secure in the world.

"I can't find it," he said.

"Run your fingers along the left outside of the frame and you'll find a small nook. The key should be in there."

Jake felt along the door frame and then his face lit up. "Found it!" he exclaimed happily. "This is exciting! It's a little like archaeology, isn't it?"

"Yes," I agreed. "I guess it is."

He then put the key in the old door and turned it. There was a click. He looked back at me and triumphantly exclaimed, "It worked!"

"Yes, it did!" I replied, trying to sound surprised. "Are you going to open it now? I'm a little nervous about opening it."

"You don't have to worry," he assured me. "I'm here to protect you."

"Okay then," I said. "Go ahead and open it."

He turned the knob and cautiously pushed open the door. "Come on," he then said to me. "You don't have to be afraid."

"You're so brave, Jake," I tell him as I follow him just inside the room.

"Is there a light switch?" I ask.

"Found it," said Jake, switching it on and revealing the partially finished basement room with its naked joists ceiling and raw drywall walls. It was rough looking, but it was clean. I always kept it clean.

"Look over there!" Jake shouted.

I knew what he was pointing at. On the far wall there were three oversized cardboard boxes that had been placed neatly side by side. Jake immediately ran over to them and looked inside. "Wow!" he shouted excitedly. "Presents! They are full of presents!"

The boxes *were* full of presents. Some were wrapped in birthday paper. Some in Christmas paper. Many of them obviously for a child.

"That's amazing, Jake!" I said. "Imagine finding such a thing and on your birthday too!"

Jake picked one of the gifts from a box and looked at the tag. "With Love to Matty," he read aloud. "Who's Matty?"

I took a moment to choke back my emotions and then said, "Perhaps, he was the old lady's grandson."

"Yeah, I think you must be right," Jake agreed. "Or maybe her son."

I tried to keep my mind focused away from the memories by telling myself this was only a play. It was just part of the script. Nothing but theatre. And all I had to do was keep in character. I must stay in character. I couldn't let reality in. "I suppose she put them in this room and then forgot about them," I told him. "That kind of thing can happen to old people. They sometimes become forgetful."

"Do you think the old woman would want them back?" he asked. "Should we find Matty and give them back?"

"It was many years ago when I bought the house," I explained. "The old woman would have passed on a long time ago and there is no way to find her grandson. Even if we could, they likely would not be of much use to him now. I think we can safely assume those presents no longer have any owner."

"So then would they be yours?" he asked. "Because you own the house."

"I guess they would be," I replied. "But since it's your birthday, I'll give them all to you. And besides which, you're the one who was brave enough to find them."

"For me?" he laughed. "That's a lot of presents."

"Yes, it is," I said.

"Can I open them now?" he asked excitedly. "There must be about a million presents here! I wonder what they are!"

He was so happy. I had made a very hurt and sad little boy happy. I must think only of this and not about myself. "Why don't we take them a few at a time upstairs and you can open them there."

"Good idea," he said, quickly grabbing up as many as he could carry.

I reached into the box and picked out three gifts to carry. Holding them tightly to my chest, I could feel my heart beating against the carefully wrapped packages. I knew what was in each one. I had not forgotten any of them. Every single gift had been thoughtfully and lovingly chosen. I could not possibly forget what was hidden beneath the wrapping paper.

"We'll open these and then come back for the others," said Jake. "This is exciting!"

"It is exciting," I agreed as I followed him to the stairs.

Before I placed my foot on the bottom step, I quickly tucked one of the gifts into a dark corner down the side of the staircase. This was a special one wrapped in shiny red Christmas paper. I had spent hours searching the stores hoping that it would somehow make a difference. It would somehow make things better. The perfect gift that would change things.

"Are you coming?" asked Jake who was already at the top of the stairs.

"Yes, I am right behind you," I tell him thinking about that one present I had hidden. Jake could be made happy with all the rest, but I needed that one—I needed to keep something for myself if I were to get through this.

Seventeen

"Hello," he said softly as he slowly moved close to her. He was now worried that she may try and flee if he were to make any sudden moves. "It's me again and I know I have a lot to explain."

"Yes, you do," she told him, feeling that strange and confusing pull between them. This was all so new to her.

"I'm sorry for calling you 'Clarissa'. I know that is your awake name only. We don't know each other's name here, do we? I mean our real names. Our real names are hidden."

"Here, a name is not a word. It is so much more. It is a shared intimacy of the highest order. Perhaps though, for practical reasons we could use our awake names sometimes since our awake-selves are aware that we exist."

"That seems like a good idea. It's a confusing situation. Each of us being two and each of us being one at the same time. It's our great paradox, isn't it?"

"It is everyone's paradox. It's simply that most people are not aware of it."

They then both went silent in contemplation and remained that way for a short time. This was not something unusual in the dreamworld, but in this instance, she could feel that his silence was rooted in his trepidation to speak. He was fearful of sharing the truth with her.

"You need explain yourself," she finally said. "If we are going to move *forward on this, you need to explain yourself. Otherwise, whatever it is you require from me—from Clarissa, will not work."*

"Yes, of course. I understand," he replied. "I'll try to explain as best I can. First though, let's go somewhere nice. It's better if we go somewhere that means something to me. That way you'll be able to feel the truth of the circumstances. You'll be inside a part of me. I want you to know me— to know Jonah. I don't want my words to be misunderstood. Please, take my hand."

She reached out and when she touched his hand, his warm presence coursed through her. It was puzzling how it all seemed so natural. So right. Then, in an instant, she found herself sitting beside him in soft green grass at the top of a hill. The sun was shining in a blue sky speckled with soft downy clouds. She then took her hand away even though she didn't want to.

Down below them was a mostly forested area. It was autumn and the trees created a magnificent tapestry of greens, oranges, reds and golds. Beyond the trees she could see a beautiful clear still lake, its perfect surface mirroring both the sky and the land around it. A world reflected upon a world. At the edge of the lake closest to them, a brown roof was visible. There was also a wooden dock protruding into the water. "Where are we?" she asked.

"It's my cabin...well, it's Jonah's cabin. It's where he has always gone to escape it all. It's his sanctuary from the pressures of the world. He can't go there now, of course. It's too dangerous. There are likely militias hiding out in those hills now. Possibly occupying the cabin, itself. Even people who worked for the CIA are not safe anymore."

"This is a very nice place," she said. "I can feel how much it means to you—to Jonah. But we may not have much time so please tell me why you have found me and what you want. You said you spied on Clarissa. Is this true? You are Clarissa's enemy?" At that point she thought about dashing away and forgetting she ever met him.

"Please remain here beside me," he said, sensing her alarm. "I'll try to *help you understand. But please, please keep an open mind—let your light stay open to mine. I am not your enemy and Jonah isn't your enemy either. It's not like that."*

"I'm listening," she said, prepared to stay. If she was going to learn anything about this confusing situation, she needed to hear him out. And the fact that there was second weapon meant she could not simply run away from this.

He absentmindedly reached down and picked a wild daisy growing in the grass. Gently holding it in his hand, he stared down into its soft yellow center. She could feel how uncomfortable this was for him and also sensed his desperate need to be understood. "Allow me to start at the beginning and go back to how Jonah came to work for the CIA," he said.

"That's not necessary," she replied, now feeling a little annoyed that he seemed to be avoiding the crux of the matter. "Just explain why you would do such a horrible thing. Why would you spy on Clarissa? She's a very nice and kind person who doesn't deserve that. I don't understand how you could do it?"

"It's complicated," he sighed.

"I'm so confused right now. You tell me that your awake-self is a terrible person and yet you are shining so brightly. What is this about? Terrible people have pitiful dull lights. And the way you feel—your presence. What is that? How can I be so drawn to you?"

"But I'm not a terrible person!" he exclaimed. "And Jonah's not a terrible person. We are truly not. It's simply that my father—Jonah's father was CIA, and so Jonah was expected to do the same and that's what happened. We all make choices when we're young and youth is very short-sighted, and the awake-world is a world full of deceptions. We make choices— choices that cannot be undone. Jonah made the choice of following in his father's footsteps. That's how his life happened in that way. Later he had many regrets."

"I still don't know how you could do it—spying on innocent people," she

said. "Surely, you didn't have to do that. You could have just quit. Jonah could have just quit."

He laughed nervously. "No one quits the CIA. Once you're in, you're in it for life. But more than that, I couldn't leave that particular job. I couldn't transfer to a different department. If I did, terrible things would likely have happened, and Jonah could not have lived with himself after that."

"What do you mean?" she asked. "Would Jonah be in danger?"

"No, not Jonah," he told her. "But bad things would likely happen to those we spied upon."

"I don't understand. Please explain."

"I was head of what they called the Tree Huggers Squad. That's not the official name, but that's what they called it unofficially. We were considered a bit of a joke around the agency even though our mission was no joke. We were supposed to treat our suspects as potential terrorists."

"Clarissa was a terror suspect!?"

"Like I said, there were millions of suspects. Most of them were just nice people who took social justice very seriously. They were also mostly pacifists. Not really the terrorist type."

"And no one in the CIA could see that it was a waste of time and money to spy on these people?" she asked.

"It's not about that," he explained. "It's not about logic or reason. It's a paranoid obsession with control. That was the culture within the agency. Just a paranoid obsession. And you couldn't fight it. You could only work around it. So, that's what Jonah did. He worked around it."

"So, he was the head of what they called the Tree Huggers Squad? How did that come to be?"

"It was far from the most sought-after job at the agency," he explained. "That's for sure. The truth is that Jonah wasn't really the type of person the CIA usually hired. He would have never passed their psych-tests. But because of his father's influence and power, they had to accept him. Not only that, but also, Jonah was born into a very privileged New England family. He had the pedigree, so to speak. Their unwritten rules of social hierarchy dictated that they needed to find him a place that was important enough, but not too important. He was given that particular department because it wasn't considered very important on a practical level. Mostly we were spying on Quakers and nuns."

"So, they didn't expect Jonah to take the job all that seriously?"

"Oh no," he exclaimed. "They expected Jonah to take it very seriously. Which brings me to why I could not leave that position. The people hired to work in that department were chosen for, among other things, their lack of empathy and ability to not feel guilt. Many of them were psycho or sociopaths. They not only spied on innocent people, but they were expected to interfere in their lives wherever possible...make things more difficult for those they spied upon. They were mostly bullies. The CIA hired bullies for these positions."

She felt sickened by what he has just said. "Did they interfere with Clarissa? Did you interfere with Clarissa?" she asked.

"Absolutely not!" he exclaimed. "I would never do such a thing. I protected Clarissa. I protected a lot of people. That's why I couldn't leave. If I left, they would have brought in someone truly terrible. I kept control of the department. I found ways to fire those who were excessively cruel. I lost certain files. I did my best to keep humanity alive in that place."

"So, Jonah was a guardian of sorts?"

"Yes, I suppose he was. He had to be. The light that I am demands it. Even though Jonah wanted to leave, he couldn't. He couldn't leave all those unsuspecting people at the mercy of cruel bullies. He couldn't leave Clarissa unprotected."

She was silent for a moment as she thought about what it must have been like for Jonah, stuck in a life he didn't want but continuing to remain for the greater good. "Now, I understand," she said. "I understand how it is that your light shines so bright even though it appears as if your awake-self has chosen darkness."

"I'm so glad," he sighed in relief. "Thank you for understanding. I was afraid maybe you wouldn't. And then I don't know what I'd do. You see,

I'm alone here—my awake-self is alone. There's a second weapon and Jonah has infiltrated the group that intends to deploy it. He didn't go looking for them. It just happened. An acquaintance from within the agency introduced him to them. It all happened very quickly. And now here I am, in the midst of darkness with no sure way to communicate with others who could help. That's why I came to find you."

"You were looking for me in particular? Why me? What can I do?"

"You don't understand. When I was working at the CIA, I used to follow Clarissa online almost every day. I enjoyed reading her posts. And she had a way of attracting people that needed to be noticed."

"What do you mean?"

"I mean, you—or rather Clarissa, had a way of attracting the people who needed to be arrested. They would come to her to insult or argue and when Jonah looked into them more closely, he'd find they were up to terrible things. Although his department didn't handle people like that, he'd send the information to others. Clarissa helped thwart numerous terrorist attacks and arrest various criminals. I don't know how it happened, but it happened."

She thought for a moment about what he had said, then told him, "Yes, there are elements in this world that don't like me being here. The darkness does sometimes feel threatened by my existence. It then feels drawn to me in anger and frustration. It tries to attack through its conduits. Those people had made life choices to become the conduits of that darkness."

"Oh, I see," he said. "That explains why it happened. The funny thing is that Jonah became known among many in the CIA as an expert at finding these criminals and passing on important tips. People in other departments would come to him looking for leads. But I never told them that they all came from you. I couldn't let them know about Clarissa."

"Thank you for that," she said. "Thank you for protecting Clarissa."

"And because Jonah knew Clarissa so well and she had unknowingly helped him so much, it was Clarissa he thought about when he suddenly found himself alone and in need of help. He just wished so hard that she could help him again the way she helped him before. That's when somehow, awareness happened, and my awake-self and dream-self suddenly remembered and knew each other. And shortly after that is when I wandered through a dream one night, hoping to find you and then saw you there, helping that singer. I couldn't believe it when I saw you! I was wishing for you more than anything and there you were! Clarissa's creator! The purest brightest you! But I was also afraid of what you might think of me, so I turned and fled."

She sighed. No wonder she had been so drawn to him. He saw her. He actually saw her for everything that she truly was. No one had ever really seen her before. They had only ever glimpsed small pieces of who she was and then filled in the rest of the puzzle with their own limited imaginations. But he saw her, and he knew her.

"I need your help, now," he told her. "And I need Clarissa's help. I need both parts of you. Not just for me but for the millions of people whose lives are at stake. Terrible plans are in place, and it must be stopped! Death and destruction are imminent unless we do something! We can't let them unleash all that pain—all that suffering. The world needs you now, more than all the singers that have ever lived needed you. Please, you must help! You must!"

Eighteen

"Today the International Criminal Court will hear more testimony against the ex-President of the United States. The President is expected to testify in his defence sometime next week..."

I turned off the television not wanting to hear anymore. There were now far bigger problems to be concerned about. There was a second weapon out there and someone was planning on using it. Jonah said he had infiltrated the group. What did that mean and how much did he know? Would I really be able to help him and how? It was frustrating knowing I'd have to wait to find out. How could I possibly distract myself in the meantime?

As I sat there thinking about whether or not I should try to lose myself in my thesis, if that was even possible right then, I heard a knock at my back door. I knew it had to be either Zeke or Jake. Who else would be in my backyard? I walked into the kitchen and could see Zeke's smiling face at the window. When I opened the door, he held out a colourful bouquet of mixed flowers. "For you," he said.

A little surprised, I took the flowers in my arms. "Uh...thank you."

"It's not much but I just wanted to let you know how grateful I am to you for making Jake's birthday a special day," he explained. "He had such a good time unlocking the secret room and then

"

unwrapping all those gifts. Were they really left behind by the previous owner?"

"Yes, they were," I said not skipping a beat. "I told Jake I had never gone into that room, but that wasn't the truth. I knew the gifts were there. I just wasn't sure what to do with them. I purchased the house from an estate—the woman had passed away months earlier. There were a number of things the beneficiaries left behind. I bought the house 'as is' with whatever items were inside. I'd given a lot of the stuff away, but I wasn't sure what to do with those wrapped presents. In the end, they turned out to be quite useful."

"Well, he loves all his new toys. And some of them seem really expensive too. I don't know who Matty might have been, but she must have loved him very much. I wonder what the story was and why they were left there," he said.

It's possible Zeke suspected that I wasn't telling the truth, but it didn't matter. I had to keep up the charade regardless. "I know that in her final years she did suffer from dementia," I said. "It's very possible that she was buying gifts and forgetting about them or buying them for a son who was already grown or even one she imagined. Who knows?"

"Who knows?" he repeated. "All I know is that you made Jake very happy, and I appreciate that."

"You're welcome," I said with a smile. "And really, thank you for these lovely flowers."

"My pleasure," he replied. "Now, I'd better get back to Jake. I promised I'd watch a new documentary with him. You're welcome to join us if you like. It's about them digging up some old temple somewhere. Not sure where it is exactly but Jake is very excited about it."

"Well, as tempting as that sounds," I said, "I need to work on my thesis tonight. I'm afraid I've gotten a little behind in my work. But thank you for the invitation." At that moment, I didn't really want to be around other people with all that was on my mind. I would not have made good company.

"I hope it's not our fault. I'd hate to think we were making you fall behind."

"Oh no!" I exclaimed. "Not at all. It's just me and my amazing ability to procrastinate or end up down some rabbit hole on the internet when I should be working. I've always been one of those last-minute people."

"That's good," he said. "I mean that's not good, just good that it's not our fault."

We both laughed.

"Anyway, I'd best get back to Jake. Have a nice evening, Clarissa and thank you again for all those presents. They really did save the day."

"You have a nice evening also," I told him as he turned to go.

I closed the door and watched as he headed back to the apartment. I really liked Zeke and didn't like lying to him, but I had to. Matty was my secret—my secret burden. And it's not as if the lie was harming anyone. It was only protecting me, and I needed to keep myself protected. For the sake of my own sanity, I had to keep this hidden away.

∞◇∞

"There are several languages of God. Music is the one I've focused my thesis on but there are others. All of the arts are languages really. Math and science too. Of course, not all music is an expression of God. Not all art. Not all science. There's plenty of bad music, bad art and bad science. But perhaps math is a given, for the most part anyway. I'm not a mathematician but I don't think you can fake math. You can use numbers to support false conclusions or make up numbers to suit your own interests, but the math in and of itself is incorruptible. Some days I wish I was born a mathematician."

The class laughed.

"So, if God has languages, what does God have to say?" asked a usually quiet man who was now more vocal since our change in professor.

I thought about it a moment, then answered, "The Omnipotent speaks of everything that is eternal. Everything that is not corrupted. Everything that is pure. It's a call. The language of God is a call to souls—a call for souls to strengthen in a world that sets out to decimate our spirits."

"That's interesting," said Professor Comay. "Do you think you could give us an example of how this works? You said that not all art authentically expresses the language of God. So, how do we know when we are hearing The Call and not experiencing some cheap fakery or illusion?"

"Only on a personal and individual level could anyone ever really know that for certain," I explained. "It comes only from inside. There is no empirical proof. No logic. For example, when we look at a majestic mountain or the waves of the ocean or the starlit sky, we see beauty. This is something that is universal. But there is no reason for us to find these things beautiful. We are not taught they are beautiful. They do not serve any basic human need or want. There is no explanation. We simply feel they are beautiful...and not just a little beautiful. We feel their intense beauty. We desire to stare at them—to be enveloped in the experience of their wonder. These things call to us because they are the Words of God. 'Let there be Light. Let there be Water. Let there be Land'."

"So, none of this can be proven. It's all just about feeling?" said Mr. Prove-the-existence-of-God. I was surprised he spoke up as he had gone mostly silent since the change in professors.

"Nothing in philosophy can ever really be proven. That's simply not the nature of this discipline. It's not an exact science or a mathematical equation. And when people have treated it as one, they've come up with ridiculous ideas like Aristotle believing women having fewer teeth than men. Logic is merely a tool used in philosophy and is not at all removed from feeling. In fact, nothing is removed from feeling. You are sitting there now completely engulfed in feeling. We all are. Constantly feeling. And sometimes logic is a part of that, but feeling is who we are."

I could see he didn't like my answer but also that he couldn't come up with a rebuttal. Talk about feeling. This guy was furious. Nonetheless he was now silent which was a good thing.

"Well, that's all for today," said the professor. "Please note that my office hours have changed for next week, but I am still available if you need any help."

As I was packing up to leave, I felt a sharp bump against my chair. I looked back and saw Mr. Prove-the-existence-of-God heading for the door. Had he really sunk that low? Going from passive aggressive insults to actual physical violence?

I followed after him, and when I was close enough, I said, "You shouldn't have done that."

He turned and looked at me, smirking. "What are you talking about?"

"You shouldn't have done that," I repeated.

"You're a crazy old woman," he said, then turned away.

"That's the end for you," I found myself saying not knowing why I said it. Those words just came shooting out of my mouth like they had a life of their own.

He looked back again and was just about to say something more when he suddenly stopped. Perhaps he saw something in my eyes—in my face. I'm not sure, but at that point he said nothing more and simply hurried away.

Nineteen

He was sitting on the end of the dock with his pants rolled up and his feet dangling in the water.

"We are meeting at the cabin again?" a familiar voice said from behind him.

He turned to see her standing there—her light seemed brighter than ever.

"This is where I feel safe. Where Jonah feels safe," he told her. "Both him and I need this."

"Yes, it's a good place," she said, sitting down beside him, tucking her skirt underneath her thighs and placing her own feet in the water. It felt warm yet cool and refreshing at the same time. "I can see why you want to be here. It is calming."

For a while they just sat in silence taking in the beautiful view and, in their closeness, enjoying the warmth of each other's light. All lights flow out into the awake-world like nourishing rivers, but when two lights come together like that, it is even more special. Such moments are gifts to both worlds. It brings the worlds closer—harmonizing them. If they could stay like that longer, they would have but there were important matters to discuss.

"I wish we had more time to enjoy this place—to enjoy each other," he said, breaking the silence.

"Yes, we could create such a beautiful dream together," she agreed. "But

we cannot think about ourselves right now. There is so much to figure out. Tell me, what exactly does Jonah know?"

"As I told you, Jonah was recruited by the terrorists. They wanted him because of his CIA background. They thought he'd be a useful asset. He's managed to gain their trust—well mostly and has learned a great deal. Their ultimate aim is to reestablish the United States as a world power, but they don't want to restore it as it was before. Instead, they want to redesign it."

"How do they plan to do that?" she asked.

"Their first move is to deploy the weapon," he said. "They want to use the weapon on the northeastern coast. Their main target is Washington DC."

"Oh no!" she exclaimed. "I can't believe anyone would want to try that and after all that has happened."

"It's true," he said. "Their plan is to destroy what is left of the American government and also strike enough fear into the world so that no one would dare challenge them."

"But they don't even know how much damage could be done. How many states they could destroy."

"The thing is, they don't care. They don't care about the amount destruction or the number of deaths. They only want what they want, and what they want is complete control. After the devastation is over, their plan is to establish a new government centred in Texas. They even have plans to eventually annex Mexico and Canada."

"But if they have only one weapon, after that is gone, what power would they have left? They do only have one weapon?"

"Yes, there is only one weapon, but they intend to bluff their way into power by claiming there are more. Plus, in the ensuing chaos, they have plans to gain control of the nuclear arsenal in Texas. They believe the world will be in such a state of shock that it will be an easy thing to accomplish."

"How can they be so foolish? Even aside from their desire to kill millions, why would they even think they could control the outcome this time? Don't they realize they could also easily destroy themselves?"

"Terrorists are not reasonable people," he said. "These men are convinced that they now understand how the weapon works and what it was that went wrong. They believe they can prevent another mistake. Their arrogance blinds them to the reality that they don't know what they are doing. They also don't care about any of the people who will be killed. They only care about establishing their fantasy of America as a single world power. They tell themselves that it must be done for the greater good— what they imagine to be 'the good'. It's the same excuse used by evil powers throughout history. The supposed greater good excuse."

She thought about it a moment then asked, "I know you are new to consciously experiencing the dreamworld, but have you tried to access their minds from here? Things can be manipulated in the awake-world. I have done it myself many times."

"I considered that," he told her. "And I looked for them, but I can't find them. I found you but I can't find them. Why would that be?"

She thought about it. He should be able to find people he knows, especially people he is in close contact with. There could only be one explanation. "They must be too dark," she said. "We find each other in the dreamworld because of the light. Their lights must be almost extinguished, making them unfindable. Light can destroy darkness within, but it cannot see darkness without. That is why in this world we exist as two separate beings. The awake being and the dream being. Our lights cannot identify and battle darkness head on. We need to be cloaked in flesh and mind to do this. Those two things are our armour, our conduits and our weapons. We serve the Pure Light—the Highest Light. And the Highest Light cannot exist within the same space as the empty darkness."

"Yes of course, that makes sense!" he said. "Part of me was hoping we could easily change everything from dreams, and you would be able to show me how to do it. But I suppose, deep inside of myself, I always knew that wouldn't work."

"Hope is never a bad thing," she told him. "We need to hope—both our dream-selves and our awake-selves need to hope."

"But hope isn't enough," he replied. "We need a plan."

"Yes, we do," she agreed. "Jonah has the knowledge. He has the knowledge and training to create a plan. Do you know what he needs from me—what he might need from Clarissa? What do we need to do in the awake-world to try and stop this?"

"First, we need proof," he said. "And we need to somehow get that proof to the Canadian government. Jonah is already gathering proof but getting it safely across the border and into the hands of people in authority is another matter. There are just so many challenges and so much risk."

"Please explain."

"It is very complicated."

"Why would it be that difficult?"

"Because I can't be sure of the extent of the terrorist network. It seems to be just a handful of men, but it could extend further and there could also be sympathizers. You see, before everything fell apart, the U.S. had filled the Canadian government with spies. Civil servants at all levels. That's what they did. They wanted as much control over Canada as possible. It is true that most of those spies likely just assimilated after the weapon was detonated. They resolved to live their lives as Canadians devoted to Canada, but one of the terrorists has suggested that they might have connections in your country. He didn't indicate where they could be positioned, and it was just a passing remark, but that possibility presents too great a risk. If we sent information just randomly to the Canadian government, it might fall into the wrong hands. It must be passed secretly and to someone with direct access to the Prime Minister's office. Any other way and it would pass through too many hands first and maybe end up in the wrong ones.

"I'm also concerned because for decades the CIA worked to keep the Canadian secret service agencies weak. They made certain that incompetent people were scattered throughout the organizations and even in the highest offices. In this way they could ensure their own dominance in

North America. And although the CIA has now been disbanded, the Canadian secret service agencies are still riddled with incompetency because of what was done in the past. I have to be very careful when giving them information that could be deadly if mishandled."

"Do you think they would detonate the weapon early if they suspected they'd be found out?" she asked. "Is that what concerns you?"

"They would, without hesitation. They would deploy the weapon early if they felt cornered. Even if it meant their own deaths, they would do it. They are just that single-minded."

"This will take some thought," she said.

"Jonah has already been constructing a plan in his mind. He knows that to be believed he must provide some undeniable proof. It can't just be hearsay, or it may not be believed. It needs to be actual physical proof. And this information can't simply be sent over the internet either because the web is not secure. Even though the NSA has been officially closed down, this terrorist group could possibly have ex-NSA sympathizers who may still have access to most every online activity in both countries. No, it has to be audio proof hidden in jump drives. It's the safest way. It's the only way. That's why we have to get jump drives from the U.S. into Canada without anyone knowing about it."

"Are you certain there is no easier way?" she asked.

"This is the best way," he said. "For it to be successful it has to be done in the most secure way possible with absolute secrecy. The terrorists cannot find out that there is a leak. This whole thing has to be handled so carefully."

"What do you suggest?" she asked him. "How do we get the jump drives into Canada? Border security is very strict these days."

"The old-fashioned way," he said. "An old trick they used to do before the internet."

"And what was that?"

"A mule. We need a mule."

"A mule?"

"*Yes. Some unsuspecting person who will unknowingly receive the information and pass it on to a contact Jonah has in Canada?*"

"*Jonah has a contact?*"

"*He does. But this contact is well known in the secret service circles and considered a traitor by the terrorists. So, there cannot be an easily recognized trail from Jonah to him. This contact has access to someone, who has access to someone, who has access to the Prime Minister's office. It's still a bit risky but this is the best we have.*"

"*Do you want Clarissa to do it?*" she asked. "*Do you want Clarissa to be a mule and get the information to the contact?*"

"*Oh no!*" he exclaimed. "*Clarissa must be protected. You must be protected. You know too much, and I need you. The mule must be unwitting fool who has no idea what is going on and whom no one would ever suspect. The information must be hidden within some inconspicuous object, make its way across the border and then be picked up somehow by my contact without anyone knowing...anyone but us. Do you have any ideas how to do this?*"

"*She thought for a moment. "So, you need someone who would be completely oblivious...someone who could be easily fooled into passing on the jump drives without any idea about what was happening?*"

"*Yes, that's right. That's who we need.*"

"*Then yes,*" she told him. "*I believe I do know someone... But I have a question for you. Does Jonah paint?*"

"*Paint? You mean like walls?*"

"*No,*" she laughed. "*Like pictures.*"

"*Jonah once got a 'C' in high school art class. He only took the course because he thought it would be an easy credit. So no, I would have to say that Jonah doesn't paint.*"

"*It would be better if he did,*" she said. "*But he could always try and fake some abstracts. Do you think he could do that?*"

"*I suppose,*" he replied. "*But I don't know if it would fool any experts.*"

"That's okay," she said. "For what I have in mind, fooling an expert won't be a requirement."

Twenty

"Oh Issa, this is such a great idea!" chirped Traci. "I've never been to an art gallery opening before. Thanks for inviting me along. I needed an excuse to dress up and have an evening out."

I opened the glass door and allowed Traci walk in first.

"Wow, this is amazing! It's all so elegant and beautiful!" she exclaimed.

That's something I loved about my friend. She found everything amazing. Almost everything. I, on the other hand, couldn't help but notice the forgotten nail hole, or the scratch in the wall, or the hastily way the false ceiling of ribbons had been installed. I saw through things. She saw things in fulfillment of their potential.

A hostess in black heels and a tight black dress walked up to us carrying a silver tray filled with sea blue champagne glasses. "Good evening and welcome to the grand opening of the Asherah Art Gallery!" she said with a dazzling smile.

"Hello!" replied Traci. "And thank you."

"Would you care for some champagne?" the girl asked holding out the tray a little farther.

"Oh yes! Thank you!" said Traci, taking a glass in her hand.

"None for me, thank you anyway," I said. "I'm driving."

"Well, enjoy your evening." The hostess then moved off to greet some other new arrivals.

"Oh, isn't she lovely and so elegant," exclaimed Traci.

For me, I only saw a wannabe actress or model, still trying to pay off the plastic surgery, and just happy to get a paying job to make her rent this month. But I kept that to myself. Traci was having so much fun and I was not going to ruin it for her.

"Oh, look at that one!" she exclaimed as I followed her over to an unusual landscape hanging on the wall. The colours were not what they were supposed to be. Trees were the colour of flowers. Flowers were the colour of trees. Land the colour of sky. Sky the colour of land. "I love it!" she said. "It's just so different! I wonder how much it is."

"It's a steal at three thousand," said a voice from behind us. "And it's absolutely beautiful! Such a piece is really worth far more, but the artist is just beginning her career. As she becomes more known the value will go up, up, up. It would be a worthwhile investment."

We both turned to see a gentleman with an immaculate short box beard that perfectly matched his closely cropped silver hair. He was dressed in a black tuxedo with a black silk necktie and a red rose tucked into the lapel. His face had the relaxed confidence of someone who had always known privilege. "Good evening, my name is Maximilian Graystone, owner of this humble but gracious salon, but please call me Max," he said. "I'm just so glad you ladies could attend my gallery opening."

"Hello, Max," I replied. "My name is Clarissa, and this is my friend Traci."

"It's so nice to meet you both," he said with a perfectly practised smile.

"You're American!" exclaimed Traci. "I can tell by your accent."

"Oh my, guilty as charged. I hope you won't hold that against me."

"Of course not," Traci replied. "I work with the American Refugee Project and Clarissa is a sponsor."

"That is so generous of you both. My fellow Americans have suffered so much. Thank God for wonderful Canadians like yourselves."

"Have you been in Canada long?" I asked him.

"About three years now," he answered. "It has always been my dream to open an art gallery and now, starting a whole new life in Canada has finally given me the incentive to take the plunge."

"Well, it's a beautiful gallery," said Traci. "I'm so happy for you."

"Thank you. I really appreciate that. There have been so many challenges in getting it all set up, but I think in the end it has all been worth it."

"Yes, it's beautiful what you've done," said Traci. "And there are so many beautiful paintings here."

"Now, if you really like this particular work, there are more by the same artist on the far back wall. You will definitely want to view those as well. I'm certain you'll find them just as magnificent," Max said.

"I'd love to see them!" exclaimed Traci.

"Why don't you go and have a look, and I'll join you shortly," I told Traci. "I'd like to talk with Max a little more about the gallery."

"Oh," said Traci with a big smile, "Of course. I'll just be back there looking at all the artwork and you can find me whenever you're finished. Take your time because I am perfectly happy to sip champagne and enjoy paintings all night long."

I realized then that Traci thought I was checking out Max as a romantic prospect, so she was more than happy to leave us alone.

As we stood side by side pretending to stare at the painting in front of us Max said, "So Clarissa, it's serious, isn't it? Jonah and I communicate but not directly. It's an old way. We used to do it just for fun. We'd send each other messages through code by posting things on the internet. Mundane things no one would suspect were actually messages to each other. But the code is limited as it was never something we planned to use professionally. It was just for our personal amusement. Because of those limitations, all I know is that you are my contact and that he needed me to open this gallery. What can you tell me? What is this about?"

"There's a second weapon," I said, feeling it was best if I went straight to the point.

"What!" he said a little too loudly but then quickly followed it up with a laugh so it could only be interpreted as part of a boisterous conversation.

"How? Why?" he whispered in concern while keeping a smile on his face.

"It's a rogue cell. Ex-CIA, military and others. They plan to use it."

"No, no, no!" he said. "They can't! Why? Why would they do something so stupid?"

"They think it will make the United States a world power again...a single world power."

I could see Max was trying to keep his composure and maintain his façade as the happy art gallery owner.

"We have to do everything in our power to stop them," he told me.

"Yes, we do," I agreed.

He then asked, "And who exactly are you? Do you have a background in secret service? Is that how you know Jonah? He never mentioned you before."

I laughed. "I'm a nobody just caught up in the whole thing."

"Well, nobody, I'm not going to ask too many questions because it's always best to limit your knowledge to only that which is necessary to know. It makes things much easier in the long run. What else can you tell me? Do you know Jonah's plan? He's communicated that he is sending something that I must ensure is passed to the highest Canadian office possible. How's he going to do that?"

"It will be hidden behind paintings," I told him. "Jump drives—carefully hidden. These paintings will come to you through an unsuspecting party—a middleman. The name of the artist is Melody Beaumont. She's a young American artist looking to make a breakthrough in the Canadian art world. You're going to love her work."

This made him laugh a little. "I've known Jonah a very long time and if he has put his trust in you, I know that I can too."

Just then a couple with champagne glasses in hand approached us to look at the painting.

"This is so interesting," said the woman. "I love what the artist has done with colour. Just look at the eloquence of how light and shadow are used in juxtaposition to the symmetry of the technique."

"You have such an astute eye, Madam" said Max, pouring on the charm. He then offered his hand and said, "Hello, my name is Maximilian Graystone, owner of this humble but gracious salon, but please call me Max, and welcome to the Asherah Art Gallery. I'm so glad you could make our grand opening."

The woman blushed. "It's a lovely gallery!" she exclaimed, shaking his hand. "Something we really needed in the neighbourhood."

At this point I thought it was best if I rejoined Traci. "Thank you, Max," I interrupted. "I should go find my friend now."

"It was very nice to meet you," he said. "And I shall definitely look into that artist you recommended."

"It was very nice to meet you also," I replied then turned to go find Traci.

As I walked to the back of the gallery, I couldn't help but be a little worried. Although my plan seemed simple enough, I had yet to put everything into place. This was something I had not shared with Max. Yes, I had told him to expect the paintings but what I did not tell him was that I had not yet made arrangements for those paintings to get to him. That still had to be done. Melody Beaumont was still just a name. Somehow, I'd have to bring her to life. Was I really going to be able to do this? Clandestine operations were not something I ever imagined I'd ever have to do. My personality is not suited to such things. I liked truth above all else. But there are times in our lives when we have to step outside of ourselves. There are times when we are called upon to find strengths we did not know we had. And with the magnitude of all that was at stake, this was definitely one of those times.

∞◊∞

Professor Comay entered the classroom a few minutes late. She set her books on the table but did not pull out the chair to sit down.

"Before we begin," she sighed, "I have some sad news. This class has already been dealt terrible news with the passing of Professor Wagner, so I feel rather reluctant to have to tell you this, but it has to be done."

We all sat silently wondering what it could be.

"One of our students, Windsor Hudson, has met with an accident. And I'm afraid he is in very bad shape. It's highly unlikely he will be returning to class. It was a horseback riding accident. Very tragic."

Even though the class consisted of only seventeen people, none of us had really got to know each other's names. We did not know who Windsor Hudson was. So now, all of us were looking around trying to figure out which face was missing. It was then that I realized Mr. Prove-the-existence-of-God was not present. In that moment, I felt strange. There were no words to describe it. Just very strange.

"I thought maybe it would be a nice thing if we all chipped in to send him some flowers and a card," said the Professor. "But only those who can afford it. Don't feel pressured if it's not in your budget. Do you think that's a good idea?"

Several students murmured their approval.

"Alright then, next class we'll do a collection and I'll bring a card for you all to sign."

She then pulled out the chair and sat down. Placing her folded hands on the table in front of her she said, "As Kierkegaard once said, 'life can only be understood backwards but it must be lived forwards' so with that in mind we move on to our next scheduled topic, *spiritual philosophers and the relationship between God and nature.*"

At that point, the professor's voice faded away, and all I could think about was what I had said to that man after the last class. Telling him his end was coming. Was it a co-incidence or did I somehow know it would happen? A vision? A premonition? A prophecy? Or could my dream-self have made it happen? Was I capable of such a thing? And if I was, was this an evil act? I felt the emptiness—the vacantness of his being. He had a violence deep within him. Not a surface anger but a deep violence in his very foundation. But I don't decide life and death. How could I? Was it Karma? God's judgment? Do I have a role in that? Does my dream-self have a role in that? Could both a giver of life and an angel of death co-exist within me? Oh, I don't know who I am. For all the things that I know—for all the secrets I have learned, I still don't even know who I am or what exactly I'm capable of. Sometimes I frighten myself.

Twenty-One

I stood in front of the wooden door preparing myself for what I would say. This was not the kind of thing I'd ever done before and now everything hinged on my being convincing. Taking in a deep breath, I then knocked three times. "Enter," came a voice from inside.

When I opened the door and stepped inside, I saw him sitting behind his desk head down, glasses on and reading something. He took his time before looking up, then exclaimed, "Clarissa!" as he dramatically removed his glasses.

Before I could say anything, he brusquely told me, "If your young man has left you and you've now come to apologize, you must know that I am no longer interested. I've moved on, and now devote all my free time to my attainment of level six. And I am proud to say that I have mastered more than halfway attainment at this level. Not an easy feat."

"That's wonderful Crawford!" I exclaimed. "I'm not surprised you are reaching level six so quickly. A man with your focus would certainly be able to face such challenges head on, but I'm not here about me."

"Oh?" he said sounding a little suspicious.

I shut the door behind me, walked over and sat down on the

chair in front of his desk. "Crawford," I said, in my best matter-of-fact voice, "let me get straight to the point. You know how I've been doing work with the American Refugee Project?"

"Yes," he replied curtly. "I believe you mentioned you were volunteering."

"Well, it is that volunteer work that brings me here today. You see, I've been messaging with someone...an American, who is in dire need of help. She's a very talented artist who needs a Canadian connection. Unfortunately, I can't help because what she needs is a well-renowned art expert. And for that reason, I'm coming to you Crawford. I know how deeply you are devoted to bringing refreshing new artworks to the world, and I also know what a generous man you are."

"An American?" he asked. "An American needs my help? I don't know if I could. I have to think of my reputation."

"But she needs you, Crawford," I replied. "You are so well-known and so respected, and she is just a poor victim of the fallout. This poor girl is so young. Only twenty-one. And a sensitive thing the way true artists always are. She's just barely coping with the difficult situation she's in. And she's so very talented. I mean—it's not that I know much about art. Not like you. But she has received such praise for her work. Before everything fell apart, they said she was a prodigy and the next great American painter. Her work has been compared to Jackson Pollock's."

"Really?" he said scratching his beard.

I reached into my bag and took out a piece of paper. "Here is her CV. When I told her about you and how you could possibly help, she told me to make sure you saw this before making any decision. She understands how politically delicate things are right now and wants to ensure that you felt comfortable in your choice." I handed him the paper.

He put his glasses back on then seemed to be taking a good long look at the photo at the top of the page. I was glad of that having spent a long time, first, searching for just the right image, and then manipulating it to ensure it could not be traced back to the original. I used The Lady of Shallot for my inspiration.

"Hmmm...she is lovely," he said. "Melody...Melody Beaumont. Such a lovely name too. Everything about her does appear to exude art."

"Yes, she is a lovely girl. And so talented. But unfortunately, she's stuck in the U.S. and there's nothing there for a young artist. It's such a hopeless place right now especially for someone as talented as her. What she needs is to be able to get her artwork into a gallery here in Canada," I told him.

"Oh!" he suddenly exclaimed. "It says here, she follows the teachings of Guru Durjoy!"

"Yes, isn't that a marvellous co-incidence!" I exclaimed. "When she told me about her attainment of level two and how she was working towards level three, I thought of you. It just seemed such a perfect fit. Professor Kravitz, a mentor in both art and spirituality."

"Do you have pictures of any of her works?" he asked.

"Of course," I said, reaching into my bag. "Here are two of her latest paintings." Jonah had placed the photos on the internet for me to easily find.

Crawford took them in hand and began to carefully examine them under the light of his desk lamp. When after a few minutes, he didn't say anything, I worried. Did he realize that he was looking at amateur work? Was this whole plan now going to fall apart?

"The problem with photos," I said, "is that they don't do the works justice. The camera, as you know, changes the colours, the shape and creates shadows. It's not the same as seeing the actual work itself. I'm sure the paintings look so much better in real life."

"No, no, no," he said waving his hand at me while not taking his eyes off the pictures. "These do in fact show great talent...great talent indeed."

"Oh, I'm so glad to hear you say that Crawford," I said in honest relief. "That's why I came to you and not someone else. With your expertise you can see things from a purely artistic viewpoint. You have a natural gift for recognizing greatness."

"So, tell me, how can I help this poor girl?" he asked removing his glasses and looking straight at me.

"You're really going to help?" I asked, trying to sound surprised.

"Yes, of course. It would be imprudent of me not to assist an artist as talented as Melody. The world needs to know about her."

"Oh Crawford, I'm so glad! You're just such a generous man! Thank you."

"It is my duty, Clarissa. Above all the things I am, both academically and professionally, a lover of art, and a lover must always sacrifice for his love."

"That's beautiful—just so beautiful. You are definitely what Melody needs. Now, just to let you know, I've already found a gallery to take her paintings. So, the hard work has been done. But because she's American, and the gallery owner was previously American, he's worried it might discredit him to accept the paintings directly. For that reason, he won't take them without a reputable sponsor here in Canada. He's nervous about, among other things, violating trade restrictions, and I can't blame him. He said that she needs a sponsor and not just some random person, otherwise I could do it myself. She needs a sponsor who is an expert in the field. The artworks must be moved through you as they need to be approved by a qualified expert."

"Hmmm, I see," he said. "That makes perfect sense."

"So, this is how it will work. Melody will send her paintings to you. And as you are an avid well-known art collector, there should be no problem getting them through customs. They will then be delivered to your home where you will have to sign for them. When you receive them, you'd have a chance to approve them of course. Although with her work being so beautiful, I don't see how you'd ever disapprove of any one of her paintings. From that point on, you would then send them with a letter of reference to the gallery. All the i's dotted and all the t's crossed. In this way no legal issues could arise."

"Yes, I see. This could easily be done."

"I know it seems like a lot to ask especially for a busy man like yourself," I said. "But it would mean the world to this poor girl. She has no one else to help her."

"Clarissa," Crawford said, clasping his hands together and resting them on his desk. "I'm so glad you came to me. At first, I was ready to send you away with some harsh words, but this dear girl needs my help. I must do something."

"Oh, thank you!" I said meaning it. "Melody will be so happy to learn she has the well-respected Professor Crawford Kravitz on her side."

"When can I speak with her? I'd like to get better acquainted," he said.

I knew he'd ask, and I was prepared for it. "That's a problem," I told him.

"How so?"

"We have to be very careful to operate entirely within the law," I told him. "The trade restrictions are very strict. They have agents analyzing everything coming across the border. If your relationship to Melody is seen in any way as personal, they might shut us down. Melody's career would end in a tattered broken country and your reputation could possibly suffer. No, there cannot be any risk of them assuming that you have more than just a professional relationship with her. This must be handled very delicately to protect both of you. We need to get her paintings safely across the border, and we need to get her established in a gallery before there can be any one-on-one exchanges."

"Yes of course," he said sounding disappointed.

"But eventually," I told him. "Once she has established her name here in Canada, you will not only be able to discuss all the things you have in common—especially the followings of the Guru, but you will be able to meet with her in person. She hopes to move here and make a new life for herself. She's so young with so much ahead of her."

"Things worth having are things worth waiting for," he said.

"Uh yes. Yes, they certainly are. And in the meantime, I'll serve as your go-between. I'll be able to give you messages from her and I'll also be able to pass on your messages in return. You will still have some contact, but it will have to be through me. If we are to get her paintings and then Melody, herself, safely into Canada, we will have to keep everything looking as above board as possible."

"I understand," he said. "It is a complicated situation, but I am willing to go that extra mile in the name of art."

"Perfect!" I exclaimed. "You don't know what this means to Melody. She will be so grateful. These paintings are like her very soul. They are her future, and you, Crawford, are making that future bright for this beautiful young lady."

"I just wish we could speak directly. I'd love to help her with her levels of attainment. Assisting with that is something that is best done in person."

"And you will speak with her one day," I assured him, "but just not yet. Right now, you have to help her get established in the Canadian art world. Once that's done, and with my contacts at the American Refugee Project, we will be able to bring her here and she can then thank her benefactor in person."

"That will be a glorious day!"

"Ah yes, sure, glorious. But now, I'm already late for an

appointment. The name and address of the gallery along with the name of the owner are on one of the pages I gave you. You can expect the first painting to arrive at your home as early as next week. Is that okay? It's not too soon for you, is it?"

"Not at all. I shall be waiting with bated breath," he replied.

"Okay then. Send me a text if there is any problem. Do you still have my number?"

"Yes," he replied. "But not because I was going to try and contact you again."

"Well, it's good you kept it. It's there in case of a problem or when you want me to pass on a message to Melody. Right now, I'd best be on my way." At that point I got up and turned to go.

"Clarissa," he said, just as I had reached the door.

I turned around and looked at him.

"Clarissa, I just wanted you to know that I don't think it would have worked out between us. We are just too different," he told me.

"You're right, Crawford. We are just too different. I'm so glad you realized that rather than stringing me along. I don't need a heartbreak at this age."

"Ah, the heart. What a delicate thing the heart is!"

"Thank you again Crawford and remember to call me at the first sign of a problem."

"Rest assured, I will," he said. "The last thing I want is to let our beautiful Melody down."

Once outside the door I let out a huge sigh of relief. Did I really just do that? Fool Crawford into becoming our mule? Not a deceptive person by nature, I wasn't sure if I could really pull it off, but I did. And I didn't feel bad about it either. It's not that I enjoyed deceiving him, as many people do enjoy deception. I actually enjoy forthrightness. That is where I am most comfortable. But this whole thing was just too huge. The terrorists had to be stopped and if it meant pulling the wool over Crawford's eyes, so be it.

Twenty-Two

"Why music?" Professor Comay asked as I sat in her office for my thesis consult. "Is it a personal interest of yours?"

"Yes and no. I'm not really musical, if that's what you mean," I explained. "I don't play an instrument and I'm not a talented singer. Like so many people, I just like to listen."

"I can relate to that," she said smiling. "My mother did force me to take piano lessons as a child and that put me off trying any other instrument after that, but I still love music. I suppose the piano and those lessons by the stern Mrs. Humphrey completely ruined the playing part for me," she laughed.

"For me, there were times throughout my life when I wanted to learn an instrument, but it just never happened," I told her. "Other things got in the way."

"It's funny how that is," she said. "Our lives just have a way of working out in ways we least expect. Despite attempts at planning, we are often just carried along by some wild ride anyway, never knowing where we might end up."

"Do you believe in fate?" I asked her.

"I'm not sure," she answered. "If fate is real, then where does it end and freewill begin? I mean, we can't deny freewill. Everything can't just be fate."

"Kierkegaard said 'life is understood backwards' but even that—how much can we really understand. We can see it in our memory but trying to make sense of the 'why' is so challenging. How can we understand it without understanding the 'why'?" Yes, the 'why'. Why Matty? Why did it happen that way? Why?

"That's a good point," she said. "Understanding life may in fact be an impossible task."

"Then should we stop trying?" I ask. "Should we stop bothering completely with philosophy. Is it all pointless?"

"I hope not," she laughed. "Or I'll be out of a job and all that work on your thesis will be for nothing."

"Perhaps, asking 'why' is more than a question," I said. "Perhaps it's our duty as human beings. I mean, is there something important lost when we stop asking 'why'? Or is hanging on to that question just a way of punishing ourselves for existing?"

"Hmmm...interesting. Are there people who never ask 'why'? Perhaps it is simply a part of human nature."

"But the question of 'why' as it pertains to existence isn't just about explanations and meaning. Isn't it also about desire? The desire for something better. You ask 'why' when you feel cheated. When you feel like life has cheated you out of something. Like the prophets of old pleading their case before God. Is asking 'why' about slashing things open—about opening a space for the possibility of divine intervention?"

"Fascinating idea," said the professor. "But I think that might be a whole other thesis."

"I suppose it is," I laughed. "Sorry for digressing. Sometimes I just find myself going down these paths."

"That's good," she told me. "Philosophy is a maze of endless corridors. It's important to explore."

"Finding meaning in a maze of endless corridors is not easy, is it?"

"This is true," she agreed. "And it's a truth we've been grappling with a long time."

At that point, I almost felt like telling her what I knew about dreams, but I also knew I couldn't. Despite how open minded my professor was and how our friendship had grown, she wouldn't understand. How could she not question my sanity if I shared this bizarre knowledge with her? Doing that would cause me all kinds of new problems. Living in two separate worlds at the same time was not easy. Pretending that one did not even exist was even harder.

∞◇∞

The calm crystal lake sparkled in the gentle morning sun. No longer was it surrounded by trees of red, orange and gold. Now those same trees created a magnificent palate of various shades of green. In some places they splashed in contrast and in others they blended together. The world looked alive and fertile with promise.

"It's summertime!" she exclaimed when she saw it.

"Yes, I got tired of the fall. I thought we could use a little summer—a little extra warmth," he replied.

"It's beautiful," she said leaning back in the yellow Muskoka chair and feeling the gentle breeze on her face. He sat beside her in a matching chair. "Thank you for sharing this with me," she added. "It's nice to be here with you."

"You're very welcome," he replied, smiling as he turned his head to look at her. "I'm delighted to be able to share it. Being here gives Jonah sweet dreams and he needs that. He's under a great deal of pressure these days. More pressure than he's ever experienced before, and he has known pressure in his life."

"Is he alright?" she asked. "I can't imagine what it must be like for him."

"It's very difficult," he went on to explain. "Every day he has to work at keeping up the perfect façade while making sure to record them and

their activities, all without them catching on. And these men have been trained to catch on. It's not easy for him. Jonah was never really trained in covert field work. He had studied the basics in the introductory program years ago, but it was never a part of his job. He was more of a manager rather than a spy. Right now, he's just learning as he goes along which is frightening for him. But he's not afraid for himself. He's afraid because of all that is at stake. He's afraid for all of those innocent millions."

"He's a good man," she said.

"Yes," he agreed. "He's always been a good man. Not perfect but good."

"Who is perfect? Even when our lights shine bright, we are still not perfect."

"Not perfect but we aspire to it. We move forward toward the Light of Lights."

"Yes, we do," she agreed.

"And that is another reason why it is so hard for Jonah," he said. "Having to spend so much time in the company of these vacuous agents of darkness is taxing. The darkness, always there, always threatening to consume life and light. There's just not much time left to get away from it all and be himself. That's why I want to meet here—in this spot. This place brings him relief. It's a sanctuary in his dreams. And you here—with your beautiful light—well, that just reassures him. It reassures him about the power and fortitude of light when he's submerged in a world so dark and so threatening—a pit filled with hollow vacant men—the valley of the shadow of death."

"I understand," she told him. "I understand how difficult it must be, and I feel for him."

"That's comforting," he replied. "Having someone who understands is very comforting."

"I'm glad we are here together," she said reaching over and letting her hand melt into his. They closed their eyes and savoured the moment as their lights briefly joined.

"We are compatible," she said releasing his hand.

"Yes...yes, we are," he agreed "This will help us in our mission. It will help Clarissa and Jonah too. Us coming together is a good thing."

"About our mission," she said, "Did Max send word that the first painting had arrived?"

"Yes!" he exclaimed. "Jonah did see his message, and it all seems to be going according to plan. Max has passed the flash drive on to his contact, and shortly the Canadian government will become aware that there is a terrorist group in the U.S. who have in their possession a second weapon. At this point though, we can't give the Canadians more specific information. Not until Jonah learns the real names of these people and where the weapon is hidden. None of them go by their real names. They only identify as numbers. Jonah is number twelve, the last one to join the group."

"Could not the authorities simply go in there now and arrest them?" she asked.

"I wish it were that easy," he told her. "The truth is, we have to proceed with the utmost caution. Unfortunately, we need to protect against any possible bad decisions by government officials. These terrorists are ex-CIA, ex-NSA and ex-military. They have the training and have planned for most every eventuality. If the Canadians blindly charge in there without all the information and a foolproof plan, those terrorists will certainly detonate that weapon, and I can't let that happen."

"Yes, I understand. So, when can we expect the next painting?" she asked.

"Jonah has already finished the next one. If he sends it off tomorrow, it should arrive in about three or four days if we are lucky."

"Good," she said.

They then sat in silence for a while, relishing the warmth of the sun which they both knew was really the warmth of each other's lights. This would help Jonah. Being together like this would make him stronger.

After some time had passed, they realized it was almost time for both of them to awaken. But before they parted, there was something she wanted to ask him. "Do you think there could be more like us?" she asked. "Those *who have become aware of the reality of the dreamworld? For a long time, I thought I was alone. I thought I would always be alone."*

"Possibly," he replied. "But it's also likely very rare. What I do know is that we must never let anyone in the awake world find out about us. It's a powerful secret and we don't know how they would react. We don't know what horrible things they might try to do in an attempt to harness that power."

"Yes, you're right," she agreed. "If others in the awake world knew about this, it could be very dangerous for us—for Clarissa and Jonah. We can't allow that to happen. I still have a lot to learn about everything, but I do know that the darkness that dwells within the awake world would be jealous and try anything to try and steal this power even though such a thing would be fruitless. Darkness cannot take the power that is in light," she told him. "But that's never stopped it from trying."

"Yes of course, that makes sense," he said having realized something new. "Any attempt to try and take that power would certainly be in vain. Darkness is jealous of the light. It wants the light for itself, but it is darkness. How can darkness possess light? That's why it causes so much chaos in the awake world. And so much needless destruction. It is out of impotent frustration." He loved learning new and true things.

"Yes, we both can see that. We both feel that too," she sighed. "It's such a relief to be able to share knowledge and understanding with someone capable of receiving it—to not have to work at explaining all the time. Before you, that's what it was like. Endlessly trying to explain and them getting it all wrong every time. It's freeing to be with someone who understands. Sharing knowledge is pleasure."

"Yes, it is," he agreed. "Knowledge is pleasure. I'm so glad I found you."

"And I'm glad you found me too."

∞◊∞

"Issa, it's me Traci! You bought me the painting! They just

delivered it!" she exclaimed on the other end of the phone. "You shouldn't have. It's too expensive."

"First of all, I can afford it," I told her leaning back in my kitchen chair. It was late morning, and I was finishing up a cup of tea while contemplating some new supporting arguments for my thesis. I was happy she called. I needed a little break. "And second, you just loved it so much that I wanted you to have it. You've been a good friend for a long time, and I just wanted to show you my appreciation," I told her.

"Oh Issa! You're too nice. And here was I thinking that you wanted to talk to Max alone to get to know him better. Actually, I'm a little disappointed about that," she laughed.

"You'll never stop trying to match me up, will you?" I said.

"Would I be a real friend if I didn't?" she asked.

"Well, you certainly wouldn't be you, if you didn't," I laughed.

"I'm going to hang it in the living room over my couch. It'll look amazing—and the colours! Oh, I love the colours! Theo loves it too!"

"I'm so glad you're both enjoying it. Somehow, I think it was made for you."

"You're the best friend ever!" she chirped. "Really, you're the best!"

Was I though? Was I the best friend ever or did I buy the painting just because I felt guilty about not being honest with her? Could both be true? Could I be a best friend even if I hid things from her? Or did any of it even matter when just the act of buying her that painting made her so happy? If she knew that I was hiding things from her, would she even be bothered, considering the importance of what it was I was hiding? Traci was one of the most reasonable people I had ever met. She was also one of the most forgiving. No matter what might have convinced me to buy the painting, I knew she'd never hold it against me. Perhaps that was the only thing that really mattered.

"Have you spoken to Zeke today?" she asked.

"No, I haven't seen Zeke or Jake today."

"He got the job!" she exclaimed. "He got the job at the university! Isn't that great!"

"That's fantastic news! I'm so happy for them!"

"This means that the Refugee Project will be ending their support in three months' time," Traci said. "I thought you should know."

"I already told Zeke that, even if he got the job, they would be welcome to stay in the apartment rent free as long as they needed. They've been through so much and I really don't mind helping them out for longer than I'm required."

"Oh thanks, Issa! It would be better if the program supported them for a longer transition period but there are just so many refugees on the waiting list. Hopefully once this border thing gets figured out the Canadian and Mexican governments can take over and it will mean fewer people in need."

"Let's hope," I replied.

"I just don't understand it," said Traci. "How could they do that? Even though they ended up killing people they didn't intend to kill, they were still trying to kill and destroy a whole country full of people. What evil is in them to even think of such a thing? I've been watching the International Criminal Court trials and it's just heartbreaking. All those politicians and generals on trial. Any of them could have stopped it. It could have been prevented. But they all went ahead with it anyway. How can people be like that, Issa? I just don't understand it."

"I don't either," I agreed. "All I know is that evil exists and somehow we have to fight its existence."

"And how do we do that?" she asked. "How do people like us do that? We're nobodies."

"We are certainly not nobodies," I told her. "Look at all the good work you do—all the lives you have changed. And you don't even know the half of it. There are lives out there that you have affected positively that you don't even know about. You are somebody important in this world, Traci. Without people like you, where would we be? All you have to do is hold up your small corner and somewhere else somebody just as wonderful as you will be holding up their small corner and before you know it, good people everywhere are holding up this planet. Do what you do and know that it's important...that you are important! Don't ever forget that."

For a moment, Traci was silent then said, "Thanks Issa! You're right. I have to keep doing what I'm doing and believing in what I'm doing. We are not nobodies. We are important. I see that."

And there is the thing I learned about dreams. All those ordinary people in the world who look as if their roles are small and insignificant, may have more power than even they know. In dreams they might do things that alter the course of history. They might possibly bring down entire nations with their desire for goodness and justice. That's the truth. From the awake-world, we don't know who they are or what they are capable of. They're protected by their ordinariness. They are hidden from the evil forces in the temporal world. In the day, they shop at the grocery store. They pick up their children from school. They pull weeds from their gardens. But at night, when their heads hit those pillows, they become their real selves, free to go anywhere in the world. And it is there, from that world, they hunt down the wicked in this one. As they have done since the beginning, they bring evil to its knees. That's who we are and what we do.

Twenty-Three

The day seemed so perfect as I walked through the park on the way to my car. The sun was brightly shining, and all the stars seemed to be aligning. My class had been extremely enjoyable with so many interesting ideas and exchanges. The professor really challenged us to think. She was a campus rarity—an authentic teacher, not a simple lecturer. The best in the Socratic tradition. Each lesson was a carefully designed pathway towards knowledge. She drew our minds out and opened us up to new potentials of thought. That day, I even had a small epiphany in support of my thesis.

After class I stopped in to see Crawford. I did this twice a week to give him 'personal messages' from the young, beautiful and talented Miss Melody Beaumont. I assured him that I did not read the messages, as they for his eyes only. I simply printed them out then folded them over and placed them in envelopes. I thought the envelopes were a nice touch. I even sealed them. It just made it much more dramatic, and he seemed to get an extra thrill out of using his letter opener.

He in turn would give me carefully folded hand-written notes complete with personalized doodles to send to her. "I love this secretive note passing," he told me at one point. "It exudes the aurora of the romantic period—the mysterious sweeping lines and muted colours—the melody of the visual feast!" He was definitely smitten.

Although he instructed me not to read the notes, I had to, of course. How else would I know how to respond? Stopping at a park bench, I sat down and took out the note he had given me. Oh, it was awful. So, over the top and filled with innuendos. I couldn't believe he dotted the i's with little hearts. Would a young woman ever fall for such drivel? But who am I to talk? I was young once and had made a terrible mistake.

Just then, a short slightly hunched woman who looked maybe a few years older than me approached the bench. "Do you mind if I sit?" she asked.

"Of course not," I replied. "Actually, I was just leaving." I tucked Crawford's note back into my bag and went to get up to leave.

"Please don't go!" she exclaimed. "Can you sit for a moment. Please! I just don't want to be alone right now. Just for a moment! Please!" She then sat down beside me, perhaps a little too close for strangers on a public bench.

I immediately sensed a selfish want within her. She wanted something from me. She wanted to unburden herself—to ease her load by searching for attention and pity—to spread her sadness into other places. But at the same time, I also sensed her deep distress. Despite her personal flaws, something horrible had happened to her and I knew that I had to show her mercy. So, I stayed.

For a moment she remained silent, but then said, "This park was one of the last places I saw my son."

I didn't know what to say and I knew it didn't matter anyway. She wasn't interested in hearing me, she just wanted someone to hear her, and I was convenient and looked approachable.

"I remember how we walked together over there near that statue," she continued. "It was a nice day, just like this one. He was telling me how he was going to propose to his girlfriend. To be honest, I didn't particularly like her. She was too crude and too bossy. And I asked him if he was sure about it. I told him it's not a decision to take lightly. His response was that he loved her and knew she was the one. What was I going to say? He was thirty-two at the time. A mother can't make decisions for her son forever. So, I accepted it even though I knew it was wrong. And many times after that, I tried to make him see that I was right, but he wouldn't listen. He was going to marry her anyway."

I shifted a little on the bench. A mother's tragedy that involved her son. I didn't want to hear it. I didn't want to know about it. But I was committed now. I couldn't just get up and leave. I wanted to but my duty to mercy wouldn't allow it. So, I listened.

"As the wedding got closer, my husband told me to try hard to show support for our son. He said I'd drive him away if I didn't. He badgered me. For days he kept insisting. 'You're going to lose your son', he told me. And finally, I gave in. I decided that I'd make a grand gesture so that no one could say I didn't do my part. Nobody could say that I was the bad guy. I'd give them an expensive engagement gift so they couldn't claim I wasn't supportive. I was a good mother.

"That's when I came up with the idea of a trip. In the end I thought a trip—a lovely trip would be best. So, that's what I did. I bought them a beautiful vacation package—an all-expenses paid trip to Florida."

She didn't have to say any more. I knew what had happened. I knew she had lost her son because of the weapon.

"I tried phoning him and he didn't answer. I thought maybe he was just ignoring me but then I saw it on the news. I saw what had happened." She then began to weep loudly.

"Who's to blame!" she suddenly screamed. "Am I to blame? I was only trying to do something nice. Is my husband to blame? He told me to do it. I didn't really want to, but he pushed me. And where the hell is God!? Is God to blame? Why would God hurt me like this? What have I done to deserve this?"

I didn't even try to answer her questions. And I knew she didn't really want any answers. She only wanted to scream it out to the universe. She wanted to try and release her pain somewhere. And there is no greater pain than a mother who has lost her child. I knew that.

"Oh, my son! My beautiful son! I love him so much! Why was he taken from me? Why? Why? Why?" she cried out in agony.

Just then something deep inside of me suddenly welled up and I too burst out crying along with her. The intense suffering of a mother's loss had triggered my own. I was now also weeping uncontrollably.

The surprised woman forgot her own suffering for a moment and turned to me. "Did you lose a child too?" she asked.

I could only nod yes at this point.

"Then you know what it's like. You know," she said.

Again, I nodded. But that's all I could tell her. If I told her the truth, she would be angry with me. I knew that. Her son was gone forever, and she would have to live with that overwhelming burden for the rest of her life. In her mind, she felt she had opened her heart to me. She had cried in front of me. And now she felt that we had connected through the same suffering. We were sisters bonded in horrible misery. So how could I tell her the truth? How could tell her that my son—my son, whom I lost years ago, was still alive?

∞◇∞

That night, as I laid my head upon my pillow, I thought about Matty just as I did every night. I tried to imagine where he was and what he was doing. I envisioned all kinds of things about how his life was going. Positive things. Happy things. I thought, maybe if I did this, it would make these things come true for him. I wanted him to be happy. I wanted him to have a good life.

Many would think it funny that I never searched him out on the internet. Scouring the world wide web for photos or any snippet of information. But the thing is, I couldn't. First of all, I knew it wouldn't help make anything better. Everything would still be the same. And secondly, to see him out there in the world—so un-reachable—so untouchable, would be agonizing. I couldn't bear that much pain. So instead, I just imagined him.

And I don't know why I could never find him in my dreams. I desperately wanted to try and fix everything and believed my best hope was to be able to do it from that world. But no matter how much I called out to him and searched through that mysterious shifting sea of spirits, I could never find my Matty. Why this was, I didn't understand. Was it because he didn't want me to find him? Can an awake-self hide away their dream-selves from others? All I knew was that every night I searched and every night he continued to elude me.

Oh, the irony! Here was my dream-self, so powerful and self-assured, saving millions of lights who were in dreaded peril. Moving minds to help ensure that hope and progress are given fertile ground in the awake world. Helping fill the planet with music and art—the magnificent healing languages of God. Doing everything that could be done to secure the continuation of human beings who were always on the edge of annihilation. But yet, when it came to Matty—the one person I loved in this world more than anyone, I was helpless. Even my powerful dream-self could do nothing. That woman who lost her son was right to ask God why? Why did it have to be like this?

I rolled over on my side and stared out into the darkness of my room. Sleep was near and there was much to be done in that other world. Some of it I knew about and some of it I would be guided into. But before that happened, I'd have a little time to swim through that spiritual sea and search. As I closed my eyes, I felt the beginning of the transitioning. My awake-self, Clarissa, was beginning to sink into the background while my dream-self began rising to the surface. In that moment I thought, "Maybe tonight, Matty. Maybe tonight I will find you and I can tell you everything. And you'll understand. And you won't be angry anymore. You'll understand and it will all be alright—it will all be alright."

Twenty-Four

The lake was warm and comforting as they floated side by side on their backs, softly bobbing in the gentle waves. He reached over and took her hand in his. Their lights instantly merged and the sky above them suddenly filled with flowing silky vermilion clouds. "This is peace," he said. "Glorious, beautiful peace."

"Peace," she said. "All things must move towards peace."

"Yes," he replied. "Peace must reign overall."

For a few moments, they just floated there silently, enjoying the calm they found in each other and in that place. Staring into the beautiful sky, they watched as a flock of vibrant turquoise birds flew overhead. "Those are not from Jonah's cabin," she said laughingly.

"No, but they are beautiful," he replied. "And they do look amazing against the sky, don't you think?"

"Perhaps, Jonah's paintings have made you more interested in creating with colour and image."

"Hmmm...that's very possible," he agreed. "I just know that I want a place where we can go and feel good about everything. This is important to help support Jonah and Clarissa. The awake world is very stressful. The dreamworld can offer us sanctuary."

"How stressful is it for Jonah?" she asked suddenly concerned about him. "Is he coping? I hate to think of him being among those dangerous men."

"He's actually doing quite well, considering his situation," he assured her. "A lot of that has to do with you. You strengthen me and I strengthen Jonah. Without you, I don't know where we'd be. I don't know how Jonah would manage it."

"I'm glad I'm helping," she said. "I want to be there for the both of you."

"There is one thing though," he suddenly admitted.

"What is it?" she asked, sensing that this was something he was hesitant to tell her.

"It's nothing really. And I don't want to worry you but there is something. It's simply an added stress on Jonah. One of the more dominating members of the group doesn't like or trust him. Jonah secretly calls him The Rat. The Rat is intimidated by him because Jonah's intelligence and expertise far exceeds his own. This base jealousy has caused him to scrutinize every move Jonah makes. The Rat is looking for anything that can be used against him. Because of this, Jonah has had to be even more cautious while gathering evidence. The good thing is that The Rat doesn't suspect he's a spy. It's all just envy and petty politics for now, but if he were to notice something and raise suspicion among the others, there's a good chance Jonah would be in danger. And if they all came to believe that Jonah posed a threat, they wouldn't hesitate to kill him."

"Oh no!" she exclaimed upset at merely the thought. "We must protect Jonah!"

"Please don't be too alarmed," he told her. "Jonah will stay safe. He has to. It's not just for his sake but for the sake of millions of other lives too."

"Is there anything I can do? Is there anything Clarissa can do that she isn't doing already?"

"No, there's nothing you can do. The Rat is just something Jonah has to handle on his own. He's dealt with similar types throughout his career. They're common enough. Each one has his own set of peculiarities but overall, they are mostly all the same. Jonah just has to find the balance between standing up to him and not antagonizing him too much. The Rat is cunning, but cunning is simply a base instinct. A predatory instinct but still just an instinct. It's not an intelligence. Jonah can always out-smart him. It's about being able to know where The Rat is both physically and mentally—making sure he's not coming up behind you with a knife whether figuratively or literally."

"He sounds like a very terrible and dangerous man," she said.

"He definitely is, but please don't worry. Jonah knows what he's doing. Yes, The Rat is complicating things, but Jonah can handle it. He's strong."

"Yes, I can feel that, through you. He is strong. I'll try not to worry and to keep focused on my part of things," she told him.

"It is nice though," he said.

"What's nice?" she asked.

"To have someone who worries about you. Our connection is growing stronger, isn't it?"

"It is," she replied. "I'm surprised. I didn't expect this. Especially when I first learned who you were."

"I'm not sure what I expected when I found you," he said. "I guess I didn't think too much about it. I just wanted your help and would be grateful if I got only that. But this connection—it keeps growing. And we keep growing."

"We do. It's helping us both. We are evolving."

"And we're really going to do this, aren't we? We are really going to stop the devastation. Do you feel it? Do you feel that it is our destiny?"

"I have no doubt," she told him. "We will save those millions of people and protect the future of the world. That is who we are and that is what we must do."

∞◊∞

"Did you hear!? I got the job!" Zeke stood at my open kitchen door with a massive smile on his face.

"Congratulations! Traci did tell me about it."

"Would you like to celebrate with me?" he asked holding up a bottle of wine.

"You do know, I'm supposed to be working on my thesis tonight," I replied. "But...maybe just one glass."

"Yes!" he shouted and then walked in before I could say anything else.

"I'm just so excited and needed to share this good news with someone. I mean besides Jake who right now is more interested in watching a show about Egyptian mummies rather than talking to me about my new job."

"Take a seat," I said gesturing towards the kitchen chairs. I then turned to get a corkscrew out of the drawer and two glasses from the cupboard.

"This'll be a new start—a new start," he said pulling out a chair and sitting down. I walked over, set the two glasses on the table and handed him the corkscrew.

I then sat down opposite him and watched as he happily uncorked the bottle. "Only half, please," I said as he began to pour the first glass. "I need to get back to work later."

"That's okay," he proclaimed. "All the more for me!"

After sliding my glass over, he filled his to nearly over-flowing. "Oops," he said then, without lifting it, leaned over and noisily sipped the wine. "Sorry, that's so rude of me."

"It's fine," I laughed. "No need to apologize. It would have likely spilled all over if you didn't do that."

He then lifted his glass and announced, "Here's to new beginnings!"

"To new beginnings," I agreed, clinking my glass to his. After taking a small sip I then set my glass down on the table.

I looked across at Zeke, but he wasn't looking back at me. Instead, he was silently looking down at the glass in front of him. I waited a moment before I asked, "Are you alright?"

"I'm fine," he replied. "Nothing to worry about."

He then looked up and I could see there were tears in his eyes. He was not fine. He was in pain.

"There's definitely something wrong," I said.

"No. Everything is alright. I guess I'm just too excited about the new job is all. It's just a bit overwhelming."

"Zeke, remember how you told me that you were a talker and that talking made you feel better? Well, start talking," I told him.

For a moment, he just stared down at the table, and I waited. Finally, he looked up and said, "Oh, I'm sorry. I'm so sorry, Clarissa. I should just go. I thought I could do this but look at me. I'm falling apart. I thought that coming here—drinking a little wine—making jokes—talking about my new job—enjoying your company—all of it would make me forget, but it isn't working."

"What's not working? What's the matter?"

"No, I should just go. This was a bad idea." He went to get up.

"Sit where you are," I told him. "You cannot leave without telling me what is wrong. Please Just talk to me."

He then sat back down in the chair and took another sip of wine before he said, "This is not a good day for me."

"Yes, I can see that."

"I've had a lot of good days lately. More than ever. But today is bad. Really bad. You see, today is our anniversary. Tara and I were married ten years ago today. We had an ongoing joke about this day. The tenth is tin—or aluminum. Tara used to joke that on this day, she was going to buy me a Tin Man costume and I told her I'd get her one hundred rolls of aluminum foil. But we didn't make it. We didn't make it to the tenth. We just didn't make it. I'm so sorry. I should go now." He then put his head in his hands and began to cry.

"No, you stay where you are," I told him. "You can't go back to Jake like this. Drink your wine and we'll talk a bit. Whatever you'd like to discuss—whatever you're comfortable with. If you want to talk about Tara, we will talk about her. If you want to talk about something different, we will do that. But you must only drink that one glass. That stuff can make it all worse."

"You're right," he said, now looking up at me. "I have to get myself together—for Jake's sake." He then wiped his eyes and added, "Actually, do you have a cup of your wonderful coffee? It's likely better if I just stick to coffee tonight."

"I'll make you a cup," I told him getting up and going over to the kitchen counter. "And I think maybe I'll join you with a cup of tea."

"Thank you," he replied. "I appreciate it."

"It's no problem, Zeke. This is a very challenging day for you—I understand that and I'm happy to help," I said as I switched on the kettle and dumped the ground coffee into the press.

For a while Zeke was quiet but then he suddenly asked, "Have you ever been married, Clarissa?" He then quickly followed it up with, "Now, if that's too personal a question, you don't have to answer. I just wondered. I mean, there must have been loads of men who wanted to marry you. Not that I'm suggesting you've had loads of men. Oh, why did I just say that? I'm really not myself tonight. Sorry."

I laughed while pouring the boiling water into the coffee press and then my cup. "Don't worry. I know you didn't mean anything by it. And the answer to that question is, yes. Yes, I was married once and then divorced."

"Was that recent?" he asked.

"Oh no. It's been a very long time," I answered carrying the tray with tea and coffee over to the table then sitting down.

"Are you still in touch?"

"No. He's passed on now," I said. "He passed on about ten years ago."

"Oh, I'm sorry. I didn't know," Zeke replied.

"No need to be sorry," I told him as I plunged the coffee press. I then poured the coffee into the cup and set it in front of him.

He picked it up, blew on it a little then took a sip. "Ahh...just what I needed—a little something to clear the head not something to fuzzy the brain."

"You can drink the wine another time when you're feeling better," I told him removing the teabag from my cup. "When you're down is not the time to drink."

"Yes, you're right. I don't know what I was thinking," he said taking another sip of the hot coffee. "There's just so many things happening—lots of good things. And not having Tara here to share them with me. It's just hard. It's hard to feel so good and so bad at the same time."

"Life is absurd and you're just trying your best to survive. We're all just trying to survive the things that get thrown at us," I replied.

"You're a wise woman," Zeke smiled, taking another sip of his coffee. "How did your husband ever let you go?"

"Oh, believe me, he didn't want to," I found myself saying while not being entirely sure how much I wanted to share with Zeke. I'd only ever talked in detail about my marriage to Traci—of course leaving out the part about Matty.

"Hmmm, so are you saying that he was controlling? Was he the controlling type?"

"Well...yes, he was. But at the time, I didn't realize it. I was young and extremely vulnerable. You see, at the age of eighteen, I lost my parents in a car accident."

"Oh no, that's terrible!" Zeke exclaimed. "I'm so sorry, Clarissa. That couldn't have been easy."

I wrapped my hands around my warm teacup and said, "It was a difficult time. Very difficult. And because my parents had me late in life it meant my grandparents had already passed on. And my parents being only children as far as I knew, meant there were no relatives left at all. At one of the most challenging ages, I found myself entirely alone in the world."

"That's sad—so sad."

I wanted to stop there. I didn't want to share too much more, but somehow my story seemed to be making Zeke forget his own pain. So, for that reason, I kept going.

"Not only was I then without my parents," I explained, "but they had left nothing behind to help me. Once their debts were paid off, there was only three thousand dollars left for me to start my life alone. I mean, they say eighteen is an adult but it's not. You're still a child in so many ways. You're so vulnerable at that age even when you have support. To find yourself alone like that...well..." I paused for a moment as I gathered my thoughts. What to say next? How much to reveal?

"I don't know how I did it," I continued, "but somehow, I managed to rent a room in a house and enrol in university. I got a small government grant to help me, and I also had a job working nights and weekends in a restaurant. So, I was making it on my own, but it was hard, and I was still trying to deal with the emotional impact of losing the two most important people in my life.

"It was shortly after my nineteenth birthday that I met Matthew. He came in and ordered a beer and fish and chips. He started flirting with me, so I flirted back because that's how you got better tips. It reached the point where he was coming in every shift I had. If things weren't busy, we'd chat a bit. He was twelve years older than me and at the time seemed to know so much. Eventually, he asked me out and the next thing I knew, we were married. I thought I was in love, but I think the truth is that I just needed something, and I thought Matthew was it. He had stability in the world when I felt like I was just treading water. But I'm not talking about financial stability. I'm talking about the bigger picture. He had a place in the world—a mother and father and two sisters. He seemed to know who he was and had a job he identified with. At the time, he also seemed to know so much about everything. He had a place in the world and that's what I wanted—a place to set my feet firmly on the ground.

"It was wonderful for the first two years, but after that I began to realize something was wrong. Matthew just didn't seem the same as he did before. But he hadn't changed. The truth was that I was the one who was changing. I was quickly outgrowing him. And to make matters worse, he became more and more controlling as he sensed my moving away from him. I tried to make it work despite everything, but it was all so unworkable. And his family was awful to me. Matthew was the youngest—a late life baby for his parents. They were all very protective of him, his parents and sisters, and they didn't like me at all. They didn't do anything overtly nasty. It was mostly snide passive-aggressive remarks. But I kept quiet about it to keep the peace. For some reason they imagined I married Matthew for money even though he had nothing but a car loan. But that didn't matter. They saw me the way they wanted to see me—as the outsider.

"Shortly before we reached our fourth anniversary, I knew something had to be done. It took me three years after that to get him to sign the divorce papers. He didn't want to let me go despite the fact the naïve teenager who once adored him no longer existed. He hated me for that—for growing up. He hated me intensely.

"After the divorce, it was hard. I had left university shortly after marrying and so my career options were limited. I found myself working jobs far below my abilities. It was always low-grade office work in toxic environments. I looked for better things, but the economy was bad at that time and I just couldn't catch a break. Those dead-end jobs were all I was able to find, and with the bills due every month, I just didn't have much choice. I felt so trapped, but I kept going.

"Six years after my divorce I got a letter from a lawyer informing me of an inheritance. This was a surprise. It seems that my father was not an only child after all. He had an older estranged brother whom he never spoke of. I was the sole heir of his estate which was quite sizable. It meant that I'd never have to work at another meaningless job again."

"Well, that was some good news!" Zeke said genuinely happy for me. "Finally, you did get a break."

"Yes," I said, "it was a great relief to no longer have to worry about paying rent or the food bill." At that point, I didn't tell him how the money was both a blessing and a terrible curse. Instead, I just let him believe that this was the good part of my story. All stories need a happy ending.

"One of the first things I did after getting my money was to quit my job and enrol in university. That's what has kept me busy ever since. Right now, I'm working on my fifth degree. My Master in Philosophy."

"That's a lot of degrees!" he laughed.

"It may seem a bit silly, but I enjoy it," I told him. "It keeps me sharp and I'm always learning new things. If I'm going to have a hobby, this is the one that makes the most sense—to me anyway."

"Well, I'm glad something good came your way. It's important to be able to do what you love," said Zeke. "I love being an engineer and I know I'm really going to love teaching it to others."

Just then there was a little knock on the door and Jake walked in. "Dad the show's over. Are you coming home now? I'm hungry. Can you make one of your special super sandwiches?"

Zeke laughed. "You know, I'm kind of hungry too. Maybe I'll make a super sandwich for both of us. How about you Clarissa? Do you want a super sandwich?"

"As tempting as that sounds," I said, "I need to get back to work. But thanks for the offer."

"Alright then Jake, it looks like you and me get all the super sandwiches! Let's go!"

Jake ran out the door and back to the apartment.

Before leaving Zeke turned to me and said, "Thank you, Clarissa. Talking to you helped me tonight. I really appreciate that. Also, I'm sorry for what you've been through, but I'm glad you're in a better place now."

"Thanks, Zeke," I told him. "I'm happy to have helped."

At that he turned and left.

As I poured the glasses of wine down the sink, I wondered why I had told Zeke so much about my past. I didn't mean to. I meant to keep it vague without too much detail. Somehow though, talking to him felt so natural and it just all came out. And it did, after all, seem to help him—hearing about someone else's tragedy. That's the thing that bonds us—the need to be connected. Especially in sadness and misery, we need to know we are not alone. Our flesh divides us, but our flesh also makes coming together possible in important ways.

Twenty-Five

"Don't be alarmed but Jonah had a close call today," he said not wanting to hold back anything from her.

"Oh no! What happened? Is he okay?" she exclaimed, suddenly realizing that any threat to Jonah's life had become of deep personal concern for her. Her emotional connection to him had grown beyond merely the dreamworld.

"Yes, he's fine," he reassured her. "It could have turned out very badly, but he's safe."

"Tell me what happened?"

"It was The Rat. The Rat is becoming increasingly paranoid. He's been pushing the group towards tighter and tighter security and scrutinizing everything said and done. I think he's even gone so far as to spy outside of their homes. At least Jonah was sure he saw him one night sitting in his car outside of his building. The Rat has become a real problem."

"What did he do?" she asked, desperately wanting to somehow help but also knowing her power in this case was limited. The Rat could not be reached from dreams. None of those men could. They were too dead inside.

"It happened at the meeting this evening," he told her.

"Did Jonah expect it? How high risk are these meetings?" she asked.

"Before now it hasn't been a problem. The meetings are quite straight forward. By order of their number, each member is given a turn to arrange it. That person chooses a different time and a different remote location. The location is not divulged until a few hours before it happens.

"Yesterday morning Jonah received instructions to go to an abandoned farm outside of the city just before sunset. After driving up the long dirt lane, he parked his car in line with the others not far from an old caved-in Dutch barn."

"They use their cars! What about license plates?" she asked. "Could Jonah not find their identities from those?"

"They all use stolen license plates. With the bureaucracy in such a mess and local law enforcement mostly absent, it's no problem to do something like that these days. There's no one to pull us over or question it."

"Oh, I see. I'm sorry for interrupting. Please tell me what happened. I am concerned about Jonah's safety."

"I know you are," he assured her reaching out and touching his hand to hers. "I feel your concern."

He then continued, "So, when Jonah got out of his car, he was curious to see the group waiting not far away on a path leading to an old wood-frame farmhouse. The last man drove in shortly after him and then they both walked together towards the group.

"That's when The Rat accused Jonah and the last man of arriving together, something which was against the rules. Of course, it wasn't true, and everyone knew it, including him. They all saw us drive in separately. Jonah told him as much and he backed down. But that wasn't the end of it.

"Jonah then learned that the reason the men were all still standing outside and not yet inside the house was because The Rat was insisting on adding an extra security measure. He wanted everyone in the group to be searched by two other members to ensure that no one was a traitor to their cause. Jonah could see that the others felt insulted and uncomfortable with the idea, but if anyone objected it would just bring suspicion upon that person, so, they all agreed to the searches.

"All guns and phones were already left at home during meetings as that was one of their primary rules. This search was more about finding any devices that could be used as a weapon or for surveillance purposes.

"The recording device Jonah was using was extremely discreet and easily hidden in the hand. It was a small penlight that didn't look like much else even upon close inspection. It was something left over from his days at the CIA. But some of these men are trained to recognize this type of technology. Jonah knew it wouldn't pass the test if they examined it. One of them would certainly see what it really was.

"As they discussed the best way to conduct the searches, Jonah took a moment to look around. He needed to find some way to get rid of the device before they could discover it. That's when he noticed a water filled trench right behind The Rat. If he could reach it, he could drop the penlight into the muddy water where it would never be found. But he'd have to do it without being noticed.

"That's when Jonah suddenly told The Rat, "Let's just get this over with. Why don't I start by searching you, then you can search me, then one of the others can search us both."

"Jonah could see that The Rat immediately liked the idea. He knew he would. After so many years of studying human nature, Jonah understood how The Rat would jump at the chance of trying to dominate Jonah in any way possible, even if it was something as small as crossing physical boundaries.

"So, Jonah walked over, stood behind The Rat and began to pat him down. He removed the car keys from The Rat's coat pocket and carefully examined them.

"They're just keys," laughed The Rat.

"Yes, they are," said Jonah who then held them up to show the others. He placed them back into the Rat's pocket.

"Jonah then crouched slightly to search The Rat's pants. "Excuse me but this was your idea," Jonah said as he checked between The Rat's legs. It was during this awkward moment that, with his other hand, he quickly removed the penlight from his pocket and covertly slipped it into the trench behind him."

"And no one noticed?" she asked.

"No one noticed. The penlight was black, and with the setting sun, it was dark enough not to be seen."

"That's such a relief."

"Yes...yes it was.

"Although Jonah did manage to escape with his life, it's unfortunate that he lost the only device he had for recording the meetings."

"But Jonah is alive. That's the most important thing. He's still alive," she said with a sigh. "Oh, I wish there were something I could do to help him, but these men are too dark. I can't reach them. I can only change things by reaching into the places where there is a reasonable degree of light. The most I can do is try to make you stronger so that you can at least help Jonah. I feel bad that I cannot do more for the both of you."

"You are doing so much already," he said, holding her hand tighter and watching their lights melt into each other. "Do you see it? Do you see how much brighter my light is then when I first found you? I'm so much stronger because of you, and Jonah is so much stronger because of me. We can do this. You, me, my Jonah, your Clarissa. We can do this together."

"I believe we can," she told him. "And I have noticed how much stronger you are—how much brighter. I am worried a little about the time though. Here, in this world, we have no use of time but for Jonah and Clarissa and all those lives at risk, time is crucial. How much will this lost device set us back? Will we still be able to stop them?"

"The good news is that losing the device is a just small setback as the authorities have already received enough recordings to verify that this is real. What we need now are names and the information about where the weapon is hidden. These are things that will not be found by simply recording the meetings anyway."

"So how will this affect you sending information to Max?" she asked.

"It's still not safe to simply send anything across the internet given all *that's at stake. Instead, whatever new things Jonah discovers will have to be written down on paper. It will be in code—a code that Max will know. There are a lot of other people that are familiar with that code but it's still better than nothing at all. It's still an added level of security. And the information will still be hidden behind the paintings. Max will pass it on the same as he always has."*

"That weapon must be located soon," she said. "I can't bear to think what would happen if it were deployed. And Canada is in as much danger as the U.S. Both your world and Clarissa's world could be completely annihilated."

"I can assure you that Jonah has been working on it. He's been able to learn that three of the members hold three separate pieces of information that, when revealed together, identify the location. The Rat, unfortunately, is one of those three. The weapon was hidden by a high-ranking general who was involved in deploying the first weapon. He was arrested just last year on charges of war crimes and is now awaiting trial in The Hague. He's the one who set all this up. Before he was arrested, he hid the weapon and organized The Rat and the others. They, of course, don't have any contact with him now but are still very loyal. In their minds, this general is a misunderstood American hero who will be absolved when the new world order is established," he explained.

"They are so delusional," she said.

"Yes," he replied. "But evil is always delusional, isn't it?"

"It's the empty void of darkness that comes about when the mind destroys the light that is its only nourishment," she told him. "Without the light, the mind is starved and so it devours itself. Full of itself, it becomes nothing but ego, and ego leads to death. Death. Real death. The death of the body, the mind and the light is a terrible thing," she said with a sigh. "There is no coming back from real death and real death is slow and painful for whatever is left of the conscious mind."

"Of course!" he exclaimed, once again elated to learn something new. "That makes perfect sense. The more I come here to be with you, the more I

understand. And the more Jonah understands too. It's all becoming clearer now, and it's helping. It's helping with what we are doing, and I'm so grateful for that," he said. "You are the most wonderful thing to have ever happened to me."

"Knowledge is love," she told him.

"Knowledge is love," he whispered back to her. He then softly leaned his forehead into hers and their lights entwined in pure ecstasy.

∞◊∞

"Surprise!" shouted Zeke and Jake in unison. Zeke was waving two small pieces of paper in the air while I just stood there at my open kitchen door in utter confusion.

"Do you know what these are?" Zeke asked as if he was about to divulge some great amazing secret.

"Umm...no, not really," I replied laughingly.

"Tickets! Look! Take them! They're a gift from me and Jake."

"Yes, from me too!" added Jake.

I took the tickets in my hand and looked at them. My heart sank and I felt a little sick. They were tickets alright.

"But Zeke, I don't understand."

"It's a thank-you gift for all you've done for us! And I know you like his music because I've heard you playing it when your window was open. Are you excited?"

"I'm speechless," I said, because I was.

"After the accident and all, they weren't sure if he'd be back. They called it a miracle that he's singing again so soon after that. It was such a bad accident. Anyway, this should be a really big concert."

"Yes," I agreed, "It is going to be a big concert which means these were very expensive tickets...and second row too. I just can't accept such a gift. It's too much. You shouldn't be spending your money on me. Perhaps you could scalp them and make a profit."

"Don't worry about that. I didn't spend all that much. One of my colleagues from work has connections and was able to get them for me at less than face value. I got the refugee discount," he laughed. "And you should also know that a deal is very close to being worked out regarding the locked down American banks so it shouldn't be long before I'll be able to access our old savings. It won't be the full amount, but it will be significant enough. Tara and I were very good savers. I won't have to count my pennies much longer."

"But still," I said, "it's just too generous. Really, you don't owe me anything." I felt a little extra guilty as I was not being completely honest. Yes, I did not want Zeke spending his money on me but more than that, I didn't want those tickets. I didn't want to see that man in the flesh. I didn't want to sit there in the crowd pretending to be just another fan.

"It's not about owing," said Zeke. "It's about Jake and me showing gratitude. And look! Did you see? Those aren't just any tickets. Those are VIP tickets. You'll get to meet him!"

I forced a smile. "Wow, that's...that's amazing. I don't know what to say."

"Just say you're happy!" he said, grinning from ear to ear.

"Yeah, say you're happy," added Jake.

"Yes...uh...I'm just so shocked. I never expected such a thing."

"I knew you'd love them," he said beaming. "When I kept hearing that music coming from your window, I just knew it. Have you seen him before?"

"No, never."

"That's fantastic because now you get a chance to finally do it."

I felt bad at how thrilled Zeke and Jake were with the surprise gift. Those tickets really were the last thing I wanted. I couldn't imagine myself going there and actually meeting him. Standing there, awkwardly—playing the idiot fan. It would be a horrible experience. But it meant so much to Zeke and Jake for me to accept and I couldn't let them down. They've been through too much in their lives for me to do that. I knew I was stuck and thought about all the ways I could avoid it—losing the tickets—feigning sickness but none of those things would spare their feelings.

It was then that I thought of something that could perhaps make the whole thing at least a little more tolerable. Knowing that I had only one real option, I then asked Zeke, "Okay, I will accept your generous gift on one condition."

"And what would that be?" he asked still smiling.

"That you go with me."

"Me?" he laughed in surprise.

"I know it's likely not your kind of music, but I can't ask Traci because she cannot stand live concerts. The loudspeakers and bass are too much for her. Would you go with me?"

"Yeah, go Dad," said Jake.

"To be honest, I never considered going myself," he replied. "But you know what? Now that I think about it, it's been a long time since I went out and had some fun. A very long time. Sure, I'll go with you. We'll have a great time!"

"That's wonderful," I said relieved that he was willing to go. It was true about Traci disliking concerts but also, I wanted to go with Zeke. If I had to face my songbird—if I had to look him in the eye, I'd like to at least do it with a young handsome man at my side. It may seem shallow or even vain, but I just didn't think I could stand seeing him look at me in that way—just another invisible fan. After all I'd done and all I'd been to him, to then have him look at me like that, would possibly be unbearable. With Zeke by my side, at least I'd have some degree of dignity and a woman's fight is always a fight for dignity.

"That settles that then," said Zeke.

"Thank you," I told him sincerely. "For the tickets. It's very thoughtful and you're very kind—both of you."

"Oh, now you're making me blush," he said. "I'm just glad you like them."

"Me too," agreed Jake who then said, "Dad, I just remembered I forgot to set up a recording. It's a dig in the Sahara Desert. They're uncovering a really big mystery. I gotta go now."

"Better hurry then," Zeke told him.

"I'm glad you liked our surprise," Jake said to me. "Dad said you'd love it."

"I do love it!" I smiled. "It's the best surprise ever."

"Okay, the show starts soon. See you later," chirped Jake happily. He then ran off towards the apartment.

We both watched as he disappeared inside. "He's such a bright boy," Zeke said. "Always teaching me things I never even heard of before. He'll make a fine archaeologist."

"He's very lucky to have found you—both you and Tara," I told him.

"And we were lucky to have found him," he replied. "Sometimes you know, Clarissa, you don't find the people you expect to find but you do find the people that you need to find."

Twenty-Six

"Do you still make music? It's just that, we spend so much time together now. Do you still take the time to make music?" he suddenly asked her.

"Not much," she answered. "I've changed. I've grown. And also, music out there—it's not the same as it once was. The singers who are given a voice in that world are now mostly just the mediocre children of the wealthy whose parents fund their careers. The songs are mostly written by computers and marketing teams. And it's become political but not in a good way. Music used to be more about challenging corrupt power but now it only serves it. In some ways, it's not really music anymore. It's just shallow sounds, greed and empty consumption. How can you create meaningful music from that? There's nothing there for me to work with. Perhaps one day I will find something in another land, but not here. Music—the kind of music capable of moving souls, seems to have died in Jonah and Clarissa's culture."

"That's so sad," he said. "Jonah does really enjoy music. He loved listening to it while sitting around at the cabin and even sometimes at his desk when he was supposed to be concentrating on his work. But it's true he doesn't think much of the new stuff. You're right that it is empty now. There is an emptiness to it."

"I wish it wasn't true but that's what it's become. Of course, not all older music was great but there were some songs that are truly precious."

"You mean the ones you helped write?" he asked humorously.

She laughed. "Yes. I don't want to brag but the ones I helped write were the best. But that's just the way of things. It's not about ego. It's about what I am—what those songs are."

"And that singer I saw you with—what happened to him?"

"He's better," she told him. "He's no longer at risk of losing all light but he's not the same as he used to be either. I can help a little with his new song but it's not going to be a great song. He just doesn't have it in him anymore. The connection we once had—it's not there. He no longer has the ability to reach out to me in that way and create within the intensity of our coming together."

"I'm not unhappy to hear that—about the connection. Do you think that's bad of me?"

She laughed. "No, I understand how you feel. I suppose I would feel the same way."

"It makes me happy to hear you say so," he said taking her hand. She felt the warmth and comfort of his hand melting into hers.

For a while, they were silent then she suddenly exclaimed, "Would you like to go to the beach?"

"The beach?"

"Yes, Clarissa has always found peace and serenity on the tropical beach. Shall we go?"

"Why not," he replied and then suddenly they were sitting side by side in the warm sand at the edge of the water, the gentle waves lapping at their toes.

"This is nice," he said. "I'm glad you brought me here. It's peaceful."

"And just look out there! Look at that that turquoise sea!" she smiled.

"I see it!" he replied. "It's beautiful!"

"It's more than beautiful. It's a mystery. On the surface, it looks like a blue crystal table. It looks incredible but it also looks alone. Solitary. Yet it is not alone, for underneath, it is teaming with life of all sorts. The sea is not simply what we see on the surface. In truth it is a mother full

of amazing and curious creatures. And here we are—staring out at this incredible wonder and we—we too are mysteries."

"We are magnificent mysteries," he said, moving closer to her so their legs were melding together. "We are life itself!"

"Yes," she replied. "I feel it. I feel so alive when I am with you and my light shines even brighter because of it."

He wrapped his arms around her and suddenly they were no longer sitting. They were now lying together entwined in the sand. "If the tide came in and carried us out and into the belly of the great mother, would we transform? Would we become sea creatures? Perhaps we would we grow tails and fins and gills and spend our whole lives swimming until we became either too old or were eaten by a shark," he said laughingly.

"You are so silly," she smiled. "You know we walked out of that sea a very long time ago. Why would we return? What meaning is there in being a fish when we can be this—what we are now in this place—in this ecstasy. A fish may feel pleasure, but we can exist in incredible joy. We procure the light. We are the light."

"We are the light," he repeated. "And we must keep it going."

"Yes, we must ensure that the lights remain and that there is adequate space for them to brighten. Because without light, there cannot even be fish."

"Or Jonah, or Clarissa?"

"Or Jonah, or Clarissa who made us possible," she said. "And we made them possible. And now we are all together here, taking the path that must be taken."

"We'll save the world," he whispered into her ear, but it didn't sound like a whisper. Instead, it sounded like a melody. A beautiful melody.

"We'll save the world," she sang back to him. "That's what we're here for."

∞◊∞

"I hate shopping!" I complained in frustration. "When you're young, you can wear anything. Why can't it be that easy again?"

"We've only been to three stores so far," laughed Traci as we walked along the sidewalk. "Don't worry. We'll find you the perfect outfit."

"The problem," I said, "is that it's such a balance for women our age. You don't want old and frumpy, but you don't want to look ridiculous either. You want to look interesting but not too interesting, so that they assume you have dementia. You want to still look like a vibrant woman in a culture that tries everything it can to steal that from you."

"That's true," Traci agreed. "It can be challenging."

"And then, sometimes it happens that when you do spot something nice and think 'wow, that would look great', you have to suddenly remind yourself that yes, once it would have looked great but now it's just not going to work anymore. It's no longer the right shape. What was once flattering is now unflattering. Why is it that they don't make nice clothes for us? They could and it would be very profitable, but they don't. I suppose it's a failing of a youth-worshipping culture. Finding something that's both interesting and complimentary is hard."

"Stop worrying. We'll find something," Traci tried to reassure me.

"And how do I know if I'm seeing something correctly. What if, in my frustration and confusion, I just can't see it? And then I buy the wrong thing and then maybe I only realize it when it's too late. I hate shopping!"

"Oh, Issa," Traci laughed. "You always overthink things. Besides, you have me along. I'm an honest friend who will tell you if something doesn't look right. Try and relax. You can trust me to help."

"Of course. You're right," I said, happy to be reminded that I was not alone in this. "You have set me up with some questionable characters in the past, but you always have good taste in clothes. That's true," I laughed.

Traci did have an eye for tasteful fashion and would definitely tell me if I were making a bad choice. And I just couldn't make a bad choice. Not for this. For this, I needed an ensemble that would give me confidence. I needed to be able to walk right up to him and look him in the eye without feeling self-conscious or belittled.

Yet at the same time, why? Why am I like that? Why couldn't I just march up there wearing anything at all. Not giving a care in the world. Why should my confidence be tied to something as superficial as clothing? I wish it were that easy. I wish I could just turn it all off. That I would not care about what other people thought of me. Least of all him. Are there people like that? Are there people— mentally healthy people who just go through life as if nobody is looking? If there are, I wish I were one of them.

But then again, how could that possibly work given the reality? Clothing is not only protection against the elements. It's also protection against forms of discrimination. People judge harshly on appearance and clothing. And you do have to protect yourself in any society. Especially if you're a woman. So, I suppose that in the end, it's perhaps about a balance between protecting yourself from discrimination while not falling into the self-defeating trap of vanity and shallowness. And in a world where all the various aspects of female identity are often twisted and used as tools to subjugate women, that takes effort.

"Oh look!" Traci suddenly said. "Is that Crawford? Should we duck into that store ahead and hope he didn't see us?"

Normally I would be all for hiding from Crawford, but it was too late. He had already seen us.

As he approached with a ridiculous large grin on his face, I knew that grin was really about our lovely little American artist. "Good day ladies!" he exclaimed. "Isn't it a beautiful day?"

"Hello Crawford, it's nice to see you. And how are you?" Traci asked.

"I, ladies, am as happy as a cherub on the ceiling of the Sistine Chapel!" he merrily chirped. "And how are you on this fine afternoon?"

Traci laughed. "We're well," she said.

Suddenly, I got the feeling that something was not right. Crawford was just a little too happy. He was up to something, and I needed to know what it was. "Traci, would you mind going ahead into the shop and having a look around, I just want to talk with Crawford for a second," I said.

"Oh!" Traci said a bit confused. "Alright. Uh, it was good to see you Crawford."

"And you too, milady," he said with a slight bow.

As soon as Traci had left, I turned to Crawford and asked, "What's up? Something's up."

"I'm not sure what you're talking about," he said still grinning from ear to ear.

"Something's not right. I have a kind of instinct for that sort of a thing and my instincts are never wrong. You have to tell me what's going on," I insisted.

"Perhaps your instincts have failed you this time," he said with a chuckle.

"Oh no they have not. You need to tell me what's going on, Crawford. I'm serious. You cannot keep secrets from me."

"Well then, if you insist," he relented while still grinning. "There is one thing that I would have told you eventually. You see, I've decided that I'm keeping the most recent of Melody's painting. It came in yesterday. I'm not going to send it off to the gallery. Instead, I'm going to pay her directly, so that she will receive all of the money. No gallery commission. Actually, I wanted to surprise her with this news. I know she's alone and in need of funds, and I just adore her newest work. I absolutely adore it!"

"No Crawford, you can't do that!"

"And why not," he replied. "How is Max going to know? And if he does find out, what is he going to do about it. There's no contract. I want that painting and I shall have that painting."

"But if he finds out, it could be bad for Melody. She could get an unfortunate reputation in the industry. How could she ever forgive you if that happened?" I said trying to reason with him.

"He won't find out and if he does, who does he know in the art world? I have a far more respected reputation in the community than he—a mere novice and an American. My credentials are far superior, and I can certainly protect my dear Melody from any scurrilous gossip."

"You don't understand. You must get that painting to Max today," I told him. "You must deliver all of her paintings to Max the day you receive them. That's what Melody wants."

"No, I must not," he said defiantly. "And why are you so adamant about this? Is there something between you and Max? Is he paying you to do this?"

"No, of course not." I realized at that point that I needed to do something desperate and hopefully it wouldn't complicate matters. "I know what I'll do. Just let me text her now and I'll ask her directly," I said to him.

"That is a wonderful idea!" he replied excitedly. "Do that! I'd love for you to text her!"

I took out my phone and Crawford stared at it in my hands as if it were Melody herself.

"Go ahead," he said eagerly.

I then quickly texted Traci:

Copy the text below and send to me. Say nothing else...

Please tell Crawford that, for the sake of my future career, he must send all the paintings ASAP to the gallery. Also tell him I'm working on a special painting just for him and he's going to absolutely love it! I'll be bringing it with me on the day we finally meet.

After I sent the text, I turned to Crawford and said, "She should get back to me shortly as long as she's not too involved in working on her next masterpiece." A moment later the text came through. I read it aloud to Crawford and then let him glance at the message while carefully covering everything else with my hand.

"You see, this is what Melody needs from you. You have to follow her instructions," I told him as I quickly whisked the phone into my pocket.

"She's working on a painting just for me? Oh, what a wonderful woman!"

"That's just the kind of person Melody is, Crawford. She's extremely generous and appreciative of everything you've been doing for her. Before you offered to help her, she didn't know how she would ever advance her career."

"I suppose I have been a little selfish in wanting to keep the painting. It's just that it so beautifully exudes her essence, and since we are unable to communicate directly, it was like having a part of her with me."

"You could always buy it from the gallery," I suggested. "That would likely help her even more."

"Yes, of course. I could do that."

"So, you will get that painting to Max today?"

"Yes, yes," he agreed. "Anything for Melody."

"That's good. She has already seen positive things happening with the arrangement, so we can't jeopardize any of that. With everything going so smoothly, and her paintings selling so well, it shouldn't be long before we can get her to Canada."

"Oh yes! Our goal is, after all, to bring her here, isn't it? It's a good thing I ran into you, Clarissa. You've reminded me of the importance of priorities. Priorities are everything. Understanding that is part of level six attainment. I am in the finishing stages of level six, you know."

"I'm very glad I ran into you too," I told him. "And that's brilliant you're reaching an even higher level. You're a great mentor to Melody in so many ways."

"Well then, I'd better hurry off and have Melody's painting couriered over to the gallery," he assured me. "I cannot bear disappointing her even for a moment."

"You truly are her guardian angel," I told him. "And I had better get back to shopping. Traci will be wondering where I am."

"Perhaps then I shall see you later in the week when you will grace me with a new message from our Lady of the Paints," he said.

I smiled as best I could and replied, "I'm sure she'll be sending something special for you shortly. Goodbye, Crawford."

"Adieu," I heard him happily sing as I turned to go into the store.

Once inside, I quickly looked around for Traci. She waved at me from behind a rack of dresses. When I walked over to her, she asked, "What on earth was that all about?"

I already knew what I was going to tell her and hoped it was enough to keep her from asking too many questions. "Well, I didn't want to mention it before because it's perhaps a tad illegal."

"Illegal!" she said in surprise.

"Not illegal exactly but it's in the grey area. You see, I'm helping Max...you remember Max from the gallery...well, I'm helping him get paintings from the U.S. and we're doing it through Crawford."

"You're smuggling art!" exclaimed Traci. "How exciting!"

"It's not exactly smuggling. I mean—it's not illegal—just in the grey area."

"And does Crawford know he's doing stuff in the grey area?" she asked.

"He does but I kind of gave him an incentive," I explained.

"What kind of an incentive?"

"A young fictional woman."

Traci began to laugh. "So that text I sent was from the young fictional woman?"

"Yes," I confessed. "But you can't tell anyone about this—absolutely no one—even Theo."

"My lips are sealed," she said running the tips of her fingers across her lips as if she were closing a zipper. She then leaned in close to me and whispered, "Is there something between you and Max?"

"No," I laughed. "He was really nice when I bought that painting for you and I just wanted to help him out. You're the one who convinced me to help American refugees. Remember?"

She laughed at that. "Well, your secret is safe with me. I kind of like it actually—we're like spies or mastermind criminals or something. It's exciting! My life is too boring. I need a little excitement."

"Okay then," I laughed. "For now, let's just focus on finding me a new outfit. It's been such a long time since I've gone to a concert, and just I need something nice to wear."

"Maybe something that says, *stealth*," Traci laughed.

"Sure," I agreed. "That's me—a real underworld spy."

Twenty-Seven

Standing at the kitchen sink and about to start washing my evening dishes, I paused for a moment to stare out the window. Across the yard the lights from the apartment windows warmly stretched across the lawn like beacons in the darkness. It was comforting. It was comforting to know that Jake and Zeke were inside. Safe behind those walls. They were good people and good people needed to be kept safe.

It's strange how life has such a way of taking one by surprise. Jake and Zeke were definitely something I never expected. And I did try to avoid the whole thing. But try as you may to keep everything simple and stick to a plan, life does have its own ideas, and there's not much you can do about it. Sometimes the changes are small and sometimes they're good. But sometimes life hits you hard with something sudden and not so good.

Most of the time, however, life is slow and covert in its ways. And when it is slow and covert, you don't even know what is happening until it's done. Then there you are. The years gone by. Left dumbfounded. Unsure about how you got to that particular time and in that particular place. Sometimes full of regrets and 'what-ifs'. Wishing you could go back and try again but knowing that's not an option.

And life does trick you. It is the great trickster. It will even trick you into becoming its co-conspirator. Many times, you will conspire against yourself without even knowing it.

And in the end, if you become more aware, it's so easy to feel helpless and bitter about life's fickle embrace. What's much harder is accepting it for the force that it is and trying to work within the absurdity of it all. Trying your best not to let go of the things that really matter. Of goodness and caring outside of yourself. That's what's important. That's what you have to hold onto if you are to survive in spirit. And the survival of spirit is everything because the body won't last forever. What do you have if you've gained the whole world but lost your only self—that powerful yet fragile precious life-force we call 'I'.

Picking up a dirty plate from the counter, I began washing it under the flowing water. As I watched the remnants of my dinner run down the drain, I suddenly I felt a strange sensation in my legs. It started near my feet then quickly surged up through my body and to my head. I was overcome with dizziness and the dish I was holding fell, shattering against the soaking Dutch oven. My legs went weak, and my knees buckled. I quickly grabbed hold of the edge of the counter to try and steady myself to keep from falling to the floor. This was something I had never felt before and for a moment I was frightened I was having a stroke.

But then, just as suddenly as this feeling had come, it was gone. My head was now clear, and my legs felt strong again. I walked cautiously around the kitchen, ensuring everything was working properly. I moved my arms in circles, backwards then forwards, to determine if I was suffering any ill effects. I counted aloud to twenty-five. Then I counted again but backwards. Everything seemed to be normal. I didn't appear to have any symptoms of a stroke. I felt fine. But what had just happened?

In that moment, I decided there was no point in worrying about it. I would, of course, keep an eye on my health but for now, I felt perfectly fine. So, I simply put it down to just one of those inexplicable things. After all, I lived in the world of the inexplicable. Why would another mysterious experience be anything out of the ordinary?

∞◊∞

"Jonah is getting close," he said, his voice so full of hope and optimism. "He's getting close to finding all the information we need."

"That's such good news," she sighed. "The sooner he's out of there the better. I do worry about his safety though."

"He's smart," he assured her. "Most of his life he's had to deal with these sorts of people. He understands what he's up against."

"The sooner he finishes the better."

"His work is progressing fairly quickly considering all that he's facing. He's come to realize that he won't be able to get anything out of The Rat. The Rat has too much of a deep-seated hatred for him. But he's gotten closer to the other two who hold pieces of the puzzle. If all goes well, he may be able to figure out the weapon's location without that third piece. He's already learned the first name of someone in the group. One of the others accidentally let it slip. His name is William, most likely ex-military—if you think you might be able to do anything with that knowledge."

"It's possible," she told him. "Knowing the name and having connected with Jonah's mind through you, it could perhaps lead me to something or someone close to him. Every little piece of information has potential."

"That's good to know. I also have more good news. Jonah has been able to access one of the older CIA databases. It contains information on the identities of millions of Americans. Years ago, when they switched over to a more sophisticated system that included such things as facial recognition, the old database was deemed redundant. So, because it was more or less forgotten, it was overlooked by the U.N. when they dismantled the CIA spy network. Jonah has been searching through some of the possible profiles but so far hasn't had much luck. It's a bit like trying to find a needle in a haystack but it's still something. There's still hope that we can stop them. We just need to know who they are."

"I wish there was more I could do, but I'm so limited in this instance. It is very frustrating," she said.

"You are doing a great deal for Jonah in so many ways. Just by being here with me is enough in itself. Through you he grows in both courage and strength."

"I'm glad. I want to be there for Jonah and for you. I don't want to let you down."

"You won't," he told her. "You could never let us down."

"It's such a balancing act," she said. "Trying to keep both our lights shining and the world alive at the same time is not easy."

"It's a struggle," he agreed. "But think about when this is all over. The terrorists will be safely locked away, and the weapon will be destroyed. And when it's all said and done, Jonah and Clarissa can finally meet face to face."

"Oh yes!" she exclaimed. "I must think about that. It will be a great day. For them to know each other in that world as we know each other in this one—what a gift that is! The absolute complete seeing and knowing of the other. In their meeting, we will be bringing the two worlds together. What a wondrous thing that will be! I can feel it in the mere thought. The unity! The bond! The oneness that heals and nurtures our divided selves. There is no greater meeting for the beings that we are! Somehow, I know this, and I think you know it too. A coming together like that will not only alter existence for us, but it will open a door between the two worlds—a door that has never been opened before. It will change the course for every living being whether in flesh or in spirit. And, most wonderful of all, the day we meet, it will move us all forward. The wonderful progress of humanity marching onward. Unstoppable magnificent humanity."

∞◊∞

"Kierkegaard spoke of the absurdity of life, and Tillich said that we must have the courage to accept ourselves even though we are unacceptable. Does anyone have any thoughts?" the professor asked.

The class was silent the way it often happens in classrooms when the instructor poses a grand open-ended question. So, there we all were just sitting quietly in our philosophical limbo, anxiously waiting. But what were we waiting for? What were we afraid of? Not having the acceptable safe answer? Isn't that what we are trained to do? Trained to come up with something that would submit to some unseen authority. Some mediocre response that would conform to the norms of the discipline. The answer that would make us look like we fit in. So, we'd look like we know what we're talking about because we're not really saying anything new or interesting.

"Life *is* absurd," I suddenly found myself blurting out. Now, all eyes were upon me, and I wasn't sure what to say next. Taking in a deep breath, I decided to simply try and let the ideas flow and hope for the best. After all, what was the worst that could happen? I could look foolish, I suppose. But I was tired of worrying about that —of living with the burden. Surely, at this age I should be past all that uncertainty. So, I decided to keep going. "It is absurd on *all* its different levels," I continued. "Take sleep as a small example. Sleep is where we disappear. But where do we go? And why do we have to go there? Why do we sometimes see things there? Feel things there? Intensely feel things there. Why do we usually not remember much of it at all? To what purpose? We don't cease to be when asleep. We are still ourselves, but we are also something entirely different. It's completely absurd."

It was then that a young man with blue rectangular glasses, whose name escaped me, interjected. "Jung believed that dreams provide an equilibrium between the conscious and the unconscious. I think he saw dreams as a type of helper or even lion tamer for the ego."

I knew that Jung was on the right track but his ideas about sleep and dreams were unimaginative compared to the truth. Still, I couldn't say anything. I couldn't tell them the other reality. They'd think I were mad. So instead, I replied, "But Jung's theory is also absurd when you think about it. We can never escape the absurdity of life. But like Tillich said, we must have the courage to accept it. And that's so difficult sometimes—looking at your life and accepting it. Accepting yourself even though you are unacceptable. The courage to be. The courage to dream. You always need courage, but the only place to find that is inside of yourself. It's not a gift from the outside. It only comes from the inside, and the inside is a very complicated place."

"But should we care if life is absurd? Do we need to believe in God? Do we need to believe in anything at all? Does it make more sense just to be a nihilist?" asked rectangular glasses.

I looked at him and replied, "I don't believe that nihilists truly exist. How could they? How could they negate everything while still holding on to their own being? You either believe in nothing and cease to exist within that belief or you at least believe in your own existence. Anything else would be an egotist playing a nihilist." I paused to see if he wanted to add anything to this, but he was silent.

"You see," I told them, "despite the absurdity, we all have that innate feeling that our lives are important. Just continuing to be alive confirms this. In fact, life is so enormously important that perhaps the absurdity is the only way we can even possibly conceive of it. Like children who make up senseless stories because they cannot make sense of things so much bigger and more complex than themselves. Absurdity is what arises from our extremely limited ability to conceive of the enormity of it all. So, our lives are lived within this confusion.

"And belief in God is not necessary for belief in life. I'm talking about authentic life, of course, not simply a narrative of inflated self-importance that feeds the ego. There is a difference between the two.

"And as it's true that people make up their own version of God anyway, some of which are not very healthy. Considering that, perhaps belief in life is more primary to a spiritual existence. Perhaps even, God proper, cannot be experienced without believing in your own life first—in your own unacceptable existence. But it's a leap of faith, isn't it? Because life is full of pain. So much of it needless and stupid pain. It's also partly a journey of bad choices and regrets. It happens to all of us—all of us with a conscience. And somehow, in the midst of this ludicrous existence, we have to keep believing in it anyway. Keep believing that it is all worth it in the end. Keep believing, despite of all the absurdity and all of the pain. Isn't that what the Bible is mostly about? Holding to belief regardless of the absurdity and the pain? We persevere like Job and just pray that we will be rewarded in the end. We live through each day in absurdity then at night we go to another equally absurd place. This is our crazy existence that must somehow be embraced. It's who we are and, somewhere within that absurdity, is also the potential of our becoming."

∞◊∞

As her songbird softly sighed then contentedly sank into the arms of her warm light, she couldn't help but think that perhaps this would be the last time they would be together. So much had changed, and she was no longer the same as she once was. She was growing—moving farther ahead.

But she knew she couldn't tell him what she was thinking. That news would probably shatter him, and he'd already been through so much. She couldn't risk sharing this truth.

"Do you notice that I am even brighter?" he asked proudly. "He's not killing me anymore. I think it's over."

"I think so too," she agreed. "And I'm happy for you."

"It feels so good. You feel so good. What would I do without you?"

She didn't reply knowing that he may soon have to live without her. Now that she was evolving—getting larger and brighter, she may be moving past such work. Perhaps it was time for lesser lights to move up the chain and take her place. She had long ago realized that it was not possible to stay the same forever. Things had to change—to progress. Any desire to stay the same was a deception and stagnation was nothing more than a prison to die in.

"Now that he's well, he's going to sing again," he told her. "Somehow, I know that even though I still don't know him or much about his life. When he does—when he does sing, would you come and sing with him—with me? Like you used to? When he sings with you, I feel that so deeply, and it's so beautiful!"

She hesitated. Should she tell him? Should she let him know that her other self would be at the concert in the flesh, or would this give him a dangerous false hope? What kind of an effect would it have on him if it didn't work out the way she knew he hoped for? Would he regress under such severe disappointment? It could possibly set him back.

On the other hand, if she told him, it might help him evolve. Truth is progress and will always set you free, even if it's not what you wanted to hear. It was true that he shone brighter now, but that did not mean he was completely safe especially if she was not going to return to help him again. Progress of the individual is important and is always worth the risk. It was then that she decided it would be best to let him know at least that truth.

"The next time he sings on the stage, my awake-self will be there," she confessed.

"Is it true?!" he asked excitedly. "Your awake-self will really be there?"

"Yes," she told him. "And not only that but it has been arranged that my awake-self will meet your awake-self in person."

"Oh, I am so happy!" he exclaimed. "To think that he would see you—actually see you! Surely, this will make my light grow even brighter!"

She could see how elated he was, but it made her worry again. Should she try and temper his joy? Should you ever try to temper joy?

"I know that you said he would never recognize you, but I think you are mistaken. He will recognize you! How can he not? He will cry tears of joy and wrap his arms around you like you were the most precious pearl ever found! He will see you and we will be as one. I just know it! It will happen that way!"

She could see how deeply he believed in the strength of his love for her. This was good. At the very least the solidness of his faith could leach into the mind of his awake-self, making it mature to some degree. But as for making the impossible possible, she knew too much of the nature of the awake world and how it worked. She knew too much about the destructive divide and how the faith of the soul does not always reach the pathways to the mind. If his awake-self even vaguely remembered or sensed her, it would be a miracle. And she believed in miracles, but she was also very realistic about them.

∞◇∞

"I must confess something to you," Crawford said, after reading the page I had just given him. It was one of the most recent messages of thanks and encouragement from 'Melody'.

"What is it?" I asked him, not really wanting to know. I just wanted to get it all over with and leave his office as quickly as possible.

"I think I've fallen in love – in love with Melody. Do you think that's foolish of me?"

Well, yes, I thought but instead told him, "Love is a very complicated emotion, Crawford. What we think is love, maybe something else entirely."

"Oh, I realize that," he said self-assuredly. "But I've known love of all sorts and all too often. And I've even known the tragedy of falling out of love. You could say I'm an expert on the subject. I'm a love expert."

No, you're not but anyway... "What makes you think that you're in love with someone you haven't even met—haven't even honestly talked to? Are you sure you aren't setting yourself up, Crawford?"

"She's just so perfect!" he exclaimed. "She's just so perfect for me! We share so many of the same interests and are on the same wavelength in every way. It's as if she were created just for me. Oh Clarissa, maybe at your age you just don't believe in such things anymore. I mean, you're a woman and we all know what happens to women when they age. That doesn't happen to men. Perhaps you are not the best person to understand my feelings, but I swear she is my one and only—my goddess!"

Actually, things do happen to men when they age but I knew that conversation would be pointless and would not help with my greater goal of keeping Crawford useful.

"And I'm just so thankful to you," he said sincerely. "You were the one who brought us together. Without you I would have never known such a perfect woman existed."

Now I began to feel a little guilty at seeing him so head-over-heels. I began to wonder if maybe I should not have made her such a perfect fit. Maybe I should have thrown in something small that would annoy him ever so slightly just to make the inevitable heartbreak more tolerable. Oh, cursed guilt! Are you here to make an honest woman of me or to make me into a doormat?

"Perhaps, you should not get too carried away just yet," I said, trying to temper his enthusiasm. "You're a sensitive type of man and I wouldn't want to see you get hurt." But was that true? Maybe such a man deserved to get hurt. Such a moral dilemma.

"You're not jealous, are you?" he seriously asked me. "Because you know I already explained that it would not work out between us. For me, you are just not enough. And I don't mean that as an insult, it's simply that you are too different from the kind of woman I need. The kind like Melody."

Well then...yes, maybe he did deserve to get badly hurt. "No, I assure you Crawford that it is not jealousy. In fact, why should I rain on your parade? You know what? If you feel that deeply about Melody, then, I say, go for it. Make plans and daydream your life away until the day you meet and embrace like the lovers in Gustav Klimt's 'The Kiss'."

"Oh Clarissa, what a beautiful and fitting image! I'm so glad you finally understand. This thing between Melody and I is far beyond anything I've ever experienced before. She is my love. She is my life. She is..."

Before he could say anymore, I interjected. "Could you quickly write out your note to her because I don't have much time. I have a class in a few minutes."

"Of course, of course," he said taking out a pen and a piece of light blue stationary from his desk drawer. He began to jot down something then suddenly looked up at me and asked, "You don't read these, correct? You simply scan, send the image to her and then destroy it. Not that I don't trust you, but I'd just like to confirm that the messages between Melody and I are strictly confidential."

"You know that when I agreed to be your courier, I promised you that, Crawford. And I am a woman of my word. And I should remind you that Melody trusts me completely. If she didn't, she wouldn't have asked me to help her in the beginning. I have an obligation to that poor girl. She is like a daughter to me."

"Yes, that makes perfect sense. If Melody trusts you, then I can certainly trust you too." He then went back to writing.

As I sat there quietly waiting for him to finish, I began to think of all the ways I could eventually dispose of Melody. The most obvious, of course, would be death. She could die a thousand different ways. But that could get messy, especially since Crawford would want to attend a funeral or at the very least a grave-site. Perhaps it would better and more fitting if she simply fell in love with a young handsome art dealer from an aristocratic family in say —Florence. She could then, leaving only the briefest of cold-hearted notes behind for Crawford, run off to live with her newfound love in Italy. It would certainly break his heart or whatever it was that he called a heart. Would that be cruel of me, or would that be justice? I know there's a difference but it's not always easy to know what that difference is. Trying to distinguish between the two can sometimes be a challenge.

Twenty-Eight

"That was so much fun! Thank you again for the tickets," I said to Zeke, as we made our way along the hallway, following the VIP signs taped to the wall. I could still feel the vibrations of the music in my body. It really was magical finally hearing the music in person. And I did sing with him—like he asked. In my mind I sang, but also from the depths of my soul.

"Well, thank you for inviting me along. I'm having a great time too!" Zeke replied honestly.

I laughed and told him, "I noticed. And to tell you the truth, it was a relief to see you enjoying yourself. I was a little worried I had roped you into something that you really didn't want to do."

"What! No! I wouldn't have come if I didn't want to. I needed a night out and this is the most fun I've had in a long time. Believe me."

"You do surprise me, Zeke. I wasn't sure if he was your type of performer, but you seemed to be really into it."

"I'll have you know," he said in a cartoonish English accent, "that when it comes to the arts, I am a connoisseur of a variety of genres. Of course, I was into it. And do you know why I enjoy concerts the most?"

"No, why?"

"Because I am the concert whisperer!"

"The concert whisperer?"

"Correct! When I go to a concert, I don't just sit there quietly, and I don't just follow the crowd. I make the crowd follow me. Like a conductor of a symphony. I tell them when to clap, when to holler, when to stand, when to sit, and when to sing out loud. I'm the concert whisperer. The concert maestro!"

"You certainly are," I chuckled. "It was very impressive."

"Yes, I certainly am," he replied humorously as we approached an usher standing beside the entrance to a small assembly hall.

"Can I see your tags?" the usher asked, and we both showed him the VIP passes hanging around our necks. "Okay, enjoy," he said, waving us through.

As we entered the hall, Zeke looked at the long lineup. "Looks like everyone rushed in before us," he said.

"That's alright," I told him. "It's better to be at the end of the line. You don't feel so hurried." And I was certainly feeling in no hurry to face my songbird.

"Also, you don't have loud talkers, close standers or weird smells behind you," Zeke added.

"That's true," I laughed.

"I just hope he won't be asleep by the time we get there," he joked, and I thought to myself it would likely be better if he were.

Taking our places at the end of the line, Zeke said, "Did I mention that you look very nice tonight, Clarissa? Is that outfit new?"

In the end I had gone with something safe and classic. A fitted knee length black jacket, purple silk blouse, black tapered pants and some almond-toe black ankle boots with a low heel.

"Yes, thank you for asking," I replied. "It is new. Traci helped me choose it."

"She's a good friend, isn't she?"

"She is. She's a wonderful person. It was Traci who convinced me to sign up with the Refugee Project."

"Then, I shall have to say that she is extra wonderful," smiled Zeke.

"Yes, Traci is extra wonderful," I agreed then added, "And you also look very nice this evening."

Zeke laughed, waved his hand in the air and again in a silly accent said, "Yes, I do. After all, I am a VIP, and one must always look the part."

"You certainly are a VIP," I replied.

"We both are," he said, making me laugh again.

I was so glad Zeke had agreed to come with me. I'd been feeling very nervous all week about the whole thing. What would happen when I faced him in the flesh? Would it be difficult? Would it be painful? Zeke was so funny and such good company that I kept forgetting about these worries. The absurdity that brings laughter destroys the absurdity that brings anxiety.

"I have to confess," said Zeke now in a serious tone, "Although, he really isn't the type of performer I usually go in for, that one song was incredible. It just gives you chills. Do you know the one I mean? I'm not sure what it's called but it's the one that really launched his career. Do you know the one I'm talking about?"

"Yes," I said. "I know the one. It is a magnificent song."

"You know, it's funny," continued Zeke, "guys like that write that one incredible song and then after that—there's not much happening. Some of his other songs are good, but okay-good—not wow-good. Do you know what I'm talking about?" Suddenly Zeke, worried that he was being too honest, added, "I hope you're not insulted by that. I'm not trying to insult your taste in music. I'm not a music snob."

"Oh no," I told him. "I agree. That song was definitely far beyond what he ever did later."

"Why do you think that is?" he asked. "And it's not an unusual thing. These pop artists create something groundbreaking and after that, it's like they used up all their groundbreaking song tokens and have nothing much left. Any theories?"

"Must be the music angel," I laughed.

"The music angel?"

"Yes. The music angel is full of songs and poetry and visits them when they are asleep. She helps them to create these masterpieces."

"Music angel huh? So why doesn't she visit them more often? Why only once or a few times?"

"Perhaps," I explain, "she needs to be other places or can't invest all the best songs in one person. Or maybe, she just needs those song writers to be in a perfect state of mind for her to interact. Or perhaps over time, as fame and money changes them, she deems them unworthy. Who knows the way of angels?"

"Now that sounds like a song. *Who knows the way of angels?* Perhaps you could write the next great song. Put all these great songwriters to shame," he joked.

"I think I'll just stick to writing my boring old essays," I laughed.

At that point, the people ahead of us moved up farther and we followed suit.

"The line seems to be moving along faster than I thought it would," I said.

"After all these years he must have it down to a fine art. *Hello, shake hands, sign, photo. Hello, shake hands, sign, photo.* Oops, am I being too cynical? I don't want to ruin your evening with my cynicism. Tara always used to reign me in when I was being too cynical."

"Not at all," I assured him. "I listen to his music but I'm not the fan type. I'm very realistic about such things. I don't idolize anyone ever. And I don't self-identify with celebrities in any way."

"That's what I like about you, Clarissa. You're what my grandma used to call an odd cat."

"An odd cat?" I said, puzzled by the strange expression.

"Yes, an odd cat. My grandma, bless her soul, used to sometimes say 'oh, he's an odd cat', and at first, we didn't know what she was talking about. We thought she was just confusing it with the expression 'odd duck'. So, one day I said, 'Grandma, you know it's odd duck not odd cat'. And she said to me, 'Zeke, baby, I never mix up my words. An odd duck is just somebody that's odd. An odd cat is altogether something different.'

"Then I asked her, 'so, what's an odd cat'?

"That's when she told me that when she was a little girl back on the farm, they had three cows, and every morning she'd follow her daddy down to the barn to help with the milking of those cows. But before they even reached the barn, they'd be swarmed by cats. All the barn cats would gather around 'cause they knew her daddy would be carrying the leftover milk from the house. It was old and on the edge of turning, but it tasted good to those cats. He'd pour that leftover milk into the bowls for them, and my grandmother would watch as those cats pushed and fought over that old milk. Shrieking at each other, making a mess and slopping it all over themselves. It was quite the chaos.

"But there was this one cat—a calico—who would just sit back and watch them all. At first, my grandmother thought there was something wrong with that cat. Why wouldn't it go fight for some of that milk? What was wrong with it? But then she learned the truth. You see, this cat knew that later in the afternoon when all the other cats were asleep, that's when my great grandmother would put out some of the fresh cream that she had no use for. So, this smart cat waited, and when my great grandmother put out the bowl, that cat got the fresh cream all to herself. The rest just had old milk, but she got the fresh cream. She didn't have to fight for it like the others. She just lapped it up in peace. She was the odd cat.

"And that's who you are, Clarissa. There's something about you. Some secret. I can feel it. Something you know that the other cats don't. And while all the other cats are fighting over some old almost sour milk, you're just waiting for that something—that better something that comes later. I can tell."

I laughed. "Your grandmother sounds like she was a very interesting person."

"She was," he sighed. "She was the best. I miss that woman."

Suddenly the line moved forward again, and as we moved up, we found ourselves standing in front of the merchandise table. A cheerful woman on the other side exclaimed, "Hi there! Did you enjoy the concert?"

"It was stupendous!" said Zeke. "The best ever!"

"He's one of the greats," she agreed.

"One of the greats," repeated Zeke.

"Well," she continued, "as VIPs, you have a choice of one item free of charge. But you're welcome to purchase additional mementos. We have many wonderful things to choose from."

It was then that I recognized the woman. It was Angela! Much older than the photos I had seen years ago, but it was most definitely her. It felt good seeing her there. She was his compass.

"This is a hard choice," said Zeke. "Hmmm...what should I pick? What are you getting, Clarissa?"

"I think I'll have the new best hits CD and I'd like two mugs as well." I didn't really want the mugs, but I added them just because I thought the extra purchase would make her happy.

"Great choices!" Angela exclaimed. Then turning to Zeke, she asked, "And you sir?"

"Hmmm...it's a hard pick but I think I want a t-shirt. Yes, I definitely want the t-shirt. I need something special to wear to work tomorrow."

"You're going to wear the t-shirt to work tomorrow?" I asked in amusement.

"I need to prove to my colleagues that I was here," he said. "They might not believe me otherwise."

I just laughed.

"What size do you need, sir?" asked Angela.

"What size do you think I need?" replied Zeke flexing his arms flirtatiously.

Angela blushed and laughed, then pulled out a t-shirt from the box under the table. "This should fit you," she said, handing him the shirt.

"Thank you," said Zeke laying it carefully over his arm as if it was a sacred garment.

She then placed the CD and mugs in a small paper bag and handed it to me. "That'll be forty dollars please," she said, and I placed the cash on her table.

"Oh, the line's moving again!" exclaimed Zeke continuing to play the role of the excited fan. "We better keep going. Don't want to miss him."

"Thank you," I said to Angela.

"Thank *you*," she replied. "And enjoy the rest of your evening."

We moved up farther and I could now see him sitting at the table smiling and signing CDs. It was so strange to see him there in the flesh. He looked older than I imagined he would despite his obvious cosmetic procedures. And his dyed hair seemed to be thinning a little too much at the temples. He didn't really look like the same person in his photos and videos. That was of course to be expected, but still, I couldn't get over just how ordinary he appeared. I knew about his mediocre light, but for some reason, I wasn't prepared for ordinariness of him in the flesh. Perhaps other people—fans saw something different. I never really understood fandom and how it seemed to take hold of people. It didn't affect me at all.

As we finally reached the table, he then looked up at us and smiled. I stared back at him not knowing what to say. My mind was racing, and I found myself instinctively trying to reach out to him in my thoughts. Trying to connect on that unseen level. Do you see me? Do you know me? Here I am.

It was then that he suddenly exclaimed, "I know you!" And for a brief moment I thought I had reached him, but he wasn't talking to me, he was talking to Zeke. "You're Mr. Second Row!"

Zeke smiled back and said, "That's right. I'm Zeke and this here is Clarissa. We're big fans."

I secretly laughed to myself as I saw what was happening. He was adoring Zeke. Not just because Zeke was such an expert at audience enthusiasm, but also because he thought he had a Black man as a fan. I could tell he felt this gave him some type of music credibility.

"Would you like me to sign those for you?" he asked, nodding at the souvenirs in our hands.

"Yes, thank you," I replied as I removed the CD and mugs from the bag and set them on the table. When he was done, he slid the items back to me, and for a moment looked directly into my eyes. But there was nothing there. It was like he was staring at a wall. I didn't exist for him. He couldn't see me. He didn't know me.

Next, he signed Zeke's shirt and then said, "Time for the photo."

He got up and stepped in front of the backdrop that was advertising his new best hits album. An assistant guided Zeke and I over to where he was standing and placed us on either side of him. He put his arm around my shoulder, and I could feel that other being inside of him—that light I knew so well—the light I had saved from certain death. But I could also feel that the awake him felt nothing. Nothing at all. I was just another nondescript fan to him.

"Smile!" said the assistant and after three quick flashes we were done. He dropped his arm from my shoulder and took a step back.

"Well, thank you for coming out," he said, mostly to Zeke.

"It was a great concert, wasn't it, Clarissa?" I could tell Zeke felt a little bad that he had received all the attention.

"It was a lovely concert," I agreed.

"You'll receive a copy of the photo by email in a few weeks' time," said the assistant who then signalled for us to leave.

As we walked away, Zeke asked me, "So, what did you think?"

So, what did I think? I was thinking how glad I was that it was not a painful experience. That was a relief. But it was certainly a harsh lesson to witness that massive chasm between the worlds. Despite all that I meant to him, he could not see me or feel me. Not in this world. Here, it was all empty. Perhaps it sums up the emptiness of the awake-world—the way it threatens to crash inward and smother us in nothingness. A world completely blind to all the loving wonder and magnificence of the dreamworld. But I didn't say any of this to Zeke. Instead, I said, "He had a stain on his shirt."

Zeke burst out laughing. "A stain?!" he exclaimed.

"That's what happens on the road and you're eating on the run. You drip food on your shirt."

Zeke laughed even louder. "That's why I like you, Clarissa. You're an odd cat."

Twenty-Nine

**"By day the Lord commands his steadfast love, and at night His
song is with me, a prayer to the God of my life.**

This is from Psalm 42:8," I explained to the class. "Is there love
in music? If there is, does that love in music reach us when we
listen to it? Can music created in love also be a conveyor of love?" I
paused for a moment to see if anyone had thoughts on the idea.

"I don't see why not," commented a man named Johnathan. By
this time, I was able to learn and remember all of the names of
all my classmates. "That puts me in mind of Ode 6 of the Odes of
Solomon:

**As the wind glides through the harp and the strings speak, so
the Spirit of the Lord speaks through my members, and I speak
through His love."**

"That is definitely a beautiful book to read," I replied. "And that
line does relate to the ideas of love and song, but in that case, isn't'
it true that it's written as a comparison? What if it is more than
that? What if the harp strings that speak are speaking one of the

languages of God? A language of love? True and honest love? In Ode 7 it says:

Let the singers sing the grace of the Lord Most High and let them bring their songs. And let their heart be like the day, and their gentle voices like the majestic beauty of the Lord."

"Hmmm...I see what you mean," agreed Jonathan, "And just to add to that, it's true of every culture that song has always been used as a medium to reaching spirit or the Divine."

"Every culture?" asked Thomas, the young man with the blue rectangular glasses who once raised the question of nihilism.

From there many others joined in and the discussion blossomed into a lively exploration of ideas about music and the Divine.

As I sat back to let others have their say, I thought about my songbird. Oh, what music we did create! And he was certainly very far from anything divine, but yet, the music somehow transcended that. It wasn't perfect. Nothing in this world is perfect. But it offered something special. It offered people a healing love. At the concert, I saw just how much it did for the people listening. Yes, it was muddied by money and fame and people's weakness for idol worship. But at the core—deep within the music, that thing was still there. That thing called love. Love, the call to the Divine.

Shortly after the concert and meeting my songbird in the flesh, I realized that it was indeed true. I'd never see him again. Not in the awake-world nor in the dreamworld. Whatever it was that brought us together initially, no longer existed. Perhaps it was that I had changed so much in such a short time. Or perhaps it was just the way of things. In that small corner, I had done what I could to keep light shining in the world. After that it was up to him how the rest of his life would go.

I felt a little sad knowing that was the end. We would never again share the embrace of ecstasy in our dreams. And I knew I would miss him. After all, we had shared a great deal together and he was one of my early loves. But our existence as lights and as humans is fluid. We must keep moving in this ocean. We cannot stay in one place and expect to live. So, goodbye my songbird. I loved you well and you loved me as best you could.

∞◊∞

She couldn't sleep. Her mind was racing. Her anxiety strangling her every thought.

Gently pushing away the blanket, she tried her best not to wake her husband. She couldn't risk that. But then she remembered, he had taken his sleeping pills before bed. He shouldn't wake up for hours no matter how much noise she made. Thank goodness for sleeping pills.

Carefully getting out of bed, she walked quietly over to the dresser near the window, opened the drawer and took out the letter she had hidden earlier that day. It was from her sister pleading with her to come and stay. This was not the first time her sister had asked her to pack her bags and leave. That had been going on for years.

She stared at the envelope, lovingly running her fingers across it. Her sister's handwriting looked so beautiful in the moonlight. Seeing that familiar careful soft looping of each letter made her feel as though her sibling were close by. If only she could do as her sister asked. Just pack her bags and leave. What a relief it would be to no longer have to walk on eggshells, afraid of when he might explode. She would finally be free. She would be safe.

Suddenly, there was a loud grunt from the bed, and she froze. Was he awake? Would he come charging up behind her? She readied herself to feel his angry fingers claw into her shoulders and thought about the treasured letter she held in her hand. He would grab it and tear it into a thousand pieces like he did before. And then after that, he would punish her for weeks in so many little ways.

She just stood there terrified...waiting. But as time ticked by and nothing happened, she realized he was not coming. She turned and sighed in relief to see him still sound asleep. Those pills were working. Thank God those pills were working.

Slipping the envelope back into her drawer, she tucked it safely under her lingerie. Tomorrow, when he is out, she'd hide it in a safer spot. She couldn't take any chances. He seemed more on edge than usual these days and that made him even more dangerous.

∞◊∞

"Jonah's beautiful light!" she called out through the darkness. "Where are you? You must come to me, quickly."

Hearing her urgent call and feeling the intensity of her excitement, he immediately came running. "What is it?" he asked, as he flew in so close, they were almost touching.

"I've found something! I've found someone connected to one of your empty men! A wife!"

"How?" he asked.

"In dreams I thought of you, of those men, of the name William. And I found her! I visited her in spirit."

"Are you certain it was her? I know that I get so confused sometimes in this dreamworld. There are times when I don't know what is really of the world outside and what is only from the inside. And there are times when I sense the two are being mixed together. It can be so confusing."

"Yes, it can be confusing, but you must trust me on this," she told him. "I've walked in this confusion a much longer time than you, and my light is older than yours. I know my way through. I know who I connected with, and I connected with the wife of one of those evil men. I felt it. I felt it deeply."

"I understand and believe you," he said realizing that he should not have doubted her.

"When I connected, I was able to feel the things that she was feeling and see the things that she was seeing. And I saw something that will help Jonah."

"Anything you might have seen—anything at all no matter how small could be helpful."

She placed her hand lovingly against his face and he melted into it. Oh, the joy...the strength in such a union. "I have found so much more than just a small thing," she told him. "I have found a name and an address."

"Really!?" he exclaimed, shocked that she would be able to find something as huge as this. "How? How on earth did you do it?"

"It was an envelope," she explained. "She was looking at an envelope addressed to her, and I saw it through her eyes."

"A name and address were on the envelope? And you saw it clearly? What did it say?" he asked eagerly.

"It said, Mrs. Emelia Calthorpe, 66 Orchard Park Way, Washington D.C."

"Oh, this is incredible! Jonah is beyond thrilled! With this information, it will take him no time to be able to identify her husband and then perhaps to link these other men. I knew I was right to find you. Without you, I don't know what I would have done. Thank you! Thank you for everything!"

"Just go now," she told him. "Jonah should wake up and put the pieces of the puzzle together before it's too late."

"Yes, there's no time to lose," he agreed then dashed away into the darkness.

Thirty

The phone rang and I looked at the call display. It was an unknown number.

Usually, I just let such calls go to voicemail but for some reason I didn't do that this time. Instead, I picked up the phone and answered.

"Hello," I said, prepared to hang up quickly if it were just another telemarketer.

"Clarissa?" asked a strangely familiar voice.

"Yes, this is Clarissa," I replied, trying to remember where I had heard that voice before.

"It's Sandy," she said.

For a moment, I didn't know who she was. Sandy? Do I know a Sandy? Then suddenly, it occurred to me. She was my ex-sister-in-law. Why was my ex-sister-in-law phoning me when I hadn't spoken to her in well over twenty years?

"I've got some sad news," she said without sounding particularly sad. This was the way she had always been. She was always a cold one. "It's Matt. He's dead."

I wasn't sure what to say. All I could think was, 'why is she calling me to tell me this when I already know that my ex-husband died over ten years ago?'

"Him and his girlfriend went down to the States," she continued. "His girlfriend, not his wife. The wife died of the virus a few years back. I told him not to go but they went anyway. It was a bomb. Somebody exploded a bomb at their hotel. They wanted to kill tourists."

What was she talking about? She wasn't making any sense.

I then started to feel a little dizzy as I began to process what she was saying. Matt? Matt's dead. Wait, she doesn't mean Matthew. She is talking about Matty. My Matty. Oh my God! No! No! No! No! She's talking about Matty!

"Clarissa are you there? Are you still there?

Suddenly, I couldn't hear anything anymore. There was too much noise to hear anything. Someone was screaming—such awful horrible screaming. Why wouldn't they stop? Why wouldn't they stop screaming? I couldn't understand any it. Why wouldn't it stop? But then something clicked, and I realized that it was me. I was screaming! I was screaming and I couldn't stop. I put my hand over my mouth to try and stop it, but it still wouldn't stop. Matty! Oh Matty! My Matty! My sweet beautiful Matty! Then everything went black...

∞◇∞

She ran to him weeping. "Jonah's light, what pain this is! Such pain! Such pain!"

"What is it?" he asked.

"It's Clarissa! Clarissa has learned her son was killed. He was killed in a terrorist attack. How can our temporal selves endure so much? The pain is overwhelming!"

He wrapped her in his arms. "It's alright," he said surprised at how her pain cut into him too. "You will get through this. Clarissa will get through this."

"But why did it happen like it did?" she cried. "Why is that awake-world so full of tragedy and sorrow? So full of suffering? And why could Clarissa's son have not seen that he was wrong? He never even knew her. How could he not have known her—not have known his own mother for who she was? It would have been so easy for things to be set right, but it didn't happen. And now this. This awful horrible ending. Why did it happen this way? Why did love not prevail?"

"I can't understand it either," he said. "Through Jonah, I have seen so much—many terrible things, and I don't understand any of it. You are an older light and know more than me. Perhaps with time you will understand. We both will."

"What is time when the here and now demands to know 'why'. There has to be a 'why'?" She then rested her head on his shoulder and tried to sooth the stabbing pain that emanated from her awake-self.

"I will try to give you as much strength as I can, but this may be beyond my ability," he told her feeling frustrated he could not do more. "Whatever happens, know that I will be here for you. I will always be here for you."

"Thank you," she said. "Having you here is something. It makes it a little more bearable. But I just don't know how Clarissa will get through this. She's known a lot of pain in her life but never like this. Never anything as horrible as this."

∞◇∞

I opened my eyes. Where was I? What is this place?

"Issa!" Traci said. "Are you awake?"

Suddenly, I realized where I was. I was in the hospital. Why was I here? Why was I lying in a hospital bed? It was then that it all came flooding back—that heavy darkness weighing upon me. Crushing me. Matty-Matt. My Matty-Matt was gone. I started to sob uncontrollably.

"It's okay, Issa. I'm here and so is Zeke."

"Yes, I'm here too," came Zeke's voice from the other side of the bed.

"My Matty is gone," I said through my tears. "My Matty. My Matty."

I felt Traci take my hand in hers. "It's okay Issa. It's okay."

"It's not okay," I replied. "It will never be okay again. Never, never, never..."

"Should I call the nurse?" Zeke asked.

"No!" I exclaimed afraid they might give me more drugs. I could already feel them in my system, holding me down, blunting my emotional release and making everything worse. "I don't need the nurse."

"Are you sure?" asked Traci.

"Yes, I'm sure. Please don't call the nurse."

"Alright," said Zeke. "No nurse."

It was then that I began to wonder about what must have happened. How it was I ended up in the hospital? "Did you bring me here?" I asked them. "I don't remember how I got here."

"The ambulance brought you," said Traci.

"How did you find me?" I asked.

"I found you," said Zeke. "I was in the apartment, and I heard you scream. When I came running, I found you on the floor. You were unconscious. I picked up your phone and there was someone on the line. I told them there was an emergency and hung up. That's when I called 911."

"Zeke rode with you in the ambulance," explained Traci. "He called me on the way to the hospital. Oh Issa, poor Issa! I feel so bad for you."

"Matty!" I suddenly cried. "Matty is gone!" It was then I realized there was no more secret left to hide. I'd have to tell them. I'd have to try and explain.

"You must be wondering," I said to them. "You must be wondering about Matty."

"That's alright," Traci replied. "You need to rest now. There is plenty of time to explain later. Right now, you just need to try and relax."

"No," I insisted. "I need to tell you. If I don't tell you, I feel like I will die. I need to tell you everything about Matty." I was not exaggerating when I said I felt like I would die. I did feel that way. It was if something was on my chest pressing down, threatening to shatter my ribs and crush my heart, and the only way to stop it was to let my friends know the truth.

"If you need to," said Zeke, "we are here and listening."

"Yes, we are here for you, Issa," Traci said taking hold of my hand.

How to begin? How to make them understand that I was not trying to be deceptive. I was not trying to fool them. It was only about self-preservation. My mind was so hazy with drugs, I wasn't sure how to start. I took a moment to collect my thoughts then said, "You both know about my marriage at a young age."

"Yes," said Traci. "You said you were married and then divorced a few years later."

"Well, all that I told you about that was true. But what I didn't tell you was that I was pregnant at the time. That's ultimately why I married Matthew. I was pregnant. I have...." I stopped myself and choked back the sobs then added, "I *had* a son."

"Why did you keep it a secret?" asked Traci. "We're your friends. You know you can tell us anything."

"I didn't mean to keep things from you," I tried to explain. "I didn't intend to lie to you. At the time, it just seemed easier. Everything kept tidy in its own special compartment. Somehow, it seemed less painful. It could give me a place I could go that was free of the past. If you knew about Matty, I would have to tell you everything and hope that you would understand. And I would also have to say his name out loud and that would have been agonizing."

"What happened?" asked Zeke. "What happened with Matty?"

I took in a deep breath and then began to explain, "When I first learned I was pregnant, I wasn't sure what to think. Having lost my parents only a year and a half earlier, I was very confused. But Matthew was over the moon at the news. And seeing his excitement helped reassure me about everything. He insisted we marry and, even though I had some doubts, I went along with it. The idea of being pregnant and alone in the world was frightening, and Matthew made everything sound so easy—so perfect.

"When we found out it was a boy, he was even more elated and insisted we name the baby after him. I was fine with it, thinking it was a normal thing to do. And by this time, I was very excited also. I felt like something was being restored after losing my parents. Right after they were killed, it was as if I was just left floating in the middle of nowhere. Just me, in this vast ocean of nothingness. But now, I was finding a solid place in this world. I was going to have a family again.

"What I told you about my marriage was all true. How I outgrew my older husband and how he was controlling. But I did not tell you what he did to me. What he was still doing to me even after his death.

"Matthew never wanted a divorce. At first, he tried to coerce me to stay. Then he begged and pleaded. Then he became very angry. He wanted everything to go back to the way it was before. But that wasn't going to happen.

"When we separated, he went to live with his parents in a town about an hour and a half away. He just quit his job and went to live with them. I knew he was furious with me, but he did seem to be civil about how we would co-parent Matty. He agreed that our son would stay with me during the week and that he'd have him on weekends. I thought 'good, he has Matty's best interests at heart'. That's all I needed from him. As it turned out, that wasn't true.

"At first, I didn't recognize the signs. Matty was so often angry, but divorce is hard on children. I knew that. On the weekends, I would read all sorts of books on the subject, and they all told me the same thing. That what Matty was going through was perfectly normal. I tried my best to take their advice on how to best handle the situation. The primary idea was always 'patience'. I needed to be patient and it would get better.

"But it wasn't getting any better. In fact, it seemed to be getting worse. Matty seemed to be getting more and more angry at me as each year passed.

"I knew part of it was that his father had no rules. On the weekends, Matty was allowed to just run wild. During the week, we had to follow a schedule. He had to go to school. I had to go to work. I tried to talk to his father about this problem, but his response was always, "So, take me to court for loving my son". I knew it wasn't fair, but there was nothing I could do. So, I just tried my best.

"Often Matthew didn't pay his child support or was late. This put a great deal of stress on me to pay the bills and ensure Matty had everything he needed. It wasn't an easy time at all, and I couldn't always focus on Matty the way I should have. If only I had been under less pressure, perhaps I would have been more clear-headed. Maybe I could have seen the pattern. I could have stopped it. But I didn't notice what Matthew was doing until it was too late.

"As Matty got older, his attitude became even worse. At times he seemed to almost hate me. I told myself that it was just because he was about to enter puberty, and at that age, it was perfectly normal for a boy to idolize his father and move away from his mother. Of course, somewhere in my heart I felt that something was not right, but I just couldn't believe that Matthew was capable of something that evil. I couldn't comprehend that anyone could be so selfish and heartless that they would weaponize their own child.

"When I found out about my inheritance, I was thrilled! Finally, all the stresses of just trying to make ends meet were gone. I could spend more time with Matty. We could go on trips together. I could build a better relationship with him, and it would be wonderful.

"But that's not what happened. Matthew suddenly decided that he should have increased custody and I should be paying child support to him. So, we went to court.

"That's where I finally found out exactly what Matthew had done. I had to sit there, in that hearing, and listen to my own son, who I loved more than anyone else in this world, say the most outlandish lies about me. He told bizarre stories like me going out on dates and leaving him alone when he was too young to be left alone. None of it was even close to being true. During that time, I never so much as even looked at a man. I was completely devoted to taking care of my child and ensuring that he had a roof over his head and food on the table.

"The most horrible thing of all was that Matty believed what he was saying. He believed that I was that terrible mother he imagined me to be. It was the most painful thing I had ever experienced. Well...now the second most painful.

"I was just sobbing by the end of it and when I looked over at Matthew, he was grinning.

"In his verdict, the judge said, that although he did not believe that what Matty was saying was the complete truth, he was worried about my son's mental health and for that reason was granting greater custody to his father. During the week he would be with Matthew, and I was only to see him on the weekends. The judge assured me that he had seen many such cases and that things would eventually work themselves out and Matty would, one day soon, realize that a boy needs his mother. My gut told me this was wrong.

I now knew how manipulative and conniving Matthew could be, but I accepted the judgment because I wanted to be hopeful. That and I had no other choice. I wanted so much to believe that what the judge said was correct and that Matty would soon see things differently.

"I picked up Matty a few weekends after he moved in with his father, but when he was with me, he was just angry all of the time. He didn't want to do anything or go anywhere. He just wanted to watch TV, play video games or talk on the phone to his father. Nothing I did or said could get through to him. He looked at me as if I were a stranger—a despised stranger.

"Soon he wouldn't even get in the car to go home with me. I'd drive out there and he'd just refuse to even come out of the house.

"Even though Matty refused to see me, for years I'd take presents for birthdays and Christmas. I'd drive out to the house, but he wouldn't accept them. Instead, Matthew would come out to the car and tell me that Matty didn't want anything from me other than for me to leave him alone. So, I'd return home and put the present in a box in the basement hoping that something would change. But that change never came. It seemed that the more I tried to reach Matty, the more intensely Matthew poisoned him against me. I felt so helpless.

"I thought about hiring a lawyer many times and taking Matthew to court, but then I would remember what the judge had said about Matty's mental health, and I was worried about that. I didn't want to hurt Matty or to make him so confused that he might hurt himself. He absolutely worshipped his father and seemed oblivious to how he was being controlled and manipulated.

"Also, I was afraid for Matty. I couldn't be sure the full extent of Matthew's obsession. He was so determined to hurt me that, if I had won increased custody, would he then have had a complete mental breakdown? Would he do something horrible? Would he do something unthinkable to Matty? This was a real fear I had, and it terrified me. I knew that if I kept things as they were, at least Matty would be physically safe.

"So, I guess I just mostly gave up at that point. I was so worn down and broken, that I didn't even try anymore. I don't know if that was the right decision. I've gone over it a million times in my mind. Should I have fought harder for Matty? Did I choose wrongly? I just don't know. It seemed like my best choice at the time.

"Then, about ten years ago, shortly before I met you Traci, Matty phoned me. I was so happy, I cried for joy that whole day. He had phoned me to tell me his father had passed away from cancer. I told him I was sorry. He then asked if he could meet up with me.

"We met five times after that. I always tried to keep the conversation light. Never spoke of his father. I tried to go slow. I didn't want to lose him again.

"Our conversations seemed to go well. We talked about the ordinary things in our lives. He told me about his job in a furniture store and about his wife. He showed me his wedding pictures. At our fifth meeting, he mentioned how they were saving to buy a house, and how it wasn't easy putting together a down payment.

"At that point, I offered to pay for the house. Not a loan. I offered to pay for it outright. I saw it as my responsibility as his mother, and he seemed so grateful at the time. He even called me 'Mom' which suddenly made all that crushing pain from the past just disappear into thin air. I couldn't have been happier.

"The next day, he sent me a real estate listing. It was a vacant home, move-in ready. I immediately went to work on the purchase. It was Matty's house by the end of the month, and the day after closing, that's when I received his final email. I opened it thinking that he was going to tell me about how happy they were to be moving into their new home and maybe even, fingers crossed, inviting me to visit. But that's not what happened.

"The email explained that before his father died, he told Matty to have me pay for a house. He said it was a way to recoup unpaid child-support. Matty ended the email with the words, "Thanks Clarissa, for finally paying what you owe me."

"I was devastated. He still believed his father's lies. The truth was, I never missed a support payment and when he needed something extra, I was the one who provided the money. I paid for his high school trip to Europe and his three different attempts at college. I never turned my back on my son. Never. Matthew had once again stuck the knife in but this time from beyond the grave.

"After that, Matty blocked me on everything. I couldn't get in touch with him to try and tell him the truth. He just didn't want to know. That's when I began to deny that I had a son. It was just too painful to talk about—too painful to try and explain."

"Oh Clarissa," said Traci. "How terrible. I'm so sorry. I'm so sorry for all of it."

"Me too," agreed Zeke. "To have your son stolen from you like that."

"And now Matty's gone," I said beginning to cry again. "And the chance for him to ever know me and to know how much I loved him is gone too. Gone forever. I'm not leaving this bed ever again. What's the point? I'll stay here forever. Go ahead and call the nurse and let them pump me so full of drugs that I don't even know who I am anymore."

"No, Issa! You can't think like that," exclaimed Traci.

"Why not?" I retorted. "Why not just stay in this bed until I die? What's the point of ever getting out of it again? What is left with Matty gone? What is left?"

"You have to get out of that bed," insisted Traci. "You have no choice."

"Of course, I have a choice," I told her. "I can stay here if I want to. Life is meaningless. Sartre was right when he said, 'What is life but an unpleasant interruption to a peaceful nonexistence.'"

"No!" exclaimed Traci. "You can't think like that! You mustn't! You can't just give up! Listen to me! After Zeke found you and called the ambulance, your phone rang. Zeke answered it and he talked to your ex-sister-in-law. She had a lot to say that you need to know about."

"What would that horrible woman have to say that would make any difference," I said. "Please call the nurse."

"No!" exclaimed Traci. "I'm not calling the nurse and you can't just give up. You can't."

"I can," I said stubbornly.

"No, you can't," Traci insisted. "You can't give up now because you have a granddaughter—a granddaughter who needs you. Her name is Marigold. She's only five years old, and now she's all alone in this world. You can't give up because Marigold needs you."

Thirty-One

I drove through the cemetery gates and turned right onto a dirt road. Sandy said I'd find him at the very end near a row of old pine trees.

When I got home from the hospital and called Sandy, the first thing she said was, "I hope you're not going to scream in my ear again." Oh, how I wanted so badly to tell her exactly what I thought of her, but I kept silent just like I had so many times back when I was married to Matthew. I couldn't risk making her angry. At least not until I had Marigold.

Suddenly, I spotted the pine trees. As I got closer, I noticed a fresh mound of dirt in the neatly cut grass about halfway between the trees and the road. I then stopped and parked the car. For a while, I just sat there staring out and not moving. I felt frozen. 'You need to get out', I told myself. 'You need to do this.'

From the passenger seat I picked up a box wrapped in shiny red paper. I then opened the door and got out of the car. Clutching the gift tightly to my chest, I slowly walked towards the unmarked grave. This was the same present I had hidden under the stairs the day I had given everything away to Jake. I never imagined that this was what I would eventually do with it.

Wanting to be sure I had the correct spot; I checked the flat marker beside the mound. There it was—Matthew's name. Sandy told me that when he knew he was going to die Matthew had purchased a double plot for himself and Matty. He wanted to possess his son even after death. I quickly walked around to the other side of Matty's grave just to get away from what was left of my ex-husband.

Falling to my knees beside the dirt mound, I began to sob. Oh, Matty-Matt. Why did it have to be like this? Why? There were so many things I needed to tell you. So many things I wanted you to know. All those years ago did I miss my chance to change things? Did I fail you? Did I fail us both? Could it have been any different? What should I have done that I didn't do?

Through my tears, I stared down at the freshly turned silty soil riddled with tiny pebbles. I found myself thinking about how all those little pebbles used to be so deep in the earth—hidden away in the place where my Matty now was. The thought was almost unbearable.

"I brought something for you, Matty," I said, holding out the wrapped gift and wiping my eyes with my other hand. "It's a Christmas present. I bought it for your thirteenth birthday. To be honest, I wasn't really sure what to get you, but I knew that when you were little you loved space and science fiction stories. So, I got you this. Shall we open it?"

Carefully, I peeled back the paper revealing the model rocket ship I had purchased so many years ago. "It's a limited edition," I explained. "Very rare. It took me a long time to find it. I went to so many stores searching for it. Finally, it was a tiny out of the way shop where I found it. It was the last one too. I was so happy because I thought I had found you the perfect gift. I thought it would make you smile."

I then carefully removed the toy from its box and gently placed it on the mound. "Don't worry about the funeral costs or the stone. I'll pay for those. And I'll get you a nice stone too. A tall one—shiny black granite. It'll sit upright so everyone will see your name. And it will say:

Matthew
'Matty-Matt'
Beloved son of Clarissa Comfort
Blessed is the Light Within

I will do this because I want everyone to know that I love you. I love you more than anything and I don't want that to ever be forgotten."

I then picked up a pebble from his grave and held it tightly in my hand. "Sandy told me what day it was you died," I said, "and I know exactly the time it happened. Do you know how I know this? It's because in that moment, I felt it. When your body fell, your spirit moved through me like an ocean wave, and I almost collapsed on the floor in my kitchen. I didn't know what it was at the time, but now I do. It was you. It was you Matty-Matt. It was you. In the end, I think maybe you did find me. You came to me. You knew I was your mother and knew that I loved you. In the end, I think that you understood perfectly just how much I loved you. I have to believe that. I have to believe that love somehow triumphed. For both of us, I have to believe."

Placing the pebble in my pocket, I then told him, "I'm going to get Marigold now. You don't have to worry. I'll take good care of her, and I'll love her as much as I love you. And maybe, you can find me in my dreams, and you can tell me that you're alright. I'd like to know that you're alright. I love you Matty-Matt. I'm sorry how things turned out and I'm sorry I didn't find a way to make it better but know that you were my child and I loved you more than life itself."

∞◊∞

The house looked tired. No one seemed to be keeping it up any-more. Sandy was the only one left now and I guess she just didn't care. I knocked on that old familiar wooden door.

When it opened, I didn't recognize her. She had gained at least one hundred pounds and her thin grey hair was peppered with pink bald spots. She didn't look well at all. But when she looked me over in that cold judgmental way, I knew it was her. "Hello Clarissa," she said with a wisp of disdain.

"Sandy," I replied, "it's been a long time."

"A long time," she said then added, "Come on in then."

I stepped inside the modest three-bedroom bungalow that had no real front hall to speak of. It had a small closet to one side but mostly opened straight into the living room. I was a bit taken aback by the fact that nothing much had changed in over twenty-five years. It was the same furniture, now just worn and raggedy. Even the same pictures were hanging on the walls—a bunch of long ago mass-produced generic landscapes. Walking back into that house where nothing had changed after all that time was eerie to say the least.

"So," Sandy said matter-of-factly as she was never one to mince words, "Marigold was the wife's not the girlfriend's—the wife who died. Matt had only been with the girlfriend for a few months. And there's no money. Matt lost his house years ago when he mortgaged it to finance a business that didn't work out. He's been living with me for the last few years. And the mother, she didn't have any family to speak of. There's only you and me. And as for me, I'm too old for this—I've got all kinds of problems with my legs and back. I have diabetes too. This house and my pension are all I have, and kids are very expensive these days. That leaves just you."

I didn't know what to say. This woman had not even phoned

me when my son had been killed. She only decided to contact me after she realized that she couldn't pay the funeral expenses or take care of his daughter. She disgusted me more than ever, but I held my tongue.

"I'm more than willing to take care of Marigold," I told her. "She will have everything she needs and more."

"Yeah, guess all that inheritance money is still good."

"Where is Marigold?" I asked, trying to keep my tone as civil as possible.

"Marigold!" she shouted. "Your grandma's here!"

From around the corner, Marigold peeked out.

"Come on now," said Sandy. "Come say hello."

Marigold stepped out from behind the wall and stood there staring nervously. She had long black curly hair and beautiful caramel skin.

"Hello, Marigold," I said crouching down to be more at eye level. "I'm your grandma."

"Come on. Come closer. Come say hi," coaxed Sandy.

Marigold cautiously began walking towards me.

I looked at her beautiful face and could see some of Matty in her, although not much. She looked more like the photos he had shown me of her mother. As she came closer, I could see she had lovely green eyes. I smiled. Green eyes—the same colour as my own.

"Remember what I told you," Sandy said to Marigold. "You're going to go live with your grandma. That's why we packed up all your things this morning."

"I have a lovely big house," I told Marigold. "With a big yard. And you'll have your own room. It has a big window and big closet that you can walk right into. I haven't decorated it yet because I thought we could do that together. What would you like for your room? Do you have any ideas? We can paint it any colour you like."

Marigold smiled. I could see she was warming up to me. That's when I couldn't hold back my emotions any longer. I felt my face suddenly flush, my chin quiver, and my eyes begin to fill with tears. I was overwhelmed with such incredible happiness in that moment but at the same time feeling so devastated and heartbroken about Matty. How could two such opposing emotions exist at the same time? I felt as if I were breaking open.

"Are you crying?" Marigold asked looking a little frightened.

"It's alright," I assured her as I tried hard to get control. I knew intense adult emotions can be scary to children. This was not a good place or time to break down. It was important that I calmed myself. Choking back my feelings I explained, "Sometimes when adults are really happy, they cry. These are good tears. It means I'm very happy that you are my granddaughter and that you are coming to live with me."

My explanation made her giggle and she said, "Adults are funny."

"Yes, we are," I agreed with a smile.

"So, her stuff is in the bedroom," said Sandy. "It's not too much—a suitcase—a couple of boxes of toys. I can't help you load it up. It's too much for me."

"That's not a problem," I told her. "I'm sure Marigold and I will manage just fine. What do you think, Marigold? Should we go get your stuff and then go for a fun car ride? I have a movie player in the backseat with all kinds of different movies. You can choose whatever you want to watch."

Marigold clapped her hands together in excitement. "Do you hear that Aunt Sandy? Grandma has movies in the car!"

"That's nice," Sandy replied unenthusiastically.

"Come on, Grandma!" Marigold exclaimed. "Let's go get my stuff!"

I stood up and she clasped her tiny hand around mine. "It's this way, Grandma. Everything's packed up. Come on!" she said as she began to pull me along.

As I followed her down the hallway, I noticed a big smiling

photo of Matthew hanging on the wall. It was taken around the time I met him all those years ago. He was staring out with those steel grey eyes that had once charmed a young, naïve and vulnerable me, and for a brief moment, I once again felt the cold touch of his bitter anger. But then quickly I shook it off. He was not going to ruin this happy moment. This was my time with my granddaughter, and he couldn't hurt me anymore. He was gone forever.

As I followed Marigold into her room, I thought about all the secrets I knew from my dreams. About how things can appear to be one way but in fact are another. After what Matthew had done to me—what he had done to Matty and how he had cheated us both— how he had broken a sacred bond between mother and child, I knew that such an intensely cruel and selfish crime would not go unpunished in our universe. Justice may not have happened in the awake world, but I knew without a doubt that it was happening now.

Thirty-Two

"Clarissa has a granddaughter!" she told him excitedly. "Can you feel her joy? It is immense!"

"Yes, I feel it!" he beamed. "And it is all so beautiful! Just so beautiful! Almost overwhelming! And you—you are so beautiful!"

She loved to hear him say that. His words were sincere, and she was grateful for them. She had heard this same thing many times before but when it came from him, it was more genuine. His devotion transcended the dreamworld. "And did you notice that Clarissa's happiness has made me shine even brighter?" she asked.

"It has," he agreed. "I didn't know it was possible, but it has. You are brighter. You are the brightest star I have ever seen."

"Happiness is good," she said. "Look what it has done for me. We need more happiness in the world. We need to make every light shine brighter."

"We can do that together," he told her. "We can work to ensure that there is greater happiness. That will be the priority of our union."

"Yes, it will be our mission. And we must start by stopping evil from creating more suffering and death. We need to stop that weapon."

"About the weapon—that is my good news," he said. "Thanks to the information you provided, Jonah has learned the names—the names of all of the men."

"All of them?" she asked in surprise.

"Yes. All of them. Even The Rat. He knows all of their identities. By you providing that woman's name and address, he was able to identify the husband. From there he pieced together the connections through various associates and colleagues using that old CIA database. He was able to identify them all without a doubt."

"That's wonderful!" she exclaimed.

"But it gets even better," he continued. "Jonah learned that each piece of the puzzle held by the three men consisted of five geographical locations. He was then able to get two of the men to reveal those locations."

"That's amazing! How did he do that?"

"The one thing Jonah understands is people. From their profiles in the database, he was able to learn enough about their way of thinking and their weaknesses to make it fairly easy. He befriended them and played to their egos—a little alcohol didn't hurt, and in the end, it wasn't that hard to trick them into divulging the information. One of the rules of the group was not to socialize with each other but they were breaking that rule among themselves all the time, so it wasn't difficult to convince those two to break the rule with Jonah."

"They just told him outright?" she asked in surprise.

"Above all things these men are arrogant, and arrogance is a form of stupidity. It didn't take much to outsmart them. From their psych reports, their need for male bonding and peer support is exceptionally high. As long as they felt emotionally secure, they could easily be tricked into divulging what they knew."

"But that is not all of the puzzle pieces. I assume that the last five locations are held by The Rat. Is it even possible to get that information from him?"

"No," he answered. "The Rat is of the kind who would never talk. But here's the thing—with those ten geographical locations, Jonah was able to figure out the final five thanks to the general who set it all up. From the database, Jonah has learned that this particular general had a quirk for sacred geometry. It was, in fact, a major superstition for him that dominated his personal life and military strategies over the years. So, Jonah began examining the ten locations in light of this information. Sure enough, he found that the first set of five points corresponded to the five points of a pentagram. The next set of five corresponded to the points of a smaller pentagram within that pentagram. From that, he assumed the pieces of the puzzle held by The Rat would also be a pentagram, so he then drew a third pentagram in the second one. But how would this give him the location?

Knowing that all of the general's assets would have been confiscated by the authorities during the investigation against him, he wondered if there could be properties that had been over-looked? What if the general had some hidden assets in shell companies? So, he checked the database for any shell companies linked to the general. The CIA always kept track of shell companies and who owned them even though people believed these companies to be secret. As it turned out, he found several companies belonging to the general, but there was one that stood out as a real possibility. It consisted of a single piece of seemingly insignificant real estate—a large warehouse which had never been registered as being used for anything.

"When Jonah marked that location on a map, sure enough, the property was perfectly centred within the smallest pentagram. There is no doubt in his mind that this is the place. The weapon is hidden in a warehouse in Virginia."

"So, you are telling me that Jonah now has all of the names and the location of the weapon?" she asked in astonishment.

"Yes, he has uncovered all of their secrets and that information is already on its way to Canada."

"Jonah did it!" she cried. "Oh, he really did it!"

"We did it!" he corrected her. "Without you and Clarissa none of it would have been possible."

"Oh," she sighed. "Yes, of course. We did it together."

"Now, we just have to pray that no one in the awake world messes up."

"There's always a risk of that, isn't there?" she said. "We try our best *here, but sometimes it doesn't work. Like so many of my songbirds. So many of them gone. So many of them lost. It still makes me sad some days."*

"What we need is faith," he said. "Let's have faith that it will all go well. A leap of faith that all our work is part of a larger plan. Something beyond us. Let's remind ourselves that the Light of Lights is somehow a part of it too. Perhaps our faith is enough to ensure that it all goes as it should."

"Faith can be a great power," she agreed. "And I think you're correct about focusing on our faith."

He then looked deeply into her eyes and asked, "Will you do me a favour now?"

"Whatever you need, I am here for you," she replied.

"Will you hold me?" he smiled at her warmly. "Just hold me for a while. Jonah is happy but he is also very weary. There is still more work to be done and he needs me to give him strength, and I need you to give me strength."

"Of course, I will," she said without hesitation. "You need not even ask. I will embrace you and all the wonder of your light for you are strength to me as well. Let us, in this wonderful dreamworld, float together. We will float together in the sea of love where all things are renewed within pure and joyous ecstasy." She then wrapped her arms around him and for a time they became as one.

∞◇∞

"Grandma, I'm going outside now," chirped Marigold. "I'm going to play in my magic house," she said as she skipped out the back door.

It was true that I had gone overboard in buying her that enormous playhouse. It was a brilliant red with fancy white trim, a pretty front porch and working doors and shutters. Inside there were three rooms painted in different shades of green with six-foot ceilings and solar lights. Marigold loved it and insisted on setting up one of the rooms as an archaeology lab for Jake. She called it 'the-digging-up-stuff school'.

She and Jake had become very good friends, but I made a point of gently explaining to her how he would be moving soon so that she might be prepared for it. Having lost her father and been uprooted from her home, I wasn't sure how a change like that would affect her. She'd only been with me for a month but had become very attached to Jake in that time. It was a relief when she didn't seem bothered by the news. She simply told me that Jake wasn't moving far, and 'the-digging-up-stuff school' would be there for him whenever he visited.

I had to confess that I was in heaven being able to shower Marigold with so many things and with so much attention. I tried to remind myself not to spoil her but at the same time I felt like I just couldn't do enough. She had been through a lot, and she needed to know she had an adult she could depend on.

But even though Marigold had brought so much joy into my life, something was deeply troubling me. Despite all that newfound euphoria, I was also feeling sick with worry. It had been over two weeks since I had last heard from Jonah. Every night I'd go looking for him and I'd call to him, but he wasn't responding. Something was definitely wrong.

Walking into the living room and sitting down on the couch, I thought about any possible explanation. The worst was that he was dead. But he couldn't be dead. I'm sure I would have known if he were. We had shared too much. I'd at least have known that. What happened to him? He wouldn't have just left me, would he?

I looked at the blank TV in front of me and I thought about switching it on. Perhaps if I watched something mindless it would help calm my worries. It could work as a temporary distraction.

Picking up the remote, I hit the power button and it opened to the news channel. I was almost ready to switch it over to something even more mindless when I noticed the big red words scrolling at the bottom of the screen, 'IMPORTANT BREAKING NEWS'. At that point, I turned up the volume to hear what the news anchor was saying.

"...the Prime Minister will be holding a press conference later today at 2 o'clock.

Once again, ten men have been arrested in what is said to be the worst terrorist plot in history. We have been told that the seismic weapon that was to be used in the attack has been seized by the Canadian government and is now currently being dismantled by a team of experts sent by the UN Security Council. A spokesperson for the Canadian military has assured us that everything is now under control and there is no further danger to the public."

I closed my eyes and breathed in a sigh of relief. Finally! Finally, they have been stopped! Millions of people are now safe. The terrorist group has been shut down! The weapon is being dismantled! All that time, work and effort spent—all those paintings sent to Crawford—and it's done. All those risks taken by Jonah—Jonah?! Suddenly, my relief turned to something else. The news anchor had said that ten men were arrested. That's wrong! It should be eleven! Eleven men! Eleven men should have been arrested! Where is the eleventh man? And where is Jonah?

Thirty-Three

"This is going to be so much fun," giggled Traci. "I haven't been to the amusement park in such a long time. I want to ride on the merry-go-round!"

"The merry-go-round is for babies," said Jake.

"Yes, it's for babies," agreed Marigold, wanting to be like Jake. She looked up to him like he was her big brother.

Traci laughed. "Well, I love the merry-go-round but, to tell you the truth, I'm a little nervous about going on it. I'm afraid I might get dizzy. Will you both go with me?"

"Oh alright," Jake laughed. "If this is important to you, we'll do it."

"Yep, we will do it," affirmed Marigold.

"Thank you. That's very nice of you," said Traci.

"Now, you both must remember to be good for Aunt Traci," I told the children.

"Of course, of course," said Jake. "You've got nothing to worry about."

"Nothing to worry about, Grandma," parroted Marigold.

I wish that were true. I wish I had nothing to worry about. But I was very worried. Worried about Jonah.

When I asked Traci if she would take the children on an outing, I knew she wouldn't refuse. She missed having children around and

"

was just waiting for the day when she would have grandchildren of her own. Taking the children was as much a treat for her as it was for them.

For me, it was important that no one was around. I needed to sleep. I needed another opportunity to try and find Jonah. Something was wrong and I had to find out what had happened.

∞◇∞

She soared through the air. Below her, the waves of spirit swelled and rolled like an earthly ocean. "I am alive!" she cried, indulging in the infinite. It was always wonderful to experience the freedom of dream after being locked in the material world. For a moment she almost forgot why she was there but then quickly remembered. Jonah's light! I must find Jonah's light!

She then stopped where she was and tried to focus her thoughts. "Where are you?" she called out to him through the darkness. "Where are you my wonderful, beautiful companion?"

She tried conjuring up the cabin, but that wasn't working. Without him there, it could not appear.

"Where are you!" she called out again as she tried to concentrate solely on their connection. "I need you here with me! I need to embrace you!"

It was then that she felt a strange and sudden pull. This was different from all those other times she was drawn to a place. This time it harshly tugged at her, and she felt as if she were being dragged down by a strong undertow. Even though it was a little unnerving, she knew not to try to fight it. Her instincts told her that she must go with it.

When the force finally released her, she found herself seemingly alone in a dark and dingy room. What was odd was that she could feel this room was not a part of the dreamworld. This room was in the awake-world. But she knew she was not inside of anyone who was awake. She was not visiting another. She was simply there like any awake person would be.

Without knowing how, she had been pulled to a place in the awake-world and was experiencing it without the help of another.

Looking around, she could see that the square shaped room was quite large. Yet despite its size, it didn't feel roomy. It felt oppressive with its cement windowless walls and only one exit—a door made of heavy industrial steel. On the ceiling were an odd array of what looked like light fixtures. Some of them resembled spotlights and others were just strange and undefinable. None of them were lit. The only light in the room came from a large bare light bulb positioned over the door and covered by a black metal cage.

Against one of the walls were three large crudely constructed high-backed wooden chairs. For a moment she thought a man was sitting in one of the chairs but then quickly realized it was only a mannequin. Its dark curly hair framing its very realistic features was messy and ratted. The head was strapped to the chair-back and one of its eyes was missing. A raggedy smock covered the body, and the wrists and ankles were tied to the arms and legs of the chair. Four wires ran from underneath the smock to a black box sitting on the floor.

On the other side of the room was a long rectangular metal table that resembled a veterinarian's surgical table. It had five straps hanging from the sides and some dried dark stains on the surface.

Beside this table was a large metal counter with six drawers. On top of the counter was an array of objects. Moving closer, she could see it was an assortment of tools in all different shapes and sizes. Some were pointed, some had sharp or serrated edges, and some resembled pliers It was then that she fully realized what this room was. It was a torture chamber!

As she stood there slightly disoriented and trying to figure out what had brought her to this horrible place, she thought she heard a small noise come from the dark corner of the room. She moved closer and saw some-thing crumpled there on the floor—perhaps another mannequin. At first, she was not sure if what she was seeing was real. It was such an entirely new experience to see things in the awake-world without inhabiting an awake person. With careful concentration however, it all became clearer. Something was there and it was not another mannequin. It was a man! His legs were awkwardly bent underneath him, and his head was bowed. He was leaning against the wall like something broken or even dead. He was naked and it was then that she noticed his wrists were shackled to a steel anchor in the floor. As he became even clearer, she could see his white hair was matted with blood and there was severe bruising across his entire body. It was then that she felt his presence. "Jonah!" she cried.

Jonah painfully raised his head to look at her. His face was badly swollen. "Are you really here?" he asked without uttering a word.

"Yes, I'm here," she said rushing over and kneeling by his side.

"I'm not just imagining it?"

"No, Jonah. You are not imagining. I am here." She gently cupped his face in her hand, and he softly moaned.

"I was calling to you," he said. "In my mind I was calling to you."

"And I'm here now. Oh Jonah, what has been done to you?"

"It's The Rat," he told her. "They didn't arrest them all at once like they should have, and their sloppiness gave him time to escape. He realized it was me who was the informant and before he could be arrested, he kidnapped me as I was leaving my house to make my way to Canada. He has been torturing me ever since including subjecting me to sleep deprivation. That's why I couldn't reach you. I couldn't sleep long enough or deep enough. How is it that I can talk with you now? Am I asleep? But I can see the room. I can feel my body—the pain. What is happening?"

"Oh, dear Jonah," she sighed. "I believe it is because you are so close to death that the awake world and the dreamworld are becoming one for you. That is also how I can be in this room with you now. You were pulling me here to this in-between place. The place between material life and material death."

"Just tell me, did we do it?" Jonah asked. "Did we save all those lives? Did they find the weapon?"

"They did." she told him. "We saved all those people, Jonah! The terrorists are imprisoned, and the weapon has been neutralized. We did it!"

"That's all I need to know. No matter what happens now, I can rest knowing it wasn't all in vain."

She then placed her hand on his forehead and her light melted into his.

"Oh, that feels so good," he sighed. "That eases the pain."

"There's been so much damage done to your body that my light is not enough to heal you fully. And certainly not in the short time we have until Clarissa needs to awaken. We must get you help," she told him. "We must get you help from the awake-world."

"It's too late for me," Jonah said. "I'm just glad to know that I made such a difference. That I was able to save so many people from so much pain and suffering. And I'm so happy that I found you and that we shared all that we did."

"No!" she cried. "Clarissa wants you to live! You need to be alive in the awake world! The awake world needs you still! Clarissa needs you! Don't slip away, Jonah! Don't give up!"

Jonah smiled at her caring words even though it was painful. "He's here now anyway," he told her. "The Rat. He's walking towards me now and I believe he plans to finish me off."

She turned and could see the dark figure approaching. There was a deep emptiness about The Rat. He was void of humanity. A sickening shadow. It was disturbing enough to witness such beings while awake. To witness one here, where his chasm of blankness was so completely exposed, was absolutely disgusting.

"I can't let this happen," she told him.

"There is no choice here," Jonah said. "I suppose this is my fate. I did what I had to do and now it's my time to leave the awake world completely."

"No!" she shouted, jumping between the figure and Jonah. Without thinking, she instinctively reached her hand deep inside The Rat's chest. She could feel his heart beating against her energy. Matter against spirit.

There was no contest. Matter was helpless against her furious light. Grabbing the valves in her fist, she squeezed hard, and the man fell suddenly with a thud to the floor.

"What just happened?" Jonah asked in complete shock.

"He's dead," she told him.

"How did you do that?"

"I don't know," she answered honestly. "In that moment, I just knew to do it."

Jonah looked at the body then exclaimed in alarm, "What is that?" Beside the body was a dimly lit thing writhing on the floor. It resembled a parasitic worm searching for a host.

"That's him," she said. "That's the Rat. That's what is left of him—of what was once his light. Now look away quickly! It's important for us to look away now!"

She rushed over and knelt down in front of Jonah to block him from seeing.

In an instant, the room filled with coldness and dread. "What is happening?" he asked feeling the sudden presence of something completely terrifying.

"It's The Collector," she explained. "We must not look upon it. To look upon it is dangerous."

It was then that they heard a terrible pitiful whimper making them both shudder in horror. "He's being taken, now," she told him. "He'll suffer in the emptiness, then eventually, he'll be eaten. That's what happens to them. When you don't take care of your light, that's what happens."

Suddenly, as quickly as the dread had come into the room, it left, and the air filled with a strange sense of relief.

"The Rat is gone forever now," she told him. "He will no longer exist in body or in spirit."

"That is a good thing," Jonah sighed. "I can feel how this has made room. Some evil has been removed from existence which makes room for more light."

"Yes, I'm glad you can feel that. You understand the way of things," she said. "You have embraced knowledge and knowledge has embraced you back."

"Can you move closer to me now?" Jonah then asked. "I feel myself fading and I don't think my body can hang on much longer."

"Of course," she said as she leaned in and wrapped her arms lovingly around him.

He then began to weep a little and told her, "I suppose this is goodbye. Please know that I wish I had met Clarissa. I wish we could have met out there in the awake world. And even though I know that my light will go on, and maybe in that way, I will see you again, I don't think it will be quite the same. I don't know if we will be able to connect the way we once did. Perhaps, Jonah needs to be alive for that to happen. But I will miss you. I will miss you so much."

"Oh Jonah," she softly said as she held him tighter.

"We've no reason to feel bad. I die knowing that together we stopped a catastrophe. We kept needless death and destruction from happening and we opened the door to a future for so many!"

"No, Jonah!" she suddenly cried. "I can't just let you go! I won't! Tell me where are you? What is this place?"

"I don't think it will help. Even if you know where I am, you don't know anyone in the awake world who could get here in time. Max cannot help me. It would take him too long to work through his chain of contacts. And even if by some chance, someone else out there eventually believes you, it will be too late. I don't have that kind of time left."

"But I have to try!" she insisted. "You have to hold on! You can't just give up! Tell me where you are and leave it to me!"

"Alright," he relented, still feeling that it was useless but not wanting to deny her hope. "I'm in the basement of the Pentagon. It's the undocumented room where they used to train torturers. They call it the Principal's Office."

She then quickly infused him with as much energy as she could before *saying, "I'm going to get help now. Just hang on! You must live, Jonah! Just hang on a little longer!"*

∞◇∞

I leapt from the bed. Jonah! I must save him!

Running faster than I knew I could, I rocketed down the stairs and out the back door. Frantically, I pounded on Zeke's door. "Zeke, it's urgent! I need your help!"

The door flew open, and Zeke asked in alarm, "What is it? What's wrong?"

"Do you have any contacts at the Pentagon? High up contacts?"

"What? What are you talking about?"

"I can't explain now," I said, still catching my breath, "but someone needs help. He's the man who uncovered the weapon threat. He's in terrible danger and needs help immediately!"

"You're going to have to tell me more if you want me to understand," said Zeke in confusion.

"The man who saved millions of lives. He's the one who gave them information about the seismic weapon. He's the one who stopped the terrorists. Right now, he's dying! Because of what he did, he was being tortured in the basement of the Pentagon by the terrorist who escaped arrest! He's on the verge of death! We have to save him, Zeke! Please! Please help!"

"Clarissa, if what you are saying is the truth, I'm not even sure who to call or what I'd say."

"It is the truth! Please believe me! Trust me! Just call your highest-ranking contact and tell him that a hero is dying in the Principal's Office and needs help. That's what they call the place, the Principal's Office."

I could see how torn Zeke was. He did trust me, and he did know me but what I was telling him seemed like pure madness. "Please help," I pleaded. "You are his only hope."

Zeke took a deep breath and said, "I'll...I'll try. For you Clarissa, I'll try."

"Oh, thank you! Thank you so much!"

It was then that Zeke went into the Jake's room to make the call closing the door behind him. I waited anxiously in the living room pacing back and forth, trying my best to calm my nerves. I tried to think positive thoughts and send those thoughts to Jonah, hoping that would be enough to sustain him a little longer. It seemed like forever before Jake's door finally opened and Zeke came out.

"Well, I spoke to him," he said. "My contact. I spoke to him, and at first, he couldn't believe what I was saying. I didn't mention you. I just said I had information. But when I mentioned the Principal's Office, he knew it was real. Apparently, the Principal's Office is a real place that only a few people know about. Certainly, someone like me wouldn't have known about it. You are telling the truth Clarissa. The good news is, he's sending a team immediately to check it out and he'll get back to me as soon as he knows something."

"Thank you, Zeke," I sighed, as I sank down in the nearby arm-chair. I felt relieved but at the same time, I was still worried they might not be taking it as seriously as they should. If they didn't move immediately, they might not get to him in time.

"Just let me get you something to drink. Maybe some tea?" Zeke said as he placed his phone down on the coffee table. "This could take a while."

"I hope not," I said. "They have to hurry!"

"I think they will," he tried to assure me. "Now what about that tea?"

"No. No thank you," I replied.

"Water then?" he asked.

"No, I'm fine." I then looked at him and added, "I don't know how to explain to you. It must seem so strange this whole thing. I'm not sure how to explain."

"No!" he exclaimed. "Please, don't tell me. I don't want to know anything. I came to Canada to leave all that behind. No more Pentagon. No more secret stuff. I want to live the rest of my life just being an ordinary engineer with an ordinary job and no complications."

I was happy Zeke felt that way because I wouldn't have been able to be truthful with him. I would've had to make up some story to tell him and I just didn't want that. I didn't want to lie to him, but I couldn't simply divulge the secret of dreams. Knowing the secret is for those who naturally uncover it through their own will and spiritual development. It can't just be spoken about casually as if you're talking about the weather. Knowing the secret is a sacred thing.

"Are you sure you wouldn't like some water?" asked Zeke. "Or something stronger?"

"No. Really, I'm fine, thank you," I replied as I continued to worry about Jonah. How long had it been since Zeke made the call? How long had we been sitting here? My mind was racing so much that I wasn't sure of time anymore. Shouldn't we have heard something by now? Had too much time passed to save him? Were they even working on it?

It was just then that Zeke's phone rang. He sat down on the couch and picked it up. "Yes," he answered.

I watched intently for the expression on his face. First, it was a look of surprise and then what seemed like relief. He ended the call, looked at me and said, "They found him, just like you said, and he's safe. He's alive. They're taking him to the hospital now."

At that point I just put my hands over my face, broke down and wept. Jonah was alive! He was going to be okay!

Zeke came over and put his hand on my shoulder. "It's okay, Clarissa. You saved his life. Whoever he is, you saved his life."

I looked up at Zeke and said, "He's a hero, Zeke. He's a true American hero. The real kind."

Thirty-Four

"Where are we going now, Grandma?" Marigold asked.

"We just have to wait here for the moment," I replied.

"Can we go on the bridge?" she asked excitedly. "I want to see the Rainbow Bridge!"

"I don't know," I told her. "But I'll ask."

"Excuse me," I said to the border guard. "Is it possible to walk out onto the bridge? My granddaughter wants to see it."

"We don't usually allow that Ma'am, but in this case, I think we can make an exception," she said, smiling at Marigold. "Just don't go too far."

"Thank you," I responded and took Marigold by the hand. "Let's go then."

As we walked out onto the bridge, Marigold chirped, "Rainbow Bridge! Rainbow Bridge! Rain, rain, Rainbow Bridge! This is so exciting!"

"Yes, very exciting," I agreed, although I wasn't talking about the bridge.

Despite there being no traffic, as vehicles were not allowed to cross there anymore, we stayed on the pedestrian walkway where there was a good view of the river. Once we had gone far enough, we stopped, and I lifted Marigold up so she could see over the barrier.

"Wow! Look at the river! And I can see the falls too! Do you see, Grandma? Do you see the falls?"

"Yes sweetheart, I see the falls. It's beautiful!"

"I feel it too!" she added. "The falls is kissing us! It loves us, Grandma! It loves us!"

I laughed knowing that the kisses she was talking about was the gentle mist on our faces that was being carried by the cool summer breeze.

"This is the best thing I've ever seen in my entire life!" Marigold exclaimed. "And look, it's a rainbow! I see a real rainbow, Grandma! That must be why it's called the Rainbow Bridge. Do you think that's why?"

"I think you're probably right about that," I said.

"I'm only five, but I know things, Grandma."

"You are incredibly smart, sweetheart."

She was getting a little heavy, so I set her down. She was now peering through the bars instead. I then turned from the falls and looked down the bridge at the American side. There, in the distance, I saw a man walking towards us. It was him. He was finally here. "Marigold," I said, "let's walk a little way further."

As we slowly made our way along the pathway, with Marigold stopping to look out at the water every few feet, I saw the man had now picked up his pace. He was limping but limping rather quickly with the help of a cane.

"I think it's Jonah!" exclaimed Marigold finally turning from the water and noticing him. She then asked, "Is that Jonah, Grandma?"

"Yes, sweetheart. That's Jonah."

As he got closer, he slowed his pace a little. The breeze was tousling his snow-white hair and it reminded me of the foam on the Niagara River. The sun then suddenly appeared from behind some clouds, and it seemed as if he had brought it with him.

"Jonah!" called Marigold, waving frantically. "It's me, Marigold and Grandma! Do you see us?"

At that point, Jonah began to laugh. "Yes, I see you!" he called back.

He was now close enough to where I could better see his face. There were some freshly healed cuts on his cheek and his forehead. I knew this was only part of what had been done to him...what he had sacrificed.

"Clarissa," he said warmly as he walked up close to me. It surprised me how tall he was. In dreams we were always the same height.

"Can I hug you?" I asked, not sure about his wounds and not wanting to cause him any pain.

He didn't answer me. Instead, he merely dropped his cane and took me in his arms. Nothing in life had ever prepared me for that moment—for that feeling. We stood there in our embrace, melting together. Body and soul. Spirit and flesh. Heaven and earth. The wind then softly blew in, carrying with it the sweetest music. Music that touched the mind like the sweet scent of rare flowers blooming in the desert. And then the door—that door long shut to the world, gloriously flew open. And from within came the sacred message delivered in the voice of love. It echoed forcefully across the entire planet. Shaking hearts and willing lights to shine brighter. **Be wise and understanding and awakened,**" it said. "**Hallelujah!**"